COME, LET'S REACH THE WORLD

Jesus said, "Say not ye, There are yet four months, and then cometh harvest? Behold, I say unto you, Lift up your eyes, and look on the fields; for they are white already to harvest."
"Pray ye therefore the Lord of the harvest, that he will send forth laborers into his harvest."

John 4:35 and Matthew 9:38

COME, LET'S
REACH
THE WORLD

PARTNERSHIP IN CHURCH PLANTING
AMONG THE MOST UNREACHED

K.P. YOHANNAN

BOOKS

a division of Gospel for Asia

www.gfa.org

Come, Let's Reach the World
© 1991, 2004 by K.P. Yohannan
All rights reserved.

(Previous edition published under the title *Why the World Waits.)*

Scripture quotations are from the King James Version of the Bible.

ISBN: 978-1-59589-003-0

Published by gfa books, a division of Gospel for Asia
1800 Golden Trail Court
Carrollton, TX 75010
phone: (972) 300-7777
fax: (972) 300-7778

Printed in the United States of America

For more information about other materials, visit our website: www.gfa.org.

To my mother, Achyamma K. Punnose, who went to be with the Lord on August 27, 1990. She was 84. For three and a half years, every Friday, she fasted and prayed. Her request: "Lord, please call one of my children to be a missionary." The Lord answered her prayer. He called me to serve Him.

CONTENTS |

ACKNOWLEDGMENTS |

My deepest thanks to:

John Beers, my colleague and coworker, for your constant encouragement to get this book out. I am grateful to the Lord for your passion for the lost.

Bernard Borah, for your deep commitment to the Lord and your significant contribution of countless hours of research. You made this project possible and have done an excellent job.

Teresa Chupp, for the overall coordination of this project. The Lord bless you for your loyalty and labor of love.

Heidi Chupp and Claudia Edwards, for your hard work, patiently reading through the manuscript, and the endless hours you worked to make it ready for the publisher.

Mary Ruth Howes and Tricia Bennett, for your diligent editorial work.

My staff at the GFA international headquarters, USA—what would I do without your encouragement and support? You are the best.

My wife, Gisela, and my children, Daniel and Sarah—my most precious gifts from the Lord. Your love and sacrifice made this book a reality.

PREFACE |

"The future of world evangelism depends heavily on an international community of missionaries and missiologists who are able to cooperate effectively in the monumental task of reaching the world for Christ."
—Ruth A. Tucker[1]

Sitting around a folding table in a huge old Dallas church building was a small group of remarkable people. They were some of the most sincere Christian men and women you could ever meet. They gathered once a month, bringing along their brown bag lunches, to talk about what they loved most—foreign missions.

They represented many different backgrounds, both in their secular careers and Christian traditions. But they all shared two things in common: first, they personally sacrificed for missions, supporting the global outreach of the Church with prayer and finances; and second, everyone at the table was a local church leader. Most served as chairperson of their congregations' mission committees.

This was a sober, serious-minded group, each playing an important role in determining the budget and helping raise funds to support his or her church's foreign missions budget. This month they had invited me to meet with them.

As a missions leader, I knew these men and women were typical of the few thousand North American leaders who have directed billions of dollars annually into overseas missions. Because of their support, over 50,000 U.S. and Canadian missionaries currently are stationed around the world, according to the 21st-century edition of *Operation World.*[2]

Many in the room had visited the mission field, and all had heard scores of missionary speakers over the years. Some of them were pastors or had been missionaries. All had close friends, fellow church members or even relatives who were serving overseas as American missionaries. Many acted as full- or part-time local representatives for their favorite missionary board or cause.

These were the ones who "tarried by the stuff," and were promised their equal share in the victory by King David in 1 Samuel 30:24. Without men and women like these, the Great Commission enterprise of the Western church would find it difficult to survive.

I had been invited to meet with this group not so much as a speaker, but to answer their questions about the rapid growth of the indigenous missionary movement. I had been specifically asked to represent the views of indigenous mission leaders from the Two-Thirds World—the areas formerly known as "the Third World." (The Two-Thirds World is primarily the non-Western countries of Asia, Africa and Latin America. Because the citizens of these countries make up two-thirds of the world's population, it is more accurate to call them the Two-Thirds World.)

Most of them already had a copy of my first book, *Revolution in World Missions,* and I came to the meeting prepared to defend my convictions and answer tough questions.

I was shocked when, after I finished a short introduction to our ministry, one of the men stood to his feet and spoke.

"Brother K.P.," he said, "we already know that indigenous missions is now the key to the future of missions. We want to be part of what God is doing. The critical things you have to say about our programs are shocking, but we all know they're true.

"I wish everyone in my church could hear what you have to say. None of us opposes indigenous missionaries. We just don't know how we can best help. And we need to know how to answer the questions of others when we try to explain to them what's happening on the field. Tell us how to build a case for indigenous missionary support in our churches, and we'll do it."

His challenge took me by surprise. For over a decade, traditional missions thinking in North America and Europe has broken my heart. The increasingly tragic waste of energy, finances and time continues to trouble me. Here was a group of respected local mission leaders struggling with the same problem!

"Well," I asked carefully, "what kind of questions are you getting from your people and leaders?"

The questions they raised were uncommonly candid. I answered them as boldly and frankly as I could:

- How can we spot authentic missionaries and know that our support is making a real difference for Christ?
- What's really happening on the mission field? Are there qualified indigenous missionaries ready to be supported?
- Why are so many nations closing their doors to Western missions and missionaries?
- What role should Western Christians and churches play in the Two-Thirds World today?
- How do we evaluate the work of indigenous missionaries?
- How can you hold indigenous missionaries accountable?
- How much does it cost to support indigenous missionaries, and at what standard of living should missionaries live?
- Do Two-Thirds World leaders want only Western dollars and nothing else from us?
- Should Western missions be subordinate to indigenous leadership on the field?
- Why does it take our Western missionaries so long to disciple local believers and plant indigenous churches?
- If what you say is true, how can we change the national policies of our churches and denominations?

For the next two hours, as the ideas bounced back and forth, I realized these were legitimate questions every Christian leader in the West should be asking. And I also realized I knew of no guidebook available to give these key men and women the answers they needed.

UNITY IN THE CAUSE OF WORLD EVANGELISM

There is a disturbing trend within many missions-conscious churches today. Although they still desire to fulfill the Great Commission, the focus has shifted inward. Rather than answer the question, "How will the lost be reached?" they now ask themselves, "How can *we* reach them?"

It is a small but alarming change, for suddenly the emphasis is on "what works best for *us*" rather than "what will most effectively reach *them*."

But it's not about us.

This book is an attempt to bring balance at a time when many churches are in danger of falling back into mission strategies and initiatives that are actually only colonial remakes.

How will we be able to mobilize the whole Church to go to the unreached peoples unless leaders like these have the answers they need? For years I have realized that only as Christians work together in unity on an international level will we ever finish the job. But to achieve that unity, we must provide Western Christians the up-to-date facts about what is really happening on the mission field.

For years I've talked about a revolution in world missions, but during that meeting I realized afresh that church leaders in the West still have a key role to play in completing this revolution. The fact is that God has made us codependent on one another (in the positive sense of the word). As the universal Body of Christ, Christians will not finish the harvest until sending churches in Western nations join hands with indigenous missions to commission more reapers.

It's time to stop thinking about us. It's time to shed the fads, buzzwords, trends and failed practices. It's time to lay down our ambitions and give ourselves to being effective in reaching the lost world.

So that's how this book came about.

Western leadership needs answers to questions about the way indigenous missions relates to doctrine, history, theology and missions policy. Without these facts, they cannot define the cause of indigenous missions intelligently and motivate action. Although I don't pretend to be a scholar, these are the areas I want to address from hands-on experience.

TIME TO MOVE WITH THE SPIRIT

This book is designed to give some practical answers that will help church leaders deal with what may be the next great move of the Holy Spirit for world evangelism—a move that will call upon the whole Church to unite in the work ahead of us.

I have tried to make this a truly honest book about missions policy— one that communicates what thousands of Two-Thirds World church leaders would like to say to the sending churches in the West if only they could.

Everywhere I speak and travel in the West, I sit down with earnest pastors and church leaders who want desperately to move with the Holy Spirit. They sense that something exciting and wonderful is happening today in world evangelism, and they want to be part of what God is doing. These are the kinds of leaders who will, I trust, find in the following pages the answers for which they've been praying.

NOTES |

1 | Ruth A. Tucker, *From Jerusalem to Irian Jaya* (Grand Rapids, MI: Zondervan, 1983), p. 458.

2 | Patrick Johnstone and Jason Mandryk, eds., *Operation World*, 21st-century ed. (Carlisle, Cumbria, U.K.: Paternoster Lifestyle, 2001), p. 751.

INTRODUCTION |

I'd like to tell you a tale of three peoples—and of opportunity.

The first two stories, as you will see, have very different endings.

The conclusion for the third is still waiting to be written . . . and may well hinge upon the response of God's people in this generation.

The country of Japan had its first exposure to Christianity during the Middle Ages, when energetic Nestorians (Eastern Orthodox Christians) brought the Gospel to the island. By 1908 there were nearly 1,000 missionaries in Japan. But when World War II broke out, the nation was deep in the spiritual darkness of Shintoism—worship of nature, ancestors and the emperor.

During the Allied occupation at the end of the war, General Douglas MacArthur called for missionaries to be part of the rebuilding of Japan. A spiritual vacuum existed in the nation. The emperor had declared he was not a divine being, and people were looking for something to believe in. By 1953 more than 1,500 Christian workers had responded, most of whom focused on humanitarian work rather than evangelism.

Today Christianity remains a foreign religion to the Japanese mind. Sadly, less than two percent profess to follow Christ; more than 80 percent profess no religion at all. It is plain that the Church missed the opportunity set before her.

Korea also first heard the Gospel around the same time in history as Japan. By 1870, Protestant missionaries had arrived, and the first church was planted in 1884. Within a few years, a missions strategy was established that promoted indigenous Christianity and gave Korean believers leadership within the local church.

Today Korean Christians make up nearly 32 percent of the population. Over 60,000 churches exist in the country, and more than 10,000 Korean missionaries serve around the globe. Ten of the world's 11 largest congregations are located in Seoul.

When a Korean church leader was asked for the reasons behind the phenomenal growth of the Body of Christ in his country, he gave two basic reasons: First, Western missionaries had laid an excellent biblical foundation. Second, these missionaries had actively equipped local pastors and believers for ministry. In other words, they took advantage of the opportunity before them, and today the nation of Korea testifies to the fruit of their labors.

Right now there is another group of people, 250 million strong, for whom the door of opportunity is wide open. Slaves in their own nation of India for 3,000 years, Dalits ("Untouchables") have been segregated, oppressed and denied basic human rights such as health care, education and access to safe drinking water—all because of where they fall in the Hindu-based caste system.

In recent years, however, there is a growing desire for deliverance among the Dalits. Leaders are demanding justice and freedom from caste slavery and persecution. Although laws against caste discrimination have been passed, little has changed—until recently.

Dalit leaders have also recognized that true hope and freedom for their people will not be found in social revolution but in another faith. In a historic gathering that took place in October 2001, Dalit leaders met with more than 700 key evangelical Christians. They agreed to allow their people to follow Christ if they desired. The Christian leaders, in turn, committed themselves to helping this mass movement despite the risk involved.

A number of years earlier, Dalit leaders had met with certain Christians in India who had declined to accept these overwhelming numbers of people into their churches. Like their leader Dr. Ambedkar, these Dalits then turned to Buddhism. But now, by God's grace, the gateway is open for millions to experience hope and true freedom through our Lord.

In addition to the Dalits, another group of Indians is searching for freedom from ongoing discrimination and segregation because of their low caste status. Often known simply as the "Other Backward Castes" or "OBCs," they number over 450 million.

Together, the Dalits and the OBCs make up nearly 80 percent of India's population. Amazingly, they represent one out of every eight people on planet Earth. Today they stand at a crucial decision point, wide open to the Gospel. Reports have begun to come in of both Dalits and OBCs turning to the Lord by the thousands and tens of thousands.

The story of these people is not yet completed. Will we as a Church respond to this incredible opportunity? Will we share the love of Christ with them while there is still time? What kind of ending will we help write?

It is time for the church in the West to reset her priorities. We must let Christ's passion for the lost direct our agendas, budgets, goals and schedules.

God has not called the Church as an institution to farming, manufacturing or other such community development projects; He calls us to preach and teach all that Christ taught. We cannot stand by and let secondary ministries be substituted for the basic priorities of the Great Commission. The greatest enemy of the *best* is not the worst—but the *good*. And this is exactly what has often happened in Western missions. Our programs are filled with many good activities that have kept us from fulfilling His best!

This book is a cry for Christians to act. We have an amazing opportunity set before us. There has been no time in history when so many millions are as open to the Gospel as they are today. But we must see the reformation of much of Western missions. Only such a reformation will enable those in the Two-Thirds World to complete the Great Commission mandate in our generation.

The principles set forth here are radical—yet they've been around for thousands of years. But if this book does even a bit to turn us back to our first purposes, it will be worth the tears and pain that went into it. Discipline is never pleasant for the moment, but in the end it brings the godliness and righteousness we all desire to see in the house of God (see Hebrews 12:11). And only then will we fulfill the passion of Christ for this lost and dying world, enabling millions of precious souls to hear of our Savior's love at least one time.

1 | THE END OF AN ERA

T he year was 1939—only yesterday in comparison to the history
of the Church and Christian missions. Although no one imagined it then, the curtain was about to fall on more than 500
years of empire and colonial rule by the West.

In Europe, Hitler was about to launch a war against the last of the
great colonial powers. It was a struggle that would clamp Great Britain
and her North Atlantic allies into a nearly fatal choke hold. Meanwhile,
taking advantage of the situation in Asia, the warlords of Japan were
preparing to launch a war that would forever break the Western grip on
the Orient. After World War II, the bankrupt and exhausted colonial
powers would have neither the will nor the stamina to resist the rising
tide of nationalism and the Marxist communism that fueled it. It swept
around the world with intense fury. The United Nations has recorded
the birth of over 100 nation-states in the three decades that followed.

THE GREAT CENTURY IN CHRISTIAN MISSIONS

For Church historians, 1939 also marked the end of what is now
fondly referred to as "The Great Century" in Christian missions.[1]

It was under the so-called armies of colonial occupation—explorers, traders, exploiters—sent mostly from the Anglo-Saxon countries of Europe, that missionaries like William Carey and Hudson Taylor planted the seeds of evangelical Christianity worldwide. Their 19th-century followers managed in only about 75 years of actual ministry to foster indigenous church movements on all the major mission fields of Africa, Asia and Latin America.

During those years, missionaries went overseas on one-way tickets, fully aware that they might never see family and home churches again. For thousands, the decision was indeed a fatal one for themselves and their wives and children. Today their graves dot every great mission field. These pioneers considered the cost and gladly laid down their lives to plant the seeds of the Gospel in barren fields—seeds that today are mature and ready to harvest. Those missionaries demonstrated the true servant spirit of Jesus, loving the people to whom God had called them and faithfully preaching the Word of God.

During those years, there were also many problems. Some nearly fatal mistakes were made at the beginning, stemming mostly from the early "compound strategies" adapted from Spanish Catholic missions to Latin America. Nearly all Protestant mission boards experimented with some form of compound evangelism, and many maintained them well into the 20th century in modified forms.[2]

Compounds, in their original form, were something like self-sustaining Christian forts. They were buildings and land surrounded by tall walls with access only through a gate that could be locked. Often they were the only option in situations where security and treaty restrictions required them. Unfortunately, many missionary societies came to consider them standard operating procedure. Required or not, there is no doubt they were the preferred method to maintain an island of safety in the midst of an often violent environment.

Converts, who were frequently disowned by family and community, often sought shelter in these centers and thus were isolated from the rest of their society. Many worked in agricultural, educational, and medical projects that were developed around the compounds. Unfortunately, while they learned the Christian faith, they also learned alien cultures and technologies that separated them further from family, friends and non-Christian neighbors.

But despite these early experiments in witness by segregation, the Lord used the lives of these pioneers to make genuine disciples. Soon, truly indigenous churches emerged within one local culture after another. The power of the Gospel was released through indigenous witness, and today there are thriving local churches on nearly all mission fields as a result. Along with indigenous churches have come indigenous mission boards, Gospel teams and evangelistic societies. In fact, at this time, the number of indigenous missionaries is growing much faster than that of missionaries sent from the West. John Bennett states that, in recent years, "hundreds of indigenous and missionary organizations have been launched in the Two-Thirds World."[3] Ralph Winter, director of the U.S. Center for World Missions, confirms that "more missionaries are now sent from non-Western churches than from the traditional mission sending bases in the West."[4]

At the time of this writing, Gospel for Asia supports over 13,000 indigenous missionaries in India, but it is not uncommon to read reports in Western publications that list the total number of indigenous missionaries in India at about 10,000. Plainly, the correct size of the indigenous missionary force is being underreported. Although some respected sources put the 1996 worldwide total at about 28,500, the real number of indigenous missionaries is closer to 10 times that amount.[5] According to the fifth edition of *Operation World*, indigenous missionaries comprise two-thirds of the world missions force.[6]

In this sense, the work of colonial missions was an unqualified success. Those men and women laid down their lives, and as a result, the Holy Spirit is now calling out an army of indigenous missionaries, who are the products of their witness, to finish the Great Commission task. Volumes have been filled with the adventures and sacrifices of these pioneer missionaries from America and Europe. They've left footprints of suffering on the pages of history that few in the West would even consider following today.

MISSIONS AND CULTURAL IMPERIALISM

The self-sacrifice and heroism of these 19th-century missionaries are portrayed with an entirely different interpretation in the secular history books of emerging Two-Thirds World nations. There, faith in Christ is seldom described in biblical or Western terms. It is not seen as a personal choice each individual must make before God.

The proclamation of the Gospel by white foreigners is portrayed as a sinister form of imperialism. Christian missions are usually linked to every injustice or sinful exploitation of indigenous peoples during the colonial era. Critics often portray evangelism as the most subtle and dangerous incursion of Western imperialism on local society because, they say, it appears so benign. Although the Gospel is admitted to be nonpolitical, nonmilitary and noneconomic, this is the reason it is considered the most dangerous alien influence of all. In fact, the Bible itself remains one of the most feared and hated books in most Two-Thirds World countries, especially those that have embraced Marxist or Islamic social orders.

Unfortunately, there is more than a grain of truth in some of these criticisms. During the colonial era, some misguided missionaries encouraged Christian converts to change their names, manner of dress, and lifestyles to conform to the "civilized" West. Conversion to Christ too often meant accepting foreign cultural baggage and occidental prejudices as well. Occasionally, during the colonial era, some converted to Christianity for economic reasons or to gain favor with the ruling elite.

Bruce Britten, veteran missionary to Swaziland, explains how this took place in Africa:

Some problems have resulted from the fact that most African nations have received Christianity from Europeans instead of receiving it from Ethiopians or other North African Christians. Probably the main problem is that Christianity in most of Africa is now mixed with European customs. Of course, this is because the European missionaries who came to Africa brought not only the Christian faith, but they also brought their own customs.

THE END OF AN ERA | 25

Naturally, it was difficult for the people of Africa to see the difference between the Christian faith and European customs. In fact, the missionaries themselves had difficulty seeing which things really belonged to the Christian faith and which things were just their own customs. The result was that Christianity and European customs became so mixed up that the European way of singing seemed to be the *Christian* way of singing, European musical instruments seemed to be the *Christian* instruments, and European clothes seemed to be *Christian* clothes. Therefore, most of the Africans who accepted Christianity also accepted all the European customs. Often an African was not accepted as a true Christian unless he agreed to throw away his own culture and conform to European culture.[7]

It takes a miracle for most Westerners, particularly Americans, to comprehend how bitterly humiliating this colonial period was to the once-proud peoples of Africa, Asia and the Middle East. Words cannot overstate how deeply the Christian religion and colonial exploitation remain linked in the minds of millions. When we consider the anti-Western fanaticism of the late Ayatollah Khomeini in Iran, Ho Chi Minh in Vietnam and Mao Tse-tung in China, we begin to understand the hatred resulting from colonialism.

Unforgiveness Lingers

Most missionaries from the West cannot help but be aware of this lingering unforgiveness felt by so many—and the barrier it creates to evangelism. Although they have tried various social programs to bridge the gap, Western missionaries today often still find themselves unable to restore a credible Christian testimony. Therefore, with the exception of a few one-on-one contacts, many Western missionaries have retreated from open evangelistic work and direct church planting.

The following account illustrates what can happen when a Western missionary recognizes his need to identify with the national. It is by former missionary doctor Arden Almquist, the executive secretary of

World Missions of the Evangelical Covenant Church of America. Dr. Almquist served in the Congo when the country was under Belgian rule. He shares some of his impressions as a new missionary:

> I was struck at once by the sharp contrast between the splendor of the European sector—greater than that known by most Belgians in Brussels or Antwerp—and the relative squalor of the African sector. . . .
>
> Eating was largely a segregated function, except on rare occasions. Not only was it unusual for an African to be seated at a white man's table; white men, including missionaries, rarely ate at an African's.
>
> I was giving the grand tour of the Wasolo mission one day to a visiting Norwegian missionary. It was mid-afternoon, and the mission workmen were seated outside their huts after having their daily bath following the cessation of the day's work. They were drinking coffee as we walked by, and they offered my guest and me a cup. I accepted mine, served in a glass, very black, and almost syrupy from too much sugar. My friend refused with a "*Non, merci!*" then turned to me, saying in English: "Surely you don't drink with these people? Aren't you concerned about getting dysentery?"
>
> But it was not only fear that handicapped the missionary. There was a kind of conspiracy of solidarity of race and culture that made him insensitive to his own basic humanity.
>
> Christmas was an example. For weeks before and after Christmas the large SoTransCongo truck which tripled as a commercial carrier, local bus and mail wagon made its weekly stop at the Karawa post, disgorging each time a dozen sacks of mail, filled with parcels from the States—gifts for the missionaries and their "benighted" children whom the thoughtful donors imagined to be so exposed to the hazards of jungle life; and so cheated of the gimmicks of an ever-expanding affluent American society. For the African "boy" or nurse or teacher or pastor there were no gifts—they had no relatives overseas. There was tacit agreement among the missionaries—indeed at one time a station council ruling—that no individual missionary was to give a Christmas present to an African individual. Instead there was a Christmas party by the missionaries as a group for the Africans as a group.
>
> This conspiracy of solidarity included the non-missionary members

of the white race, the Belgians, Portuguese, and Greeks who made up the white community. Whatever their personal qualities or qualifications, or lack of them, they were recognized as "belonging" in a special way, although many of them showed little or no evidence of faith in Christ. Gradually, as the days became months, and the months years, one got caught up in these attitudes.

There was a conspiracy of solidarity in the African community too, as rigid as our own, as an experience toward the close of my first term of four years made clear.

We had a strike at the Wasolo station. It began when I dismissed five student nurses. Quickly the solidarity of the African community manifested itself. The workmen quit working, and all building ceased. The schoolteachers sent the two hundred pupils home. Work at the hospital came to a standstill. It was my fault—I had injured the Africans' keen sense of justice in a burst of anger. It was easy to rationalize my deed. Four of the five had stolen medications, or accepted bribes for services, or been delinquent on duty. I had warned them, but to no avail. In exasperation I had summarily dismissed the class and told them to return to their villages. But I had done so in anger, and I had been unfair to one among the five whom everyone felt to be innocent. I talked it over with the senior missionary on the station, who smiled awkwardly and told me: "It's your problem. You got yourself into it. You'll have to handle it."

I returned to my room to pray together with my wife. Then, humbled, I took a can of powdered coffee and some sacks of sugar and went down to the African village where the strikers, in a sullen mood, were sitting around their small fires in front of their huts. I told them I was sorry and asked them to forgive me. Then I invited them to add hot water from their cooking pots to the symbols of reconciliation in my hands, so that we might share a cup of coffee together and talk things over. They listened in silence, with growing interest. There were murmurs of surprise and suddenly there was joy! We shook hands all around and drank together. I agreed to review my hasty decision, and they agreed to return to work and recall the schoolchildren to their classes. There were tears and laughter, and someone said: "Doctor, this is the first time a white man ever apologized to us."[8]

NEW TWO-THIRDS WORLD LEADERS REACT

Two-Thirds World leaders cannot forget that many of their former colonial masters openly ridiculed local culture, language, religion and history. Furthermore, they blame their current economic, military and technological dependence on centuries of exploitation by the so-called Christian empires of Britain, France, Holland, Spain and Portugal. American military adventures in Latin America, Southeast Asia and the Middle East since World War II have further prejudiced many.

Today, although the revolutionary zeal of nationalism may be fading, a new generation of Two-Thirds World leaders continues to act out this inherited bitterness. Restrictions on missionary activity by foreigners is one of the easiest and most popular ways to strike back.

In China, foreign missionaries are still banned, 50 years after the communist revolution. Despite token Bible printings, it remains difficult to obtain the Scriptures in China today. China's population has now reached 1.28 billion, and worldwide over 1.5 billion people speak Chinese. With hundreds of unreached people groups, China represents the largest single concentration of unevangelized people in the world. Yet there is no sign that it will soon open to Western missionary evangelists and church planters.

In northern Africa, there is an almost universal wall against Western evangelistic missionaries. Other African nations require that humanitarian and secular skills be brought into the economy. If missionaries cannot justify their presence as relevant to the cause of nation building, visas will not be granted. In a recent article, Mans Ramstad states, "We have the challenge . . . of serving our host country's purposes so that we are welcome to stay."[9] Yet, somehow, the hundreds of unreached people groups remaining in Africa must be reached.

In Myanmar (known for centuries as Burma), Christian missionaries from the West are banned, despite the fact that mission hospitals and schools were the primary sources of social services in the nation until 1960. Myanmar, once one of the richest and most progressive nations in the Two-Thirds World, today is not only among the poorest but has actually gone back in time to an era without modern medicine or education. Yet Myanmar's nationalistic leaders apparently still prefer present conditions to the possibility of opening its doors to Christian missionaries from the outside. Even the number of tourist visas has been drastically reduced to curb any outside influence. Propaganda billboards along the road read, "Crush all internal and external destructive elements as the common enemy."[10]

Myanmar's anti-Christian and anti-Western prejudice is shared by most Asian nations from Afghanistan to Vietnam. Around the world, and especially in the Middle East, nations with Muslim majorities have almost universally banned missionaries since their independence. Shiite fundamentalists and other conservative groups are pressuring for a return to Qur'anic laws that call for *jihad*, or "holy war," against America—a nation they portray as "the great Satan" for spreading immorality in Islamic nations.

Conversion to Christianity remains a capital offense in many Muslim nations, and those who turn to Jesus Christ are cut off from family, friends and society.

Islamic fundamentalists and other reactionaries have introduced restrictive legislation against Western missionaries in 35 countries. These include in *North Africa:* Algeria, Egypt, Libya, Morocco, Sudan, Nigeria and Tunisia; in *West Africa:* Mauritania; in *East Africa:* Comoros and Somalia; in the *Middle East:* Iran, Iraq, Jordan, Kuwait, Oman, Qatar, Saudi Arabia, Syria, Turkey, United Arab Emirates and Yemen; in *Central Asia:* Afghanistan, Bangladesh, Iran, Maldives and Pakistan; in *Southeast Asia:* Brunei, Indonesia and Malaysia; in *Central Asia:* Uzbekistan, Azerbaijan, Tajikistan, Kazakhstan and Turkmenistan.

As of the year 2000, there were 1.2 billion Muslims throughout the world, and that population is growing at more than 2 percent per year. The Islamic world has 3,700 unreached people groups. Yet current relations between Muslim countries and the West seem to be worsening rather than improving, making the atmosphere for Western missionaries more difficult than ever.

Since 1947, these rising tides of Two-Thirds World nationalism have made strange bedfellows. In government and education, they have adopted secular humanistic systems of thought and economics, including subtle forms of Marxism and Leninism. A near worship of science and technology also prevails. On the spiritual level, nationalism has helped foster revivals of primitive religions.

NOTES |

1 | Ruth A. Tucker, *From Jerusalem to Irian Jaya* (Grand Rapids, MI: Zondervan, 1983), p. 109.

2 | Donald K. Smith, "Reviewing the Place of Western Missionaries for the Third Millennium," *Evangelical Missions Quarterly,* January 1999, p. 56.

3 | John Bennett, "COSIM," *Evangelical Missions Quarterly,* July 1999, p. 315.

4 | Ralph Winter, "Finishing the Task," Mission Frontiers (www.missionfrontiers.org).

5 | John A. Siewert and Edna G. Valdez, eds., *Mission Handbook,* 17th ed. (Monrovia, CA: MARC Publications, 1997), p. 74.

6 | Patrick Johnstone, *Operation World,* 5th ed. (Carlisle, Cumbria, U.K.: OM Publishing, 1995), p. 643.

7 | Bruce Britten, *We Don't Want Your White Religion* (Manzini, Swaziland: Britten, 1984), p. 25.

8 | Arden Almquist, *Missionary, Come Back!* (Cleveland, OH: World, 1970), pp. 4–14.

9 | "Making Tents or Building Churches: An Interview with Mans Ramstad," *Evangelical Missions Quarterly,* October 1996, p. 421. Mans Ramstad is the pseudonym of a veteran tentmaker in China who works with an organization that provides services to other organizations in China.

10 | "No Myanmar Trips?" November 11, 2000, ABC (abcnews.go.com/sections/travel/DailyNews/myanmar 980925.html).

2 | COPING WITH THE RISING TIDE OF NATIONALISM

The impact of the anti-Western movement among the Two-Thirds World family of nations has been devastating. Eighty-six countries prohibit or restrict Western missionaries.[1] "The whole non-Christian world appears to be growing more hostile to Christianity" was one observer's comment in 1996.[2] Currently, 3.8 billion people live in these restricted-access countries, and that number will most likely continue to increase. Even access to the airwaves is in danger of being cut off. "There are many countries in the world where you can broadcast [the Gospel] locally today that will not be open to this one to five years from now."[3]

In addition, the open door created by glasnost and perestroika is closing up. "Since 1993, the Russian Orthodox Church hierarchy, extreme nationalists, and Communists have lobbied for revisions of the liberal 1990 law on religion in order to restrict the activities of foreigners. . . . In September 1997 such a law was passed by both houses of the Russian parliament and signed by President Yeltsin . . . it seems certain to restrict the activity of foreigners."[4]

Only in Latin America, it seems, have most nations failed to restrict Western missionaries solely on the basis of a nationalistic reaction. Yet Marxism in Cuba and the revolutions in Central America have been flavored with a strong antimissionary and anticlerical fervor. Liberation theology is a sworn enemy to traditional evangelism, and most Latin American nations have documented harassment and persecution of missionaries.

Even Mexico, America's closest neighbor to the south, can be difficult for American missionaries. The U.S. Secretary of State's "Report on Religious Freedom" reveals that "leaders sometimes acquiesced in, or actually ordered, the expulsion of Protestants. . . . In many cases such expulsions involved the burning of homes and crops, beatings, and occasionally, killings."[5]

Western missionaries who have remained overseas in this atmosphere have generally found their attempts at evangelism increasingly difficult. Nationalism has created a xenophobia in which white evangelists are viewed as foreign agents. In fact, even in more open nations, such as Brazil, Colombia or Nigeria, it can be difficult for a Western missionary to do public work without accusations of being "American CIA."

White missionaries in many countries must deal with anger, bitterness or polite indifference based on the past sins of their nations.

In his 1984 exploration of African resistance to the Gospel, Bruce Britten asked this question: "Why is it that many Africans today feel they don't want anything 'white'? The answer is obvious. While everyone agrees that not all whites are the same, the fact remains that for hundreds of years many whites have looked down on and oppressed the people of Africa. It would be foolish for anyone to deny this."[6]

This reaction is comparable to the resistance white Gospel workers sense when they attempt to plant churches among the Sioux Indians of North and South Dakota. Not only are these tribes still immersed in the animistic traditions of native religion, but they are also the great-grand-children of the Indians massacred at Wounded Knee by U.S. cavalry in the late 1800s. Those memories are too fresh.

Memories of foreign occupation can be even more deadly. For most Americans, who have never been subjugated by an outside power, these kinds of feelings can be hard to understand. But African and Asian nations have their equivalent of KKK "night riders" too.

Even in 2003 the whereabouts of three New Tribes missionaries, captured in 1993 by the Revolutionary Armed Forces of Columbia, are still unknown. The kidnapping of two female social workers in August 2001 in Afghanistan and the kidnapping and death of Martin Burnham in the Philippines are recent examples of guerrilla activities in various countries that are fueled by a hatred of the West—and therefore of Western missionaries.

MISSION REACTIONS—DENIAL AND DESPAIR

Although missionaries returning to the mission field after World War II intellectually understood that they were coming back to a different world, many failed to see how permanent and serious this crisis in Western missions really was. The victorious Americans were especially unwilling to accept the coming reality of life in newly independent nations. Instead of working with the rising tides of nationalism, they called for even more Western volunteers, funds and programs!

Meanwhile, however, many secular corporations reacted in the opposite way. Sensing the depth of the change in public opinion, they sought alternate ways to manufacture and market their products to Two-Thirds World customers. The keystone of almost every successful business strategy was to find a way to adapt to nationalism by eliminating or minimizing the physical presence of foreign personnel. Failing that, they tried to maintain operations with the smallest expatriate staff possible.

Western businesses quickly trained local personnel to replace their foreign staff, promoted nationals to leadership positions, sought local investors, began joint ventures and licensed their patents to indigenous manufacturers.

But not colonial mission leaders. Many attempted to find ways to stay on, maintain as much control as possible, and run their mission compounds as before. They tried to ride out what they viewed as a temporary storm.

One eyewitness of the 1949 communist takeover of the Shanghai headquarters of one of the best-known agencies (who asked to remain anonymous) reveals a telling anecdote about this widespread attitude. As they packed their bags to leave those beautiful facilities, missionaries joked openly with one another about the impending move. "We've been through this before," laughed one. "We'll be back!"

For years they waited to return, even keeping the old name (which indicated their focus on China) Meanwhile, the communists turned their Shanghai offices into the local party headquarters! Finally mission executives realized the new antimissionary rules were here to stay. Eventually they changed their name and moved the work to nations that didn't restrict their activities. Ironically, one by one, many of these nations have closed their doors also.

In some countries, missions were allowed to phase out their operations gradually. Even then many resisted to the end—until the new nationalist governments gave the intransigent ones no other choice. They were simply ordered out. Those who had made disciples and had already turned the control of their ministries over to indigenous churches saw their ministries survive and grow. Those who had not done so lost everything. "Of the six mission run hospitals in Bhutan, [two] were nationalized in 1990, [another] in 1991, [another] in 1992, and the other three were scheduled to be handed over by 1995. All of them retain a few missionary staff, but government plans are for them to be gradually replaced by all Bhutanese staff."[7] In trying to put the best face possible on this total loss of investment, "the missions have generally chosen to view the government policy of nationalization as being 'pro-Bhutan' rather than 'antimission.' "[8] In fact, Bhutan just passed a law that all government employees must convert to Buddhism or lose their jobs.

MISSION REACTIONS—DEFENSE AND SUBSTITUTION

In those few nations that let missionaries stay, the post-World War II days presented a new challenge. They had to find new ways to continue operating and to justify their existence to their hosts. Here are some of the more common strategies used by colonial-style missions to remain on the field after independence.

CARRYING ON AS IF NOTHING HAD HAPPENED.

This "business as usual" approach is mostly used by a tiny minority of missionaries who have continued to attempt evangelism and church-planting work. They have chosen to ignore political and social change as much as possible. Some persist in difficult pioneer work, often among tribal and primitive peoples or in urban areas. Most post-colonial nations have denied them visas. In such cases, these missionaries are occasionally found in border regions or urban slums, quietly working with concentrations of refugees and students from the main people group they hope to return to sometime in the future.

It is significant that only a small percentage of North American missionaries working overseas are still engaged in this kind of traditional soul-winning ministry. In fact, the Missions Advanced Research Center in Pasadena (MARC) has stopped recording statistics on field activities of North American missionary personnel. So many agencies refuse to reply to questions on this subject that collecting valid statistics is no longer possible.

The somewhat-dated figures from MARC show that a mere 10 percent of the average missionaries from evangelical denominations are involved in evangelism or church planting. Other agencies report 27 percent (the Evangelical Foreign Missions Association), 28 percent (the Interdenominational Foreign Missions Association) and 33 percent (nonassociated missions).[9] In a detailed statistical analysis of missions activity, David Barrett reports that 409,000 missionary presence hours leads to only 12,800 hours of direct evangelism. If his figures are accurate, the math reveals that the average Western missionary spends only 3 percent of his time in preaching the Gospel to the lost.[10]

SUBSTITUTING SOCIAL WORK.

This is by far the most popular replacement for evangelism on the mission field today. Because most Two-Thirds World nations refuse to welcome foreign evangelists, many missionaries and sending agencies have changed their image in the host country. They now seek to come to the mission field as agricultural and development workers, child-care providers, medical missionaries and teachers.

But fearful that even this humanitarian work will be used as a ruse for evangelism, some nations, such as Nepal, require these missionaries to sign nonproselytizing agreements. Under these contracts, missionaries promise not to evangelize or make converts. (This is such an important subject that an entire chapter will be devoted to it.)

The late Donald McGavran, a respected church-growth spokesman, deplored this trend toward increased emphasis on health, education and economic productivity. "Missiology needs to state clearly that no amount of physical or mental advance outranks spiritual rebirth."[11]

SUBSTITUTING "PRE-EVANGELISM" MINISTRIES.

In some cases, missionaries have been allowed to stay and work in tribal areas as anthropologists and linguists doing translation and literacy work. Again, this is frequently permitted only with restrictions or under nonproselytizing contracts with various departments of host governments.

SUBSTITUTING TECHNICAL MINISTRIES.

In other cases, missionaries have turned to behind-the-scenes ministries, such as becoming audio- or videotape specialists, broadcast producers and technicians, computer programmers, engineers, journalists, mechanics, program managers, pilots and research specialists.

This is a true twilight zone of modern Christian missions. Such ministries are harder to fit into the New Testament pattern of missions. There is no doubt that the aid these specialists provide is increasingly important as mission organizations take advantage of mass media and advanced technology.

SUBSTITUTING "FRATERNAL WORKER" ARRANGEMENTS.

Many missions, unwilling to let go of the established churches and denominational structures they founded generations ago, have discovered ways to keep their missionaries in the country as advisers and counselors to the national church.

Most of these missionaries, because they control strategic foreign funds and have enormous prestige, have in effect become behind-the-scenes executives or program controllers in the national church. They frequently hold teaching positions at the Bible schools and seminaries that supply clergy to national churches. Through scholarship aid and financial grants to hospitals, publishing houses, relief organizations and summer camps, they are able to manipulate and direct the affairs of their so-called indigenous churches.

The tragedy of the career path chosen by these mission leaders is compounded by the fact that their lifestyles often are emulated by emerging indigenous leaders.

SUBSTITUTING SURROGATE MISSIONARIES.

Some missionaries and the denominations or parachurch organizations they represent have found another approach to remaining on the mission field, which they often describe as "using nationals." Unfortunately, this is an accurate description of what actually takes place.

Similar to the fraternal-worker agreement, this scenario unfolds when a wealthy missions organization plays the major role. In an effort to portray an image of success, a foreign missionary will recruit local Christians from existing ministries to staff mass-evangelism or church programs. In some tragic cases, poor indigenous pastors have actually joined a foreign denomination in exchange for a monthly stipend. These new recruits often are photographed for missionary magazines and public relations at home, thus glamorizing the activity of these national workers and especially the Western missionary behind the scenes.

Though the image of effectiveness and success can be sustained for a while, the results on the field are inevitably disastrous. First, when the compensations that first motivated these indigenous workers stop or when their commitment is tested, they often disappear. Second, and more tragic, this type of deception produces all kinds of victims. Nonbelievers in the local community have even more of an excuse to ridicule and refuse God's grace and salvation. As a result, the struggling indigenous church is weakened, and worst of all, unreached souls remain unreached.

USING SHORT-TERM MISSIONS.

There is currently a huge wave of short-term mission programs rising in the United States. The *Latin America Evangelist* website estimates that, in 1998, 450,000 short-term missionaries were sent from North America.[12] Although these trips can be valuable, there are serious issues that need to be addressed. Paul Borthwick issues a challenge to "take a hard look at short-term youth teams because of how much they cost the sending church, how much they cost the missionaries on the field, and because they can easily degenerate into 'adventure vacations for Jesus.'"[13] Rick Wood agrees, "There are many questions that swirl around the effectiveness of these short-term efforts and their sometimes detrimental effects to ongoing mission work on the field."[14] Christian University professor Jim Lo has stated, "When it comes to short-term missions, it's time to herd the cattle back into the pen."[15] He is concerned because he has "seen the damage done by individuals who go on short-term mission trips without training."[16] Richard Slimbach minces no words: "Most would agree that hit and run . . . type missions often do great harm."[17]

The obvious benefit of short-term mission trips is that they can develop a heart for the lost and a passion for the Great Commission. The problem comes when they are seen as an effective way to reach the lost, when in fact they drain much-needed resources from more fruitful methods of sharing Jesus' love with the lost billions of the world. Paul Borthwick admits that "if our goal is to accomplish certain tasks, then probably it would be better to send [the] money."[18] The amount of money it costs to take a two-week missions trip can keep an indigenous missionary on the field for an entire year. No one would argue that a foreigner staying for two weeks will accomplish anything comparable to an indigenous worker on the field for a year. Compare the two expenditures of approximately $1,500:

SHORT-TERM PARTICIPANT	INDIGENOUS MISSIONARY
Labors for two weeks	Labors for one year
Probably doesn't know the language	Knows the language
Is a layman	Is a trained evangelist and/or pastor
Is new to the culture	Knows the culture
Will leave in two weeks	Will be there for years, following up new believers and planting churches

Perhaps a better term for these two-week trips would be "vision tour." People can see the field, and God can instill in them a lifelong desire to see the fulfillment of the Great Commission. Several ingredients are crucial to creating effective short-term trips. These include training in cross-cultural sensitivity, instilling an attitude of going as a learner and servant, being leaders who model servanthood and sacrifice and a debriefing period at the end to help people process how their lives should change as a result of the experience.

USING THE "MY WAY OR ELSE" RESPONSE.

There is one more response to nationalism, though it would probably better be called a nonresponse. It is one of the saddest of all tactics to which some mission organizations have resorted. In the face of rising local aspirations, some missionaries have left the field, abandoning a ministry or project without transferring the ministry to nationals or providing transitional funding.

Two sad examples of this occurred in India. A certain colonial-style mission, which is still respected and raising funds in North America, was denied visa renewals for its last American missionary couple. The couple were actually only token missionaries, mainly left to supervise the work of a fine Bible school with an excellent native staff. The Indian staff members were long ago ready and able to keep the school going. Western missionaries were no longer needed.

But rather than release the school to the Indian church, the missions board half a world away voted to sell off the property and close the school. The native staff and national pastors involved were not consulted in the matter. The decision was a simple one to the American board: No foreign missionary in charge means no more Bible school.

Replacing that particular school will require an enormous capital investment and years of work by the indigenous churches of that language group, if it can be replaced at all. This places on the poor, indigenous church an agonizing new investment in order to maintain a training center for pastors.

In another example, one of the grand old colonial-style missions ended generations of work in North India. One of the most important services it rendered was the sponsorship of a much-needed radio broadcast in the local language. However, because it no longer had any foreign missionary in the country, the mission decided to cancel the broadcast—the only radio program at that time that was reaching over 75 million people! There was no attempt to continue sponsoring the broadcast using any of the dozens of fine indigenous preachers in that state. Like many similar societies, that mission still maintains rigid policies against supporting indigenous missionaries. Although these rules might have seemed to make sense in the Victorian world, they no longer make any sense given the situation on the mission field today.

Another fast-growing trend is for churches to bypass both traditional mission agencies and those that support indigenous workers. They prefer to be their own sending organization. The question is whether these churches have the experience and know-how to be effective. As Stan Guthrie has said, "More churches, especially the mega-churches, bypass the historic agencies, but they reinvent the wheel, fail to provide adequate training and supervision, and hinder coordinated efforts on the field because of the radical independence of their missionary force. . . . More and more missionaries are short term and 'nonprofessional'—leading to what Ralph Winter has called the 'amateurization' of Christian missions. The growth in mission boards and church involvement has not been matched by a commensurate growth in the understanding of either the mission or the church."[19] In another article, Ralph Winter states, "I fear that much of this frontier enthusiasm is ill-prepared and doomed to failure and damage to the cause."[20]

The net result for the work of the once-great missions is stagnation and possible slow death. Their bondage to self-imposed legalism prevents them from being involved in some of the most exciting Christian movements of our day, including evangelism efforts targeting unreached people groups in restricted-access countries.

For the mission that has its eyes fixed on spreading the Gospel and planting churches, there are many ways to continue impacting the Two-Thirds World. But for the mission that still has its focus on keeping Western personnel assigned overseas, there is little future.

NOTES |

1 | David Barrett and Todd Johnson, eds., *World Christian Trends* (Pasadena, CA: William Carey Library, 2001), p. 60.

2 | "Making Tents or Building Churches: An Interview with Mans Ramstad," *Evangelical Missions Quarterly,* October 1996, p. 421.

3 | Kenneth MacHarg, "Medium (Not So) Rare," *Evangelical Missions Quarterly,* July 1998, p. 348.

4 | Peter Deyneka and Anita Deyneka, "Evangelical Foreign Missionaries in Russia," *International Bulletin of Missionary Research,* April 1998, p. 57.

5 | Department of State, "United States Policies in Support of Religious Freedom: Focus on Christians" (www.state.gov/www/global/human_rights/970722_relig_rpt_christian.html).

6 | Bruce Britten, *We Don't Want Your White Religion* (Manzini, Swaziland: Britten, 1984), p. 30.

7 | Cindy Perry, "The Church in Bhutan," *Dharma Deepika,* June 1999, p. 20.

8 | *Ibid.*

9 | Samuel Wilson and John Siewert, eds., *Mission Handbook: North American Protestant Missions Overseas,* 13th ed. (Monrovia, CA: MARC Publications, 1986), p. 616.

10 | David Barrett, "The Fragmentation of Mission into 4,000 Freestanding, Stand-alone Monoliths," *International Journal of Frontier Missions 9,* no. 1 (March 1997).

11 | Donald McGavran, "Missiology Faces the Lion," *Missiology: An International Review 17,* no. 3 (July 1989), pp. 337, 339.

12 | *Latin America Evangelist,* January 2000. Available online at http://www.lam.org/lae/001/shortterm.html.

13 | Paul Borthwick, "Short-Term Youth Teams: Are They Worth It?" *Evangelical Missions Quarterly,* October 1996, p. 403.

14 | Rick Wood, "MF behind the Scenes," *Mission Frontiers,* January 2000, p. 6.

15 | Jim Lo, "What Have We Done?" *Evangelical Missions Quarterly,* October 2000, p. 436.

16 | *Ibid.,* p. 437.

17 | Richard Slimbach, "First, Do No Harm," *Evangelical Missions Quarterly,* October 2000, p. 439.

18 | Borthwick, "Short-Term Youth Teams," p. 406.

19 | Stan Guthrie, "Past Midnight," *Evangelical Missions Quarterly,* January 2000, p. 103.

20 | Ralph Winter, "Three Types of Ministry," *Evangelical Missions Quarterly,* October 1997, p. 420.

3 | THE FUTURE ROLE OF TRADITIONAL MISSIONS

W hatever methods they have used to stay on the field in restricted areas, most North American missionaries overseas will agree that the results of their labors are limited in terms of numbers won to Christ or churches established. Of course, there are a few spectacular success stories in certain places, but a close examination of these will show a strong indigenous missionary structure. Dana Robert reflects, "In retrospect, it is evident that even during the colonial period, indigenous Christians—Bible women, evangelists, catechists, and prophets—were all along the most effective interpreters of Christianity to their own people."[1]

In reality, church growth and witness on the mission field today are occurring largely within the realm of indigenous missionary work. As will be shown in following chapters, indigenous missionaries more easily understand the local culture and adapt quickly to the environment.

It would be unfair to write the obituary for traditional missions. Although many are no longer accomplishing the Great Commission task as effectively as they once were, they still are supported by the prayers and finances of a large segment of the Body of Christ. The regrettable fact is that sentimental attachment of Western believers has blinded them to the need for change.

A REVIVAL OF INTEREST IN TRADITIONAL MISSIONS

Yet, astonishingly enough, there may actually be a revival of interest in traditional foreign missions today. According to Global Evangelization Movement, 3,920 new mission agencies and service organizations have been created in the past 10 years. In an even more staggering estimate, they calculate that 24,580 missions-related groups will have been created by the year 2025.[2]

In spite of recent articles, such as "Reflections on Missionary Malaise" by Jim Raymo and "What's Happening to Missions Mobilization?" by David Dougherty,[3] there are signs of life in traditional Western missions. Missionary recruiting efforts continue at a fast pace. In December 2000, InterVarsity Christian Fellowship's Urbana convention attracted 20,000 students interested in missions and hundreds of mission organizations interested in those students. Millions of dollars were spent on the convention itself, and hundreds of thousands more were spent by mission agencies producing booths and promotional materials. Agency representatives traveled from all over the world to share their vision and burden with career-minded Christian students. The Caleb Project, one of many programs now motivating and mobilizing students into missions, has 30 full-time staff and an annual budget of about $1.5 million.

I thank God for movements such as the Caleb Project and conferences such as Urbana. We need more of these conferences to be a challenge for world evangelization. However, let us keep in mind that it is what we do after we walk out of these conferences that will make the difference in souls saved.

In addition to the hundreds of independent mission boards, societies and religious orders that are recruiting missionaries, nearly every denomination and thousands of local churches are also challenging their best and brightest young people to go out as missionary staff. According to the *Directory of Schools and Professors of Missions and Evangelism in the United States and Canada*, there are now at least 257 schools offering 3,746 mission courses in 661 degree and nondegree programs.

The cost of this missionary education infrastructure is rarely mentioned or analyzed in church and mission budgets. However, one executive officer of a major agency says he believes his mission invests about a quarter of a million dollars in a missionary from the time of acceptance until the completion of the first term of service—a period still considered training time by most missions.[4] The figure sounds more than reasonable, because many missionary educational costs never show up in mission budgets. They are borne by family and friends. A typical missionary educated in the United States, for example, spends four years in college ($60,000), two years in seminary or Bible school ($40,000), and one year raising support ($20,000). None of this shows up formally in the missions education process. These numbers double for married couples, of course, so the actual cost of training a missionary family might easily run as high as $450,000 to $500,000.

The tragedy is that many of these missionaries will not go back to the field for a second term. Robert T. Coote, in his introductory essay to the 13th edition of the *Mission Handbook,* states, "A major category of resignations is first-term casualties. . . . It is generally thought that up to half of all new missionaries do not last beyond their first term."[5] Communicating how difficult it can be for Western missionaries among the unreached, Nik Repkin writes, "Consistently, I've seen godly persons last no more than six months to a year among the unreached."[6]

In addition, thousands of students will complete missionary training and never go to the field at all. As a result, the whole missionary education process appears inefficient. There is more than a little irony involved in the fact that missiology was an unknown academic subject during the halcyon days of Western missions.

Meanwhile, mission budgets continue to grow year after year. Denominations, mission boards and Christian organizations in the United States and Canada raised $3.3 billion in 1999 to operate programs for Western church agencies—a growth of 23.2 percent over the previous three years.[7] In fact, 56 new North American mission boards have been formed since 1950. Each new edition of the *Mission Handbook* faithfully records the new mission start-ups.[8]

The challenge to complete world evangelization in the last decade of the 20th century was sounded loudly by many organizations. While the A.D. 2000 movements did much to raise awareness of the need of the unreached, some are concerned that there was more talk than accomplishment. One of these is Jay Gary, who directs the Christian Futures Network in Colorado Springs, an organization whose goal is to "help faith communities cultivate foresight." He contends that the key to completing the Great Commission is "the courage of mission leadership to recognize that it has propagated a scandal of evangelization, in raising the rhetoric of closure without changing its field deployment priorities among the unreached."[9] David Barrett reports a staggering $70 billion spent on 250 plans to evangelize the world by the year 2000. His analysis of the results of these plans is that they were an "abject failure." He states, "What subsequently happened in that decade, however, is completely different to what was promised," and he wonders why "no one has begun apologizing, let alone admitting liability."[10] According to statistics in the *Atlas of World Christianity*, we are falling further and further behind in reaching the world, because population growth is more rapid than our progress in spreading the Gospel.[11]

Another problem is the imposition of plans by Western groups on overseas churches. Bill Taylor is "all too aware of the enormous power of the North American missions machine industry enterprise—how out of goodness of heart that machine has so controlled the agenda in so many parts of the world. Here's a time to say, let's stop and lift the machine to see what is happening."[12] David Neff's analysis of the 1999 World Evangelization Fellowship consultation recounted the following: "When the mouse goes dancing with the elephant, the situation is bound to be awkward, and someone is likely to get squashed." He notes Miriam Adeney's image was adopted by many "as they talked about the continuing problems of co-operating in mission with the gung-ho giant up north."[13]

Robert Rasmussen, after talking with a Kenyan missions leader, wrote, "Many of our brothers are responding to our campaigns by 'checking out.' [They] are not responding to strategies from 'outside.'"[14]

He adds, "Non-Western nations are tired of being asked to subscribe to the big schemes of the United States and the United Kingdom. . . . Their concerns focused on ministry survival: paying rent on the church building, getting Bibles for their services, and so on."[15] What this Kenyan brother needed was not a grandiose plan and Western personnel but some simple and practical help with the church rent and some money to buy Bibles.

In the future, will we support and encourage indigenous missionary movements, or will we insist on coming in and running more programs on the backs of the nationals?

WHY TRADITIONAL MISSIONS MUST NOT EXCLUDE NATIONALS

If I were to claim that the Model T Ford was the greatest method of transportation of all time, I doubt anyone would take me seriously. True, in its day, the Model T was on the cutting edge of technology. We look admiringly back to this turning point in transportation history. But that day is over. You and I realize this, and we've moved ahead with the times to faster and more efficient ways of getting around.

Unfortunately, many colonial-style mission organizations are still clinging to their Model Ts, holding up traditional mission methods as the best way to reach the world. They have not seriously considered their practices, choosing rather to remain in the past and refusing to move forward. Here are some of the principles they are ignoring.

TRADITIONAL PRACTICES ARE NOT BIBLICAL.

The Bible teaches clearly in Romans 10:14–15 that some will "go" and others will "send" them. There is no reason whatsoever to interpret this verse to mean that missionaries must be Western. Yet this is exactly how many North Americans still unconsciously define a missionary.

I experienced this underlying resistance in my conversation with the missions pastor of a large southern California church. He had invited me to be the principal speaker at the church's annual missions conference. I was encouraged to hear of their $1 million missions budget. *This church must really desire to see the world reached for Christ,* I thought.

As I talked with the missions pastor, however, I discovered that out of the 10 members of their board, nine are retired, colonial-style missionaries. Then I learned that the missions policy of this church specifically states that it will not support indigenous or national missionaries. The only people they support are those sent out from their own church or from related American organizations. I told the missions pastor, "I'll be glad to speak at your church, but you'll have to change your policy."

He smiled sadly and said, "I don't see any hope of that, Brother K.P." Needless to say, I didn't speak at that church.

We are living in an age when over half the world's population—and the majority of the unreached people—live in countries that restrict Western missionaries. If this church is truly committed to evangelizing the world, sending out their own people should *not* be their number-one priority! Their impact on the world today would be multiplied many times over if they considered indigenous missionaries. But they are stuck in a rut of traditional missions.

TRADITIONAL PRACTICES ARE NOT COST-EFFICIENT.

Comparing figures from eight major mission organizations, the average annual cost of maintaining a Western missionary family on the foreign field is now about $61,000. This same amount of money will support an average of 60 indigenous missionaries in Asia. In most of the Two-Thirds World mission fields, where the per capita income remains about $300 a year, it is not uncommon for indigenous missionaries to live on $3 to $5 a day. Paul Uptigrove, president of Dalgrove Inc., has analyzed the effectiveness of traditional versus indigenous missions. Based on cost per missionary and number of new believers per missionary, he concludes that indigenous missionaries are between 75 and 175 times more productive per dollar spent.[16]

A world population of 6.2 billion requires hundreds of thousands of new missionaries to be sent—perhaps as many as 1 million Gospel workers in order to reach everyone. Even 100,000 new workers, at an average of $61,000, would require an additional $6.1 billion of giving to missions. This would demand a 184-percent increase in the amount of money given each year to missions. Indeed, many fear the opposite trend—that a reduction in giving will occur in the coming years due to the poor giving habits of today's younger believers.

It is hard to imagine even the richest nations on earth picking up the tab for the missionary force needed to reach a world population of over 6 billion people. In fact, finances are already a major problem in reaching the world with the Gospel. Woodrow Kroll, in the *Home Front Handbook,* states, "Tragically, those who are called and trained can't find enough financing to get to the field."[17] Missions leader George Verwer laments, "The lack of finance is a major factor in holding up the work of God."[18]

Clearly, it is no longer merely inefficient to support only Western missionaries, but it is actually cost-prohibitive. We simply cannot afford to operate under the delusion that the world can be won to Christ by sending our own people overseas. Yet this seems to be the basic presupposition of the majority in the North American missions establishment.

Please don't misunderstand me: I am *not* saying the cost involved in sending a missionary should be the highest criterion to determine who goes and who stays. However, we do need to take this factor into consideration as we move toward world evangelism.

TRADITIONAL PRACTICES PRESUME THAT WESTERNERS HAVE SUPERIOR KNOWLEDGE, FAITH, LOVE AND SPIRITUALITY.

The day of "the white man's burden" is past. There is nothing in Western Christianity or technology that makes it mandatory for the indigenous churches of Asia and Africa to import Western missionary experts.

The primary work of missions—making disciples and establishing churches—is actually often hindered by overeducated, technologically dependent people. Church planting is a work best done by simple servants who are as much as possible like the people they are reaching.

WHY TRADITIONAL MISSIONS RESIST CHANGE

If Western missionaries are not more effective on the field, why do most traditional-style mission boards still make a North American staff policy the cornerstone of their approach to world evangelism? If the following reasons are the motivation, I believe they must be challenged.

INERTIA CREATED BY DENOMINATIONAL PROGRAMS, TRADITIONS AND PAST MOVEMENTS.

In many churches and groups, the foreign missions program is a sentimental bureaucratic tradition that just can't be axed, even though the program staff may long ago have lost the zeal for world evangelism.

Without a fired-up champion to lead the missions program, it can wither and die. Unfortunately, there are always those willing to say, "We've always done it this way."

A DESIRE TO PERPETUATE PET DOCTRINES AND DENOMINATIONS.

This could be true not only of theological teachings but of church structures and programs as well. Many missions, in an effort to emphasize a particular school of thought, divide the indigenous church on the mission field along the same doctrinal lines as in the West. They introduce their "distinctives" and biblical interpretations as exclusively correct.

This is true for many groups, not just cults or individuals who have become obsessed with a specific doctrine. These divisive teachers may be biblically correct but are unbalanced in their emphasis. They gain a following by stressing a particular interpretation that would normally be innocent in itself. When any doctrine, even a correct one, is emphasized in a way to develop a personal following and divide the Body of Christ, it becomes sinful. And too often so-called correct doctrine is used as a tool to perpetuate or gain power or create a splinter group.

A DESIRE TO INTRODUCE ECONOMIC OR POLITICAL SYSTEMS.

When groups politicize mission agencies, using them to promote particular economic systems or political schemes of government, the church is divided. Many conciliatory denominations and agencies have fallen into this trap in recent years. They have found that some of their innocuous old mission organizations have been infiltrated by political activists eager to use church agencies to bring about social change secretly.

In a *Reader's Digest* article titled "Do You Know Where Your Church Offerings Go?" Rael Jean Isaac told how one United Methodist group discovered that $442,000 in church funds had gone to fund violent revolutionary movements, including the Palestine Liberation Organization.[19]

Mission agencies make excellent covers in some denominations for individuals whose private agendas would not be accepted by local congregations or even the denomination itself. Some of these have been so radically unbiblical as to include illegal support for armed revolution, political lobbying and organizing terrorism and violence.

A HIDDEN DESIRE FOR POWER.

Many mission societies continue to exist long after the cause for their formation, because the leadership refuses to relinquish control. This was already a problem in the New Testament church, where such people are described as "being lords over God's heritage" (1 Peter 5:3). These are men and women who, like Diotrephes in 3 John 9, love "to have the preeminence," lording it over the people of God and exploiting them for personal gain.

Unfortunately, some missions have provided an excellent vehicle for individuals to gain this kind of unholy respect and following, both at home (where they raise funds) and on the mission field (where they lord it over others).

A DESIRE FOR ADVENTURE, CAREER DEVELOPMENT AND ECONOMIC GAIN.

Many youthful staff, I believe, can be attracted to missions for these mixed motivations of the flesh. Some missions recruiters, eager to fill staff gaps on the field, have turned to the use of specialists and short-term workers. Instead of appealing for simple obedience to the Great Commission, some missions recruitment is turning into a giant job fair, with candidates choosing missions based on career development.

These kinds of motives, of course, exist in all of us. However, they are not worthy of the Lord and can be dangerous to the mission. Leaders who are driven by such desires can be poor decision makers. When called on to make sober judgments affecting the destiny of lost souls, multitudes of people, and even nations, their reasoning can all too often be blinded by self-serving emotions. Billions of mission dollars are too often directed to ineffective programs. Valuable young lives are being wasted by improper assignments.

Meanwhile, there are thousands of unreached people groups—billions of people among whom there is no indigenous community of believers large enough or strong enough to evangelize their neighbors. These billions of lost souls are falling off the edge into an eternity without Christ while much of the resources of the global church remains occupied elsewhere. This is one of the most devastating heritages of traditional-style missions.

It is time to reform those mission agencies that are still flexible—and perhaps close down those that have outlived their usefulness. In other words, let's look at the spiritual bottom line and take the action necessary to make missions a profitable *spiritual* investment.

I believe God continues to call His people from all over the world to reach the lost, and this includes the church in the West. It is not an either/or question of the indigenous missionary or the Western missionary. When God calls a man or a woman, he or she must obey.

During the 19th-century era of missionary activity, when missionaries like William Carey and Hudson Taylor gave their lives to reach the lost, the number-one priority for the Church was to send Western missionaries to heathen lands. But now times have changed. According to God's plan, in nearly every nation new churches are being established. Indigenous missionaries are being raised up by God to reach their own people and the neighboring unreached areas. This is the third and, I believe, the final era of missionary movement.

Thus, for the Western church today, priority number one must no longer be *going* but rather must be *sending*. Priority number two, then, should be *going as servants* to train and assist our brothers and sisters in finishing this final task.

NOTES |

1 | Dana Robert, "Shifting Southward: Global Christianity since 1945," *International Bulletin of Missionary Research,* April 2000, p. 53.

2 | David B. Barrett and Todd M. Johnson, "Status of Global Mission, 2000, in Context of 20th and 21st Centuries," *International Bulletin of Missionary Research,* January 2000.

3 | Jim Raymo, "Reflections on Missionary Malaise," *Evangelical Missions Quarterly,* July 1998, pp. 276–280, and David Dougherty, "What's Happening to Missions Mobilization?" *Evangelical Missions Quarterly,* October 1997, pp. 442–446.

4 | David J. Hesselgrave, *Today's Choices for Tomorrow's Mission* (Grand Rapids, MI: Zondervan, 1988), p. 166.

5 | Samuel Wilson and John Siewert, eds., *Mission Handbook: North American Protestant Missions Overseas,* 13th ed. (Monrovia, CA: MARC Publications, 1986), p. 63.

6 | Nik Repkin, "Why Are the Unreached Unreached?" *Evangelical Missions Quarterly,* July 1996, p. 288.

7 | John A. Siewert and Dotsey Welliver, eds., *Mission Handbook: USA and Canada Christian Ministries Overseas,* 18th ed. (Wheaton, IL: Evangelical Missions Information Service, 2000), pp. 34, 56.

8 | *Ibid.,* pp. 36, 57.

9 | Stan Guthrie, "Past Midnight," *Evangelical Missions Quarterly,* January 2000, p. 101.

10 | David B. Barrett and Todd M. Johnson, eds., *World Christian Trends, A.D. 30-A.D. 2200* (Pasadena, CA: William Carey Library, 2001), pp. xiii–xiv.

11 | "Atlas of World Christianity" (book review), *Evangelical Missions Quarterly,* January 2000, p. 120.

12 | Interview with WEF Leaders, *Evangelical Missions Quarterly,* April 2000, p. 228.

13 | David Neff, "Stepping on Toes," *Evangelical Missions Quarterly,* April 2000, p. 238.

14 | Robert Rasmussen, "Global Push or Grandiose Schemes?" *Evangelical Missions Quarterly,* July 1996, p. 274.

15| *Ibid.,* p. 276.

16| Paul Uptigrove, "Comparison of Missions Strategies" (http://www.dalgrove.com/mission_strategies.htm).

17| Woodrow Kroll, *Home Front Handbook: How to Support Missions behind the Lines* (Tyrone, GA: Operation Mobilization, 1994).

18| George Verwer, "Out of the Comfort Zone" (http://www.thinkwow.com/comfortzone).

19| Rael Jean Isaac, "Do You Know Where Your Church Offerings Go?" *Reader's Digest,* reprint ed. (Pleasantville, NY: 1983), pp. 1–2.

4 | WHITE THINK

Besides bequeathing to us the current system of sending white missionaries abroad, the colonial era left the missions enterprise of the Church with another legacy: a worldwide social services network. This welfare operation has become so bloated and so widespread that the bulk of missions giving in many churches and denominations ultimately ends up there.

In Mark 16:15, Jesus gave us His vision to fulfill: "Go ye into all the world, and preach the gospel to every creature." But it is hard to imagine churches ever fulfilling that vision until we rethink the priorities of our mission programs. Unless sending churches work to restore a biblical balance to their missions outreach, the projects and people they support will become increasingly ineffective.

To understand the damage this emphasis on social services has done to the overall cause of missions, it is important to note how this relates to the implied social mandate that colonial missionaries carried into their work. This issue is not new to missions. The apostles dealt with it in Acts 6, and it became a problem again in Victorian colonialism. The hidden social agenda of 19th-century missions was very real, even though the missionaries themselves were seldom aware of it.

I am deeply grateful for the commitment and dedication of those early missionaries who left the comforts of their homelands to fulfill the Great Commission. However, like even the most sensitive bicultural missionaries today, to some extent they were prisoners of the time and place in which they were born. To some degree or another, they carried with them the dominant worldview of the culture that sent them forth: a superiority complex toward the nonindustrialized lands that had been conquered by the West.

Therefore, it is easy to see how the typical colonial-era missionary could be sent to the mission field with a dual motivation: to convert the heathen to Christianity, thereby helping bring the benefits of Christian civilization to primitive societies. Though they seldom actually admitted it, missionaries envisioned as part of their calling a new world cast in the mold of Christian Europe.

This mentality—the "white man's burden"—had a profound impact on missionary practices and principles then, as it does in an updated form still today. This assumption of cultural and scientific superiority opened a wide door for the present confusion in the definition of what Christian missions should be about.

Such a mentality has convinced many Western missionaries that they have something better to give the nationals in addition to the Gospel. Best-selling author Gayle Erwin *(The Jesus Style)* says it is based on "white think." This system of false assumptions includes the following ideas:

- White people can evangelize the world alone.
- Third World people are ignorant of the Scriptures.
- Third World people are just plain ignorant.
- Western technology and prosperity make us better than others.
- Third World people should submit to us when we go to their countries.
- We can easily learn the truth by observing and asking questions.
- Third World churches should adopt Western customs and buildings.
- Third World people cannot be trusted with money or leadership.[1]

Erwin's list is actually longer than this, but these eight points give an idea of what "white think" is all about. In practical terms, this approach has opened the door for Western missions to add a great many programs to evangelism, including just about every trade, skill and professional training that deals with human services. Most damaging of all, this "save society" emphasis has scrambled the priorities of the sending churches. Most local church leaders and many pastors in the West cannot state the goal of their missions program.

Is social reform, compassionate concern or evangelism to be the driving purpose of missions? Tens of millions of Christians in the United States and Europe cannot reply correctly to this question. Fundraising promotions have merged the three into one, and the average Christian can no longer separate the Gospel of Christ from the various social gospels of religious humanism.

"The future of the world hinges on what we make of this word mission," writes Ralph Winter. "Yet at this moment mission is almost universally misunderstood—in both liberal and conservative circles.

"About the only people who still think of mission as having to do with preaching the gospel where Christ is not named (being a testimony to the very last tribe and nation and tongue on this earth) are the oft-confused people in the pew. In this matter, their instincts outshine those of many eminent theologians and ecclesiastical statesmen."[2]

All this confusion has a legitimate basis in history. Social justice and human need were strong motivating forces both for the early missionaries and for those who sent them. The list of outstanding social reforms that missionaries brought to the Two-Thirds World in the 19th century is a long one. In one colony after another, missionaries introduced democracy, elections, education, literacy, modern medicine, printing, sanitation and women's rights.

Amy Carmichael, who gave 55 years of service to India without a furlough, helped change the direction of a nation. The fellowship she organized in Dohnavur helped save thousands of children from the degradation of temple prostitution. In addition, her unrelenting revelations of the secret temple rituals finally pressured Hindu and government leaders to ban the despicable practice of "marrying children to the gods"—a custom that made adolescent girls available sexually to male worshipers of Hindu idols.[3]

But not all such attempts to bring the fruits of Christian civilization to native populations were as successful, especially when the tree of Christian faith had not yet had time to take root itself. The sordid history of pressured conversions and mass baptisms and the premature institution of civil religion in many parts of Latin America created some of the most regrettable chapters in the story of colonial-era missions.

No one involved in missions today, of whatever theological persuasion, can escape association with the history of traditional missions, in both its positive and negative sides.

THE RISE OF MISSIONARY INSTITUTIONS

In retrospect, many of the vast efforts at social engineering by missionaries were kind, gentle and helpful, even if they were not always biblical or effective. No one can deny that some of the most progressive changes in colonial society were wrought through the creation of thousands of 19th-century institutions. Mission hospitals, leprosariums, orphanages and schools became the most visible evidence of missionary presence during the Great Century from the mid-1800s to 1939.

The institutions founded by these earlier missionaries had a sweetness about them that seemed to charm everyone, including the missionaries themselves. Many argued that switching to the institutional approach would create a positive identity for missionaries in the community, opening unlimited opportunities for evangelism and witness.

It was argued that, as people were healed and educated by Christians, they would automatically develop an interest in Jesus, the Gospel and the church. Although history has often proved these theories to be flawed, there is no mistaking the positive public relations value these missionary institutions had at the time. Furthermore, institutional work created goodwill toward the church and missions from indigenous populations, the secular and religious media, and supporters in the homeland.

In difficult political times, these humanitarian institutions gave missionaries a legitimate and useful reason to remain in the colonies. Their economic impact was great. They created many jobs for nationals, both in the institution itself and in the surrounding community. Whole towns and neighborhoods grew up around some mission hospitals and schools. The institutions themselves often became important sources of income for the mission and national church—from outright donations as well as from fees and tuitions.

It is no wonder that, by the turn of the 20th century, missionary clinics and schools were well established almost everywhere, usually following the railways and waterways into the farthest interiors of every continent. Denominational mission boards in the sending nations and their furloughing missionaries appealed for funds to pioneer and operate these institutions, thus effectively blurring the lines between evangelistic and humanitarian programs in the minds of home-church supporters.

Except for a few brave exceptions, such as Anglican missionary to China Roland Allen and Henry Venn of the Church Missionary Society, 19th-century church leaders treated the institutional approach as normative. Allen (who would later write several mission classics, including *Missionary Methods: St. Paul's or Ours?*) was one of the lone voices who spoke out against the rising tide of evangelism by institution.

Charles Henry Long and Anne Rowthorn wrote that Allen "questioned the priority given to schools and similar institutional work over evangelism. By establishing schools and hospitals and committing to them rather than to the churches, the bulk of their budgets and personnel and missionary societies were not only trying to take 'the best of the West' to backward peoples, but they were trying to establish new cultural norms for them. In its extreme form this strategy led to the assumption that Western higher education was not only an expression of, but almost a precondition for, the life of the church."[4]

Henry Venn wrote of the "euthanasia" of missions as early as 1854 and began using the "three self" terms to describe the coming indigenous church for the first time. He argued not for institutions but for mission agencies that would create self-governing, self-supporting, and self-propagating churches and then "die out."[5]

The movement toward a social gospel was so broad in English and American Protestantism that it is difficult to put a finger on one man, one date or one movement that was pivotal. However, if one name stands out above all others, it would have to be that of William Booth.

Booth's life and ministry have challenged me to the core, and I thank God for raising up this man to reach his generation. A former Methodist evangelist, ministering to the slums of London, Booth dramatically combined humanitarianism and evangelism into what eventually became known as the Salvation Army. As one of the most famous of many new missions formed during this period, the Salvation Army concentrated solely on what would now be described as a "holistic ministry" that spread around the world in less than 25 years. Virtually every colony had a lively Salvation Army presence, and many other organizations duplicated its programming style and techniques.

Many committed evangelical leaders loaned their names and support to help found such organizations as the YMCA (the Young Men's Christian Association), and these humanitarian spin-offs of the church spread to every corner of the globe. Not surprisingly, the majority of missions and their supporting churches jumped on the social-service bandwagon to some extent.

However, the primary focus of these social organizations began to drift away from evangelism. Few stopped to compare these popular theologies with the teachings of Jesus and the apostles about the Great Commission. Social reform and charity were equated with evangelism in the minds of millions, and by the turn of the century, it was a logical assumption that social services were an integral part of missions. To many, in fact, social services *were* missions, and some missionaries were quite comfortable perpetuating this misconception. It took the offense of the cross away and gave them an easily accepted platform on which to stand.

The Tragic Harvest of the Social Gospel

Two world wars and a Great Depression later, liberal belief in the ultimate goodness of mankind and the hope of "heaven on earth" had been rocked to its foundations. The philosophical and theological underpinnings of the social gospel were gone.

Institutional evangelism had already proved itself ineffective in making converts or establishing Christian churches. It wasn't until the decades following the independence of colonial countries that missionary advocates of education, health and welfare were able to see the disappointing results of their misguided zeal. The hoped-for Christian presence in postcolonial governments seldom materialized. When it did, it was soon snuffed out by anti-Christian forces.

Far from ushering in the kingdom of God, in many cases the schools and universities founded by missionaries were themselves taken over and used as bases for terrorism and bloodshed! In what is now Myanmar, the American Baptist University of Rangoon was nationalized, along with all other mission schools and hospitals, in 1960. After the missionaries were deported and Burmese church leaders were removed, the school was used to propagate a Marxist projection for Myanmar's future. The University of Rangoon continues to turn out the ruling elite for one of the most corrupt and oppressive governments in the world.

In China, the Presbyterian Seminary in Nanjing became the headquarters of the Great Cultural Revolution, which persecuted millions of Christians and led to many senseless deaths. It became the center of the Communist Party–controlled Three-Self Patriotic Church. The YMCA in Shanghai, which was once the flagship of a vast network of Chinese Ys, was turned into a center of torture and murder by the Red Guards during the Great Cultural Revolution.

In India, as hundreds of Christian schools and hospitals came under government control, they were often used to propagate secular humanism more effectively than they had propagated Christianity under missionary control. There are also frequent stories in the Indian media of converts from these missions who have now reverted to animism,

Hinduism and idolatry. Christian hospitals and the mission compounds around them often attracted so-called "rice Christians" (converts who joined the church primarily for material gain). When the missions payroll ended, so did their "faith."

In Africa, where Christian missions are now heavily involved in providing relief, development and nation-building services, their ministries are opening few new doors for evangelistic witness.

Even in countries that have remained open to the West, continued institutional outreach has had little impact on evangelism. Two clear Asian examples are Nepal and Thailand. In both these countries, where there are extensive networks of Christian institutions involving hundreds of foreign missionaries, few Christian converts can be traced to the work of these institutions.

In Thailand, it is true, churches have been started in Chaing Mai, Monoram and Bangkok near Christian hospitals. A close examination of the work, however, reveals that most of these churches would have formed anyway, regardless of the institutions associated with them.

These are not rare examples. The story is almost the same wherever one looks. Institutions have been ineffective at winning converts or planting churches. Few missionaries working in an institutional context, by the very nature of the structural constraints, can do effective evangelism. Furthermore, by their calling and gifts, they are often unsuited for discipleship and church-planting outreach—the essential elements of any Great Commission ministry.

NOTES |

1 | Gayle Erwin, "How to Overcome 'White Think' in Cross Cultural Ministries," *Servant Quarters,* Summer 1989, pp. 1–7.

2 | Ralph Winter, "The Meaning of 'Mission,'" *Mission Frontier,* July 1987, p. 3.

3 | Ruth A. Tucker, *From Jerusalem to Irian Jaya* (Grand Rapids, MI: Zondervan, 1983), pp. 240–241.

4 | Charles Henry Long and Anne Rowthorn, "The Legacy of Roland Allen," *International Bulletin of Missionary Research,* April 1989, p. 65.

5 | Stephen Neill, *A History of Christian Missions* (Baltimore, MD: Pelican, 1964), pp. 259–260.

5 | WHAT ABOUT DEVELOPMENT AND TENTMAKING?

Missions, including even the most evangelical, seem as though they haven't learned lessons from the past failures of their social work. Many mission executives, frustrated by government restrictions on evangelistic work, still cling to the concept of institutions and social work because it is often the only way they can get visas to stay in some countries.

SOCIAL WORK VERSUS SOUL WINNING

Many evangelical missionaries still claim they engage in social work because they believe it will provide opportunities to witness. Although this may be true in some cases, year after year, many show little evangelistic results for their efforts and expense. According to missions expert George Verwer, "Statistics show that a quarter of North American cross-cultural missions are currently engaged in translation, evangelization, church planting, and teaching. Three-quarters are assigned to administration and support work . . . such as agriculture, aviation, community development, literacy, medicine, and relief efforts."[1]

Of 28,100 Christian organizations cited by Gem-werc, 24,000 (84.5 percent) are listed as service organizations, and the other 4,000 (14.5

percent) are mission-sending organizations.[2] David Barrett's article "The Fragmentation of Missions" presents numbers indicating that only three percent of missionaries spend their time doing direct evangelism.[3]

Andrew Peat, a former missionary to Taiwan, summarizes, "I just knew that there were hundreds of foreign missionaries in Taiwan who needed to raise phenomenal amounts of support. Most of them did little or no church planting or evangelism."[4]

A glance through the help-wanted lists of various mission organizations shows that only a small percentage of the open positions on the field today are for church planting or evangelistic missionaries. Instead, the need list includes an amazing variety of occupations: administrators; secretaries; health care providers; construction workers; linguists; mechanics; computer programmers; electricians; teachers of music, English, math and science; and transportation workers. These are the kinds of workers the evangelical mission boards most strongly seek. Even fewer missionary positions are offered for soul winners in the older, less evangelical churches and denominations.

For example, Bishop C. Dale White, an important ecumenical leader in New York, attacked the Mission Society for United Methodists, saying that its practice of sending evangelists overseas was "completely out of touch with reality." In an article in the *Dallas Times Herald,* he is quoted as saying that the evangelical Methodist group was a "divisive force" for suggesting a return to spiritual ministries.[5]

Bishop White's view is shared by most of the denominations of the National Council of Churches—and regrettably by some conservative evangelical church leaders as well. Yet the majority of American churches continue to send some missionary staff overseas, usually with denominations or missions historically associated with their founders. Invariably, many of these workers find themselves involved in maintenance activities of programs such as Christian education, theological education and social work.

Evangelistic missionaries are almost nonexistent in the older denominations. For example, a qualified spokesperson for the Protestant Episcopal Church in the United States, who was interviewed for this book, said that less than one percent of its overseas missionaries are primarily involved in evangelism and church planting.

Denominational leadership, both conservative evangelical and liberal, often establishes relationships with sister churches on mission fields. Because of this, there is a strong tendency to assume Two-Thirds World evangelism is complete or that it is the sole responsibility of the indigenous church. This leaves the door open for North American missionaries to put their emphasis on helping to maintain existing churches and to provide social services as a "witness" to secular society.

The National Council of Churches, therefore, focuses most of the remaining missionary zeal on the historic, mainline churches through its Church World Service (CWS) division. The CWS website indicates that its $69.8 million budget in 2001 went for an array of social-economic programs, such as:

- The HIV-Positive South African Choir tour
- An agricultural rehabilitation program in Sierra Leone
- Gender-inclusive initiatives in India

Development is the current buzzword used by the missionary social workers involved with conciliatory associations. Rural development includes many programs so secularized that entire staffs are not even nominally Christian, such as the Muslim workers hired to run so-called Christian credit unions for Indonesian villages. Many of these highly politicized programs go far beyond the simple charitable and relief efforts, which are the thrust of emotional fundraising appeals. So, by design, they are almost always separated from proclamation of the Gospel.

WHAT ABOUT MISSIONARY TENTMAKERS?

In addition to direct missionary social work, there is a popular movement today urging Western Christians to go overseas as bivocational "missionary tentmakers," again mostly as advisers, educators, social workers and technicians. The term *tentmaking* comes from the apostle Paul's practice of supporting himself in the tentmaking industry while preaching the Gospel.

Nearly 10,000 North Americans are teaching English in China at this time, according to Teri McCarthy in an article in the *Evangelical Missions Quarterly*.[6] Tentmakers who were interviewed in China repeatedly said the Chinese government prefers Christians for these positions.

Unlike missionary social work, which directly drains support funds away from evangelism and church-planting work, most of these tentmakers are supposedly earning a regular salary overseas and therefore should not have to raise support from sending churches. These tentmakers should be witnessing in their daily lives, as every Christian is called to do, and to the extent that they do so, they certainly deserve the prayers and encouragement of mission-minded congregations.

However, the following flags of caution must be raised whenever this kind of outreach is loosely labeled as "missionary."

Are they really cost free? Steven Rundle observes that many businesses that are set up as a front for doing evangelism lose money and therefore "actually add to the cost of missionary work." Ruth Siemens, quoted by Rundle, goes even further: "Phantom businesses sooner or later bring shame to the name of Christ."[7]

Are tentmakers adequately prepared? Rundle laments that "almost nothing has been available, until recently, that adequately prepares the student in both business and . . . evangelism skills."[8] Finally, he concludes that some of the blame for the problems of tentmakers rests on "a schizophrenic church that is more confused than ever about . . . how to appropriately mobilize, train and support tentmakers."[9]

How free will the tentmaker be to witness? Many Muslim and other closed countries insist that such workers sign nonproselytizing agreements. How can a tentmaker sign such an agreement with a clear conscience? Mans Ramstad observes, "Every tentmaker wants to use the title 'missionary.' Regardless of the title used, the question is whether they want to work toward traditional missionary goals of evangelism and church planting. We suspect that for various reasons, many don't."[10]

How much free time will the tentmaker have available to spend in discipling converts and forming churches? Often tentmaking work for foreigners involves high-level job responsibilities that intrude into free time, preventing the tentmaker from having enough unscheduled time to do true missionary work. Any successful bivocational ministry overseas requires that the tentmaker have long periods of free time. A secular job would distract from one-on-one disciple making, small-group meetings and the other extended periods needed for witnessing and follow-up.

One tentmaker reflects, "Tentmaking, like communism, is a good idea in theory. . . . It worked for me once when I didn't have kids and a serious full-time job. But usually, we tentmakers are a lot more like active laypeople than like Paul, our erstwhile inspiration."[11]

How much freedom will the tentmaker have to move openly in local society? Unless the tentmaker lives in a dormitory or in another intimate situation, such as a private home, crossing cultural and language barriers may be extremely frustrating. Many tentmaking positions require the expatriate to work in isolated and difficult circumstances, separate from the people of the land. Tentmaking positions in management often require the foreigner to be involved in local politics and require him or her to avoid involvement in religion and the lives of the common people.

Some English teacher tentmakers in China have had extraordinary opportunities to witness for Christ and have even started small Bible study groups on campus. There is no doubt that many tentmakers grow spiritually during their time there.

But a word of caution: Cross-cultural missionary work should not be undertaken as a time to "discover one's own ministry" or to experiment with personal callings at the expense of Two-Thirds World populations! Gayle Erwin has said it well:

> If you have not developed your capabilities and proven your ministry here at home, do not expect that you can do so over there. To be a tourist and observe might be appropriate, but to go to another country to "find" your

ministry is to become an instant burden to them.

First of all, your thoughts are inward as you still develop and find yourself, and you are unable to be truly others-centered.

Second, you absorb their energies as they try to figure out just what to do with you without hurting you. Just because you are white does not mean that other countries welcome you with open arms. Most countries will not give you a long-term visa unless you have skills that are needed and in short supply. The kingdom is not in short supply of people trying to "find" themselves.[12]

To summarize, the most important question to ask yourself is this: *Can I tentmake and still preach the Word?* We need to remember that in these tentmaking or "social work" situations, nothing ever happens for God until somebody presents the Gospel. The missionary must have freedom and time to present the Word of God clearly and openly. Disciples must first be made and then be formed into living churches. This alone is valid New Testament missionary work and is the only kind that should be considered for financial support from sending churches. Though the apostle Paul at times supported himself making tents, his primary activity was evangelistic.

Despite these difficulties, tentmaking holds exciting promises, and it will be interesting to see how this kind of outreach develops over the coming years.

NOTES |

1 | George Verwer, "Out of the Comfort Zone" (http://www.thinkwow.com/ comfortzone).

2 | World Evangelization Research Center, "Status of Global Mission" (http:// www.gem-werc.org).

3 | David Barrett, "The Fragmentation of Missions into 4,000 Freestanding, Stand-alone Monoliths," *International Journal of Frontier Missions 9*, no. 1 (March 1997).

4 | Andrew Peat, "Redefining Missions," Christian Aid (http://www.christianaid.org/ redefine).

5 | "Methodist Bishop Blasts Group's Overseas Mission," *Dallas Times Herald,* July 8, 1988.

6 | Teri McCarthy, "A Call to Arms: Forming a Christian Worldview of Teaching English," *Evangelical Missions Quarterly*, July 2000, p. 311.

7 | Steven L. Rundle, "Ministry, Profits, and the Schizophrenic Tentmaker," *Evangelical Missions Quarterly*, July 2000.

8 | *Ibid.*, p. 296.

9 | *Ibid.*, p. 299.

10 | *Ibid.*, p. 292.

11 | Phil Skotte, "Confessions of a Tentmaker Turned Layman," *Evangelical Missions Quarterly*, July 2000, p. 292.

12 | Gayle Erwin, "How to Overcome 'White Think' in Cross Cultural Ministries," *Servant Quarters*, Summer 1989, p. 2.

6 | WHAT ABOUT SOCIAL JUSTICE AND COMPASSION?

Doesn't the Bible, particularly the Old Testament, have a strong emphasis on compassion, social justice and charity? Certainly. No one can deny that. Sociopolitical involvement is clearly expected by a just and righteous God. Old Testament law makes provision for the aliens, the poor and the widowed. Throughout the law of Moses, God demanded that all oppressed and exploited people be protected.

The laws concerning Jubilee, gleaning, the Sabbath and tithes show God's concern and provision for the poor in society. Some of the most terrible Old Testament judgments fell upon Israel and Sodom and Gomorrah for their exploitation of the poor and needy.

A comparison of Old and New Testaments shows that there can be no argument about the Christian's clear social responsibility (see Genesis 1:26–27, 18:25; Leviticus 19:18; Isaiah 1:17, 58:10–11; Luke 6:27, 35; James 2:14–26). Evangelism, however, is not social action. The Great Commission is not a mandate for political liberation. Disciple making is not charity, although it may involve charity part of the time.

So, although we as individuals and local churches must speak out and be involved in the work of reconciliation and compassion, that doesn't mean we should call it "missions." Nor can God's laws for justice and mercy in the nation of Israel be considered a missions mandate for the

Church to seek social justice as a ministry category.

The cutting edge of biblical, New Testament missions is proclamation, conversion and disciple making that leads to the establishment of local churches. Any time this basic task is confused with political or social action, missions lose their integrity and power.

The New Testament apostles did not turn the world upside-down by social work; they turned the world upside-down by proclaiming the Word of God, which is sharper than any two-edged sword.

SOCIAL WORK IN THE NEW TESTAMENT

But isn't social work a valid New Testament ministry? Didn't Jesus and the apostles concern themselves with the needs of the whole man? Isn't social work, even without soul winning and church planting, a legitimate ministry in its own right? Why shouldn't missionary social workers be sent overseas, because there is a needy world out there?

The only way to answer these questions is to survey the New Testament texts that have been used to advocate social work. They need to be studied in context. We need to see if these proof texts can truly be applied to the Great Commission.

DIDN'T JESUS FEED THE HUNGRY AND HEAL THE SICK, AND AREN'T WE SUPPOSED TO DO THE WORKS THAT HE DID?

Matthew 14:15–21, 20:34; Mark 7:37; Luke 8:49–55; John 9:1–7, 14:12

Those who ask this question may agree with J. Philip Hogan, executive director of the division of foreign missions for the Assemblies of God.

Many people feel that the church should engage in social assistance only for the purpose of prying open doors for the Gospel in restricted-access countries. But if that is our motive for providing assistance to hurting people, then we are the ones who need the help. . . . I want the world to know that the reason we do these things is because Jesus Christ did them.

If our providing social assistance opens doors that would otherwise be closed to the missionary endeavors . . . good! But if not, we will still continue to provide relief. Because opening doors is not our reason for sharing in other people's sufferings. Demonstrating the truth of Christ's words and sharing the love of God are our intent.[1]

Yes, Jesus again and again demonstrated His love and compassion in miracles of healing and provision, but these were only incidental to His main purpose. Our Lord's miracles of feeding and healing were basically signs to prove His identity as Messiah, as He told the disciples of John (Matthew 11:2–5; Luke 7:18–22). Jesus miraculously and symbolically showed compassion to the sick and needy, but His mission here was obviously not to end hunger and disease. If He had wanted to do so, He could have ended all hunger, injustice and disease at any time with a single word.

In Luke 19:10, Jesus clearly stated His primary mission: "For the Son of man is come to seek and to save that which was lost." Jesus knew that the main problem of mankind is sin, and that's why His primary mission was to die on the cross to deliver us from it.

The Great Commission, repeated five times in the Gospels and Acts, stresses preaching and teaching as the main activities of the first missionaries. Obviously, social action and compassionate ministries should not deviate us from the priority of preaching the Gospel and calling sinners to repentance.

DIDN'T THE EARLY CHURCH SELL ALL THEY HAD TO PROVIDE FOR THE NEEDY?

Acts 4:32–37

Yes, it is obvious that the New Testament church, at least in Jerusalem, had an extensive program of social services for widows and orphans within their own membership (see Acts 6:1–3 and 1 Timothy 5:1–16). But the emphasis in these passages is never on meeting the needs of the world or on using social welfare programs as an evangelistic technique.

In fact, when Peter and the other apostles were asked to get involved in social work in Acts 6:4, they actually declined! "But we will give ourselves continually to prayer, and to the ministry of the word," said the Twelve. Prayer and preaching were their missionary priorities, although it is clear they made provision for this important ministry of the local church.

The apostles, our first missionary examples in the Bible, appointed deacons from the local body to oversee social work. How ironic it is that we today have switched this around, so that we are in effect sending our "deacons" abroad to provide social services for people who are not even Christians, let alone members of our local churches!

DIDN'T PAUL COLLECT EMERGENCY RELIEF FUNDS FOR THE SAINTS IN JERUSALEM ON HIS THIRD MISSIONARY JOURNEY?

Romans 15:25–26

Yes, but once again, here is an exception rather than the rule. This was the only time Paul collected relief funds in an emergency, and he did it to help others in the Body of Christ. In 2 Corinthians 8–9, we see that these funds were collected for the brethren and not collected for outreach purposes to the world, as is so common today.

Does this imply that emergency relief and assistance to unbelievers are wrong? Of course not. But we also cannot say that disaster aid and famine relief are required as part of the Great Commission. Nor dare we somehow imagine that rice shipments or milk supplements are evangelism. To argue that such aid is a viable Christian witness, some form of evangelism or even biblical Christian missions is at best fuzzy theology. Its worst case comes when such social aid is presented as a reasonable substitute for evangelism in our church mission budgets.

Surely we cannot ignore human tragedy, such as the famines that kill thousands in Africa and other parts of the world, the AIDS epidemic and the millions who suffer through civil war in our generation. We, as the Body of Christ, must do everything in our power to show His love by taking care of these needs. These are precious people made in the image of God. And our Father cares about them.

But my plea to the Body of Christ is while we must do all we can to meet the needs of the suffering and dying millions, we must not see these activities as a substitute for evangelism and establishing churches among the unreached. A recent editorial in *Mountain Movers* says it well:

> Ministries of compassion are temporal remedies at best. The Church is not here to make this present world better, because this present world is condemned. And Jesus never commissioned His Church to clean up this world. He commissioned His Church to snatch men's hearts out of this world and set them on a path to another world—an eternal, spiritual world.
>
> So we tenaciously follow the pattern of the early Church. They cared for suffering humanity. But they were careful to make certain that those ministries did not replace their primary reason for being—the preaching of the gospel.
>
> Unless their corporate activities ultimately led to the winning of souls and the planting of indigenous churches, they altered those activities. And any activity that supersedes that objective today must also be expunged from the Church's agenda.[2]

DIDN'T JESUS SAY THAT WHEN YOU HELP THE POOR, IT IS THE SAME AS HELPING HIM?

Matthew 25:40

This verse is frequently taken out of context, especially for missionary offerings and appeal letters. Jesus said that when you assist "the least of these my brethren, ye have done it unto me." Who are His brethren? Jesus made it clear in Mark 3:35 that His brethren are those who do the will of God—not everyone in the world, as is frequently heard in the mission appeals for relief. Therefore, social work cannot be justified as an evangelistic technique that requires that we operate billion-dollar relief and development programs in the name of Christ. Of course, every Christian is required to show compassion for other believers who are hungry, in need or imprisoned.

WHAT ABOUT JESUS' PARABLE OF THE GOOD SAMARITAN? DOESN'T THAT
TEACH US TO HELP OUR NEIGHBORS?

Luke 10:30–37

There are many lessons in this parable, but the main point is a warn-
ing against religious legalism and hypocrisy. Any God-fearing believer is
an incredible hypocrite if he or she obeys the letter of the law but breaks
the spirit of it by ignoring a needy person. The Pharisee and lawyer here
put religious ceremony and ritual ahead of love, perverting the whole
law of Moses. That was the main lesson Jesus was trying to make in this
passage.

Again, these verses and others do not establish missionary development and relief ministries as such. Yet today billions of dollars are
involved in this so-called missions work. Charity has been turned into
a business that often dwarfs the ministry of true missions. Whenever
this happens, those in leadership must bring back the correct balance.
Proclamation and teaching must be restored to their primary place.
Then, as the Gospel changes lives, individual Christians will play their
normal role of "salt and light" in society. This method in the long run
brings far more beneficial social change to a community than short-
term programs that seek to force radical change on already established
structures.

RESTORE THE BIBLICAL PRIORITY

As billions of dollars continue to be siphoned off into secondary mission programs, it is time that remedial action be taken to restore the
biblical balance to current mission programs.

The challenge facing leaders of any reformation in missions now is to
separate frontline evangelistic mission efforts from social work. As long
as there are over *2 billion* lost souls who have never heard the Gospel—
and 12,000 unreached people groups without a witness—the need for
New Testament missionaries is overwhelming.

Plainly, the focus of missions must concentrate on placing qualified evangelists and church planters among the hidden people groups and in the unreached areas of the harvest field that have been neglected for too many centuries. Modern mission agencies have confused this still-incomplete pioneer work with maintenance programs for existing churches, with support services and with humanitarian-aid programs.

A gross error, of course, would be to deny the validity of these other ministries. They have a place, but it must be a subordinate one to the central work of presenting the Gospel. The crisis in missions today is not that temporal needs are being neglected, quite the contrary. Any analysis of the trends in our mission budgets will show that we are majoring on the minors. Modern missions has been seriously sidetracked, and it is important for those who understand the necessary balance to restore biblical priorities.

If church and mission leaders in the West don't act soon, those in the pews must. A women's group in a mainline denominational church spoke out through their checkbooks when they discovered where their mission dollars were going. They notified their denomination's women's division that they were withholding half of their yearly pledge. Their reason: concern over where their mission dollars were going.

The conclusion is simple but not easy. Every believer must reexamine every cause and mission that gets his or her support. Learning how to make valid judgment calls and establishing systems that will send support to the missionaries who are really doing pioneer work—these are the challenges of the 21st century.

Satan has presented us with an alluring array of substitutes for the Great Commission. We need to wait humbly upon God for discernment about the validity of the mission causes that get His tithes and offerings.

NOTES |

1 | J. Philip Hogan, "Because Jesus Did," *Mountain Movers,* June 1989, pp. 10–11.
2 | *Ibid.*

7 | WHO IS A MISSIONARY?

I was trying as best I could to comfort a dear Christian leader in our Carrollton, Texas, office. He sat across from me in shock and despair, completely devastated by rejection. As an Indian citizen, he had recently earned his doctorate in theology at a leading seminary. A brilliant Christian teacher, he is one of those rare geniuses whom God has gifted with a command of four languages.

His family had been converted to Christ through the ministry of a leading colonial-era denominational mission that had been in India for generations. Mission officials had encouraged him to leave his wife and children in India and come to the United States for further education. In fact, leaders of his denomination pointed to his achievements as a "trophy of grace" and as one of the triumphs of their long missionary labors in South Asia.

So it was only natural that my Indian brother would want to return to his homeland as a missionary to his own people and that he would apply to that same denominational missions board for support.

Because Americans from the society can no longer receive missionary visas for India, he assumed the mission would want to send him back to carry on and extend the work. He was in for a rude awakening.

His application was graciously received by the American board. They wrote back an effusive letter of praise, affirming the brother and expressing sympathy and moral support for his calling. However, they "regretted" that they had to refuse his application because sending out an indigenous missionary, no matter how qualified, "conflicted with their bylaws."

Although their bylaws didn't say it in so many words, they confirmed in writing the popular definition of a missionary; that is, the person must possess North American citizenship.

WHAT SHOULD DETERMINE MISSIONARY QUALIFICATIONS?

Who is a missionary? What are the basic qualifications for missionary service? Before we look at what the Bible teaches, let us look at some modern definitions and qualifications. In the real world of missions today, New Testament standards for Christian service play such an insignificant role in missionary selection that the Lord Jesus Himself, and probably most of the apostles, would not even get through the screening process for their first interview. Ironically, the well-connected, educated, middle-class, affluent and politically oriented Judas might have "the right stuff" to score well on his application.

The screening procedures for much missionary service today remain rooted in the colonial-era concept of missions. So it should come as no surprise to see that the qualifying process is often prisoner to some of the most prejudiced cultural norms of the 19th century. To be perfectly honest, many mission societies make their staffing decisions much as the Pharisees did in Jesus' day, when they added the Talmud (a book of commentary and interpretations of Scripture) to the Torah. These modern-day Pharisees have added a code of standards and rules to Scripture that are formed primarily by Western culture, so decisions are based not on the Bible but on the traditions and interpretations of men.

The following are six major examples of unbiblical standards.

HAVING EDUCATIONAL DEGREES.

Most missions require a Western liberal arts education for all new candidates, or at least a college degree and some minimum amount of

Bible school training. Many mission boards now give preference to those with master's or other advanced degrees.[1] Such degrees have little to do with successful pioneer missions work. In reality, a Western university education, or even theological training, is often more a hindrance than a help on the mission field. In frontline situations it can erect another barrier that has to be overcome in relating to lost souls. Indeed, most native Christians find that a Western education has to be consciously unlearned before they can begin to minister to their own people!

How different is this emphasis on formal education from the practice of Jesus and the disciples? Jesus was a home-schooled rabbi who didn't train in the leading seminaries of Jerusalem. Rather, He worked with His hands as a common carpenter. Like most of the disciples, who were also blue-collar workers, He lacked a formal education. The Pharisees, in fact, criticized the first missionaries as "unlearned and ignorant men" (Acts 4:13). Actually, they were not ignorant or unlearned because they had studied three years with Jesus, the Son of God, but by the standards of men, they appeared to be such.

My point is not that ignorant missionaries are desirable. We must never stop learning. Missionaries need as much practical Bible training and experience in the ministry as possible. However, we must understand that little of this kind of training comes from the formal, Western education still required by many mission societies.

BEING IN GOOD PHYSICAL AND PSYCHOLOGICAL HEALTH.

I once heard a missions executive state that his organization was not a hospital but a fighting army. (Wounded soldiers, learners and people with problems need not apply!) When problems surfaced in the life of a missionary, this brother eliminated that person from his organization as fast and as quietly as possible.

This unnatural emphasis on health and perfection in Western missions also extends to a distinct prejudice against recruiting older people. It is interesting that Jesus began His ministry at a rather mature 30 years of age—an age that would be the limit for many mission societies today.

HAVING THE "RIGHT" BACKGROUND.

Through letters of reference, interviews and phone calls, Western mission boards often select staff who are the most socially compatible with themselves. Unbiblical standards such as denominational distinctives, race, ethnic heritage, age and social class become important determining factors.

Jesus was a king who gave up His kingdom to be born as a human baby and live a life of simplicity in an obscure village. He identified with the lowest classes of His society and was not afraid to be seen associating with prostitutes and corrupt politicians. The church leaders of His day hated Jesus for this so much that they plotted to kill Him.

HAVING TALENTS AND SKILLS.

"This is the day of the missionary specialist," proclaims recruiting literature handed out at mission conventions to Christian students. The fastest-growing emphasis in Western missions today is on secular technologies and training, such as aviation, anthropology, broadcasting, computerization, construction, electronics, engineering, linguistics, marketing, media, medicine, nursing, rural and village development, sociology, social work and teaching. Thus, the emphasis is on physical and mental abilities rather than on the Holy Spirit and the inner man. This shift began in the 19th century, as pioneer missionary institutions required the first education and medical specialists.

Of course, there is a legitimate need for some skilled personnel. I am not against them, but the emphasis on them has gone so far that reliance on the supernatural appears to play only a minor role in Western-based missions.

BEING AN EXPATRIATE.

Some missiologists have gone so far as to make expatriation a part of the definition of a missionary. Unless a person actually leaves his or her homeland, they claim, he or she is not qualified to be called a missionary! Others vary this theme, insisting that one is not a missionary unless he or she is doing cross-cultural ministry.

Roberta Winter and Richard Cotten address this issue:

> A missionary is someone who is sent to witness of his faith cross-cultur-
> ally. Can he be a native? Not technically speaking. If he is a native of
> the culture where he works, then he is not witnessing cross-culturally.
> Therefore the term indigenous missionary is self-contradictory.[2]

I am saddened by this continued insistence to split hairs on terminol-
ogy. Why is the focus on where indigenous missionaries can and cannot
go, instead of helping them reach the unreached wherever they are?
What about the Lord's constant emphasis on taking the Gospel to the
Jews first? This was missionary work within His own culture, and it was
where the Father instructed Him to place the accent in His outreach. For
Jesus, cross-cultural witness was the exception, not the rule.

In fact, nowhere in the Scriptures were the apostles required to cross
cultures to qualify for missionary service. A few of the early apostles
seem to have served most of their missionary lives in Jerusalem and
Judea.

Given the reality of the mission field today, it would be foolish for
us to require all missionaries to leave their home cultures. The best current examples are in China, India and the former Soviet Union. There,
millions still have not received the Gospel in villages that are within the
cultural reach of existing congregations. Indigenous missionaries can be
sent to them without crossing cultural barriers. They also can go to close-
by cultures where the barriers are relatively weak compared to what they
would be for Western missionaries.

Few of the unreached people groups in our modern world are reach-
able by cross-cultural missionaries from the West. Even though reaching
them requires some cross-cultural work, *this is best done by those from
nearby cultures.*

After graduating from a foremost Christian liberal arts college, Vicky
(not her real name) sensed God's call on her life for missions. She left
soon afterward for the Philippines under the auspices of a leading
denominational missions agency. While she was there, she met a Filipino

believer whom I'll call "Matt," who was involved in missions work in his country. It was only a matter of time before they knew the Lord was joining their lives together.

Matt and Vicky traveled to the United States for their wedding and now plan to return to the Philippines as soon as they raise their support. However, they will not be returning under the same agency that sent Vicky. In a letter she wrote to one of our staff, she explained the startling reason: When she and her husband approached her missions board with a request to send them both to the Philippines, Vicky was told that the mission has "a policy that they do not send nationals as missionaries to their home countries. . . . [Matt] is a Filipino citizen, and therefore he cannot be sent." If Matt were to become a U.S. citizen, however, then they would be approved to work under this missions agency.

Out of nearly 170 mission agencies operating in the Philippines at that time, this denomination was one of the top 10 in terms of number of personnel, and their missions budget exceeded $15 million.[3] Looking at the level of involvement in this mission field, it appears that the agency had invested a considerable amount in winning the Philippines for Christ, both in terms of people and finances.

My question is this: If there is a simpler, more efficient, and more logical approach to reach the Filipinos with the Gospel, why is this agency resisting it? Tragically, all that stands between its ability to multiply its outreach is a man-made policy.

BEING A GOOD FUND-RAISER.

Because the average North American missionary must raise about $60,000 a year to go abroad, mission boards must choose candidates who possess excellent public relations and fundraising skills. Even so-called faith missionaries who cannot directly appeal for funds must spend a large amount of their time speaking and traveling in order to assist in the fundraising process. The same applies to denominational missionaries who are salaried and don't directly raise support.

These six man-made standards for missionary qualification have gained such widespread use that they obscure some of the most important determining factors that are truly biblical and should be paramount. These factors include, but are not limited to, soul-winning abilities, church-planting skills, past witnessing experiences, spiritual gifts and calling, and an established life of faith and sacrifice. (We will discuss these biblical criteria in the next chapter.)

The selection process for essential qualities such as these is surprisingly informal in many mission boards. It is not unusual to find missionaries overseas who have demonstrated few spiritual gifts or who have not proven themselves to be effective in local-church ministry in the homeland.

If a missionary candidate is not already a soul winner and disciple maker at home, how will going overseas change him or her? If someone has not already established a congregation from scratch in the homeland, why would we think that person will be a church planter overseas in an alien culture and with a foreign language?

THE POPULAR DEFINITION OF TODAY'S MISSIONARY

Using the popular criteria now in use, a reasonable definition of a missionary today could be stated something like this:

A young, healthy, degreed, mentally stable, well-financed, middle-class North American from a conservative, evangelical Protestant tradition who is willing to travel abroad to offer technological skills to existing Two-Thirds World indigenous churches.

With this kind of definition in vogue, it is no surprise that many in the sending churches do not see or understand the importance of the fast-rising indigenous missionary movement. Indigenous missionaries, although they are currently doing the New Testament work of missions more effectively than their Western counterparts, are not considered qualified by the most important Western standards.

Western missionary qualifications tend to perpetuate the culture, education, health, science and technology of the West. They make second-class citizens out of God's servants from other countries. The use of these false standards guarantees that this mind-set will continue to control the missionary enterprise. Otherwise qualified, effective indigenous missionaries are made to appear untrained and unacceptable to Western donors. (Perhaps this is why indigenous missionary activity is so underreported in the Western press. It also reflects why the number of indigenous missionaries appears much smaller than it really is in so many field surveys.)

What can be done to change this mind-set? There are thousands of Western missionaries who love, respect and want to help indigenous missions, but they face a tremendous challenge. They must go back to their mission boards and home churches and work for changes in the system—changes that will find new and creative ways to free up prayer and financial support for indigenous missionaries.

There is really only one practical way to show our love and respect for the ministries of indigenous missionaries: We must start using our mission support structures to send them to the unreached people.

"But whoso hath this world's good, and seeth his brother hath need, and shutteth up his bowels of compassion from him, how dwelleth the love of God in him?" (1 John 3:17).

SHOULD WE CALL INDIGENOUS MISSIONARIES BY ANOTHER TITLE?

What I am saying does not always make me popular in some mission circles. I often travel to Wheaton, Illinois, speaking and calling on friends there whom I love and respect. Wheaton is an affluent college town, upper middle class by American standards, with many outstanding Christian organizations.

One warmhearted Wheaton College student, trying to be helpful to me after I had finished my calls in the area, asked if he could drive me back to O'Hare Field to catch my next flight. I thanked him for his servant spirit, and we enjoyed a good time of sharing about world evangelism on the drive to the airport.

As we talked, I could sense he was living every day under a powerful challenge to go overseas as a traditional missionary. I knew firsthand the strong appeal many Western missions are making to young Americans today.

He had read my book *Revolution in World Missions* and had given it some thought. As we rode along, he turned to me and said sincerely, "K.P., your problems would be over in Wheaton if you just stopped calling your native staff 'missionaries.' Can't you call them something else?"

What perceptive advice! I realized immediately that this young man understood the problem exactly, even though he was offering me the wrong solution. His advice crystallized the problem in my mind as never before.

"No!" I exclaimed. "I will not surrender the word *missionary* and allow only North Americans to use it!" I became so engrossed in explaining why that I almost missed my plane! "By New Testament standards," I told him, "indigenous missionaries are just as qualified as Americans or Europeans to be sent to reach the lost. And they're often more effective. As long as the word *missionary* remains the term Western churches use to describe pioneer evangelists, I will insist that it apply equally to indigenous missionaries."

NOTES |

1 | Samuel Wilson and John Siewert, eds., *Mission Handbook: North American Protestant Missions Overseas,* 3rd ed. (Monrovia, CA: MARC Publications, 1986), p. 66.

2 | Roberta Winter and Richard Cotten, "What about National Missionaries?" *Global Prayer Digest,* July 1990.

3 | W. Dayton Roberts and John A. Siewert, eds., *Mission Handbook: USA/Canada Protestant Ministries Overseas,* 14th ed. (Grand Rapids, MI: Zondervan, 1989), pp. 124, 381.

8 | THE BIBLICAL DEFINITION OF A MISSIONARY

More than once, I confess, I have seriously contemplated eliminating the word *missionary* from my vocabulary. After all, the words *missions* and *missionary* are not found in the English Bible. Moreover, their meanings have become so muddled in everyday usage that they almost always need to be coupled with an adjective to make clear what is really meant. But because most Christians still use *missions* whenever they describe outreach to a lost world and because there is no other equally generic term, it's probably best to retain the word and try to revive its original meaning.

Although the Bible does not actually use the word, the concept of missions is on every page from Genesis to Revelation. The Bible itself is a missionary anthology, a record of messages from the "sending God" of Isaiah 61. He is a loving God who reaches out to a race of lost and rebellious sinners. Defining the concept of missions in this biblical context gives it a richer meaning and will help recover the original meaning, at least among active Christians who still use the word to describe the outreach work of the Church.[1]

The Old Testament repeatedly tells us of "missionaries" (those who were sent by God), from Abel and Noah to Elijah, Jonah, and the rest of the prophets. The New Testament provides a clearer picture of missionary calling and work, as we understand it today, describing missionaries and their tasks in elaborate detail. As we read the New Testament, we get the full picture of how the Lord intends His body on earth to carry out the missionary mandate. And the best examples of real missionaries are the first apostles. (The word *apostle* comes from the Greek *apostoles*, which means "sent one" and is the closest New Testament word to our word *missionary*, defined as "one who is sent on a mission.") Both *apostle* and *missionary* share the same primary definition of "one sent with a religious message."

THE LORD JESUS AS MASTER MISSIONARY

The apostles learned "Missionary Principles and Practices 101" at the feet of Jesus, the master missionary. There is no better place, therefore, to begin forming a New Testament missionary definition than by studying the life of our Lord Jesus Himself. The Lord, who founded the Church and gave us our missionary marching orders, was, in fact, the first missionary in the New Testament sense. "As my Father hath sent me, even so send I you," He said in John 20:21. He best models for us the work and message of a New Testament missionary. In this verse Jesus calls Himself a "sent one," or missionary, in the same way the term is most commonly used today. He is clearly saying here that additional "sent ones" are to be included in His missionary band and that these missionaries are to go and do the work of the Gospel as He did. How vital it is, then, for us to do our missionary work as Jesus did!

There is no doubt, when studying this passage and many others, that Jesus consciously modeled the missionary life of a "sent one" for those who would follow in His steps. So let us look briefly at some of the elements of His missionary life and ministry.

REMEMBER THE PURPOSE OF JESUS.

Jesus gave His own job description in Luke 19:10: "The Son of man is come to seek and to save that which was lost." He describes Himself as the good Shepherd (John 10:11), always searching to reconcile rebellious mankind to the Father in heaven.

There was an urgency to His purpose. In Mark, the Gospel of action, we see Jesus always moving on to the next village "immediately" or "straightaway" because He knew how short His time was. The cross on which He was to suffer was ever before Him. This action adverb (Greek, *euthys*), which can be translated as "at once," is used 42 times in Mark.[2]

Christ's ministry of reconciliation has now been given to us, as 2 Corinthians 5:18–21 tells us. God has entrusted us with this work, so that we are ambassadors as Christ was, seeking the lost, restoring men and women to God.

LOOK AT THE MESSAGE OF JESUS.

It is amazing to me that in the New Testament Jesus is never seen teaching the balanced, holistic Gospel we hear touted in the seminaries of the West today. In His parables and teachings, Jesus was always taking the things of *this* world and using them to point to the next world. It was as if Jesus was continually saying, "How can I help you understand the world I come from and what heaven is like?" As He taught in parables and illustrations, He was always asking, "To what shall I compare heaven, the kingdom of God?" as if there were really no way His fallen human listeners could envision the next world.

The kingdom of heaven about which Jesus taught was nonmaterial and invisible. He wanted to bring all men into an eternal kingdom that was "not of this world," as He told Pilate at His judgment (John 18: 36). How different Jesus' message is from the Marxist gospel of the liberation theologians and from the social gospel preached and taught by their more peaceful predecessors of the 19th century! Much of Western theology today brings in a worldview that is totally concerned with this material world. Jesus was far more concerned with attracting subjects from this world who would follow Him into the next!

CONSIDER THE STYLE OF JESUS.

Jesus identified fully with us. The message of Philippians 2:7–8 is clear on this subject. He "made himself of no reputation, and took upon him the form of a servant, and was made in the likeness of men: and being found in fashion as a man, he humbled himself, and became obedient unto death, even the death of the cross."

Jesus accommodated Himself to our human condition so fully that even the most fearful sinner need not be threatened by the message or the messenger. He came as a mere baby, then as a servant, and then a carpenter. Though King of kings, He came not through armies and government. Though High Priest, He came not on the glorious temple mount in Jerusalem. Though He owned the cattle on a thousand hills, He came not among the rich. He chose instead to minister as a homeless wanderer who led a life of simplicity and poverty.

Jesus chose a missionary style that incarnated the Gospel. He didn't just preach the kingdom of God; He *was* the kingdom of God. He didn't just preach the Gospel; He *was* the Gospel. Jesus was the first "living epistle," as Paul would later describe believers (2 Corinthians 3: 2–3). "I am the way, the truth, and the life," said Jesus; "no man cometh unto the Father, but by me" (John 14:6).

Paul seemed to understand this incarnation principle well. He so incorporated the concept into his lifestyle that he was able to instruct the church at Corinth to "be . . . followers of me, even as I also am of Christ" (1 Corinthians 11:1). This is the highest standard of consistent living imaginable. To Jesus, to Paul and to the New Testament missionaries, the Gospel was never an intellectual concept; it was a way of life.

REVIEW THE METHOD OF JESUS.

Jesus preferred to teach His missionary band by formation rather than by lecture and explanation. Although He frequently paused to answer questions in times of didactic dialogue, He preferred to teach by example, living out each lesson before them. That is how He taught them to be missionaries. As they went from village to village with Jesus, they observed Him doing exactly what He had commanded them: "Heal the sick, cleanse the lepers, raise the dead, cast out devils" (Matthew 10:8).

Jesus apprenticed His disciples as missionaries, rather than providing them with formal training in a classroom setting. As He eventually sent them out to proclaim the Gospel by themselves, we see that they learned from their own successes and failures. They learned to extend the kingdom of God through miracles and anointed proclamation (Mark 9: 28–29).

Most of all, Jesus showed them that they needed to abide in Him, in the same way that He dwelt in God the Father (see John 14:10–12; 15: 1, 9–10). Missionary service is based on intimate resting in God. Only as we rely on God to do the work is the task accomplished—for it is not our work, but His!

LEARN FROM THE UTTER SUBMISSION AND OBEDIENCE OF JESUS UNTO DEATH.

Jesus refused to contemplate anything less than a life of total submission to God. He chose to live a life without options. "I came down from heaven, not to do mine own will, but the will of him that sent me" (John 6:38). Jesus accepted a life of scorn and rejection. He voluntarily opened His hands to the nails of the cross. He understood that obedience to the Father's will would mean a life of suffering and sacrifice and ultimately death.

Jesus loved God more than His own life, and He was willing to die in order to save lost humanity. "God so loved . . . that he gave his only begotten Son" (John 3:16). The disciples caught this same sacrificial zeal. They had been with Jesus. They absorbed His passion for souls and went out to preach the kingdom until they, too, died martyrs' deaths.

No missionary can have the authority of God resting on his ministry unless, as did Jesus, he totally sells out to God.

DEFINING OUR TASK CORRECTLY

The modern church has failed to define the true meaning of being a missionary, because it has failed to define the missionary task according to the Great Commission in Matthew 28:19–20; Mark 16:15; Luke 24:46–49; John 20:21; and Acts 1:8. Instead, *we have defined missions and the missionary in our own cultural terms.*

Instead of submitting to the Lord Jesus, we have relied on our own wisdom and thus allowed the missionary task to be defined as an extension of colonialism, denominationalism, humanism and even materialism. The true definition of *missionary* is clear, as long as we keep it attached to the Great Commission. If we stand by this simple New Testament description of our spiritual warfare, we can readily adapt to any new weapons and strategies needed to carry on the battle in this dawn of the 21st century.

The task of the local church is *not* to serve as a missionary-sending agency. The local church is called to be a cell in the universal Body of Christ. It is that universal Church, the whole Body of Christ, that must accomplish the Great Commission in unified cooperation. The "Go ye" of the Great Commission is a command *given in the plural* (in the Greek text) to the whole Body of Christ. It must not be understood in the singular, as though it were given only to our local churches, denominations or parachurch organizations.

As we work together in this way, we will no longer feel the compulsion to send a member from our own congregation or denomination to the "uttermost parts" of the earth. In fact, we will drop the notion that a true missionary has to be sent from "here" to "there." We are free to join with others and send missionaries from "there" to "there," if that is the more efficient way to use our resources. And, of course, we will no longer insist that the missionary meet the peculiar qualifications and artificial standards of our local culture, favorite doctrines and denominational traditions. Instead, we should be able to accept and support any needy missionary from anywhere in the Body of Christ.

This true definition of a missionary is free from racial, sectarian and vocational overtones. It allows us to help available indigenous missionaries accomplish the task in an effective, efficient manner. Let us look instead for any "sent one" who is going into all the world to reach those who have not heard the Gospel. We will know an authentic missionary because he is like the Lord Jesus; He is preaching the Gospel and is a living personification of the message being preached. The sure evidence of this authentic missionary is the trail of living churches that are established in his wake.

NOTES |

1 | John R. W. Stott, "The Bible in World Perspective" and "The Living God Is a Missionary God," in *Perspectives on the World Christian Movement* (Pasadena, CA: William Carey Library, 1981), pp. 3–18. (See also other articles in section one, "The Biblical Perspective," pp. 19–127.)

2 | John Walvoord and Roy Zuck, eds., *The Bible Knowledge Commentary* (Wheaton, IL: Victor, 1983), p. 105.

9 | WHAT DOES A MISSIONARY DO?

T he Chinese street vendors didn't even look up as a thin, scholarly looking youth emerged from the gates of the enclave reserved by the emperor for the "green-eyed devils" of the foreign community in Shanghai. He wore Chinese spectacles and shuffled along quickly on his urgent assignment, carrying a precious bag of literature and books.

His shaved head and long, black pigtail, as well as the baggy silk pantaloons and teacher's robe, hid an amazing fact. This Chinese-looking doctor, wearing flat-soled shoes with turned-up toes, was Hudson Taylor, a daring young missionary recruit who was determined to do what everyone said could not be done. He was going to take the Gospel of Christ inland, up the rivers from China's port cities and into the forbidden provinces where no white man or evangelist had ever gone before.

Hudson Taylor was actually a sandy-haired lad from Yorkshire, England, barely 21 years old. He had given up everything, including the woman he loved, to go to China and do frontier evangelism. Out of his patient obedience to the Lord would eventually emerge the great China Inland Mission (CIM), the largest of all the colonial missions and one of the most successful evangelistic bands of all time.

HUDSON TAYLOR'S ZEAL FOR THE LOST

Driven by a passionate zeal for "a million a month dying without God," the impoverished youth was generally scorned and ridiculed by the older missionaries who greeted him in Shanghai. His poverty, lack of education, refusal of ordination and insistence on identification with the Chinese were not amusing or commendable to others in the carefully watched foreign community.

Starting in 1854 and for many years thereafter, Hudson Taylor was to be an embarrassment to them. They saw him as a dangerous fool who risked his own life and the lives of others to press into forbidden regions and preach the Gospel where Christ had not been named. But Taylor had a spiritual secret. He had decided that he would submit, as Jesus did, to the way of the cross. "Not I, but Christ" was the motto that would keep him moving and organizing a militant task force of Gospel teachers.

He was willing to take the risks necessary to follow his Lord into the remote provinces and villages of the Chinese interior. When it came time for him to join his Savior, 51 years later, he was preceded in death by nearly 200 who had joined the CIM and were martyred by the Chinese for trying to bring the Gospel inland. Hundreds of others, including wives and children, died of exotic fevers and the harsh life of travel. Although these itinerant evangelists knew the rigors and risks of the mobile lifestyle Hudson demanded, they also were willing to pay the price. After all, it was the souls of the Chinese that were at stake: "More than 1,000 every hour are passing away into death and darkness."[1]

Missiologist Ralph Winter says, "God strangely honored him because his gaze was fixed upon the world's least reached people. Hudson Taylor had a divine wind behind him. It took 20 years for other missions to begin to join Taylor in his special emphasis—the unreached, inland frontiers."[2]

The missionary life and ministry of Hudson Taylor were marked by four impressive achievements: *One,* he did the work of a missionary as defined by the Lord Jesus; *two,* he proclaimed the New Testament missionary message; *three* he paved the way for authentic, indigenous churches; *four,* he developed and possessed an inner life that reflected the missionary lifestyle of Jesus.

We cannot address the question "What does a true missionary do?" unless our answer includes these four basic elements.

THE LORD JESUS' MISSIONARY JOB DESCRIPTION

If your letter carrier arrived at the door one day and, instead of delivering the mail, asked to come in and fix the sink, you would know something was very wrong at the post office. That is something of the situation in Christian missions today, and almost no one is stopping to ask why. In many cases, the job descriptions of modern North American missionaries bear little resemblance to the relevant Scriptures defining true missionary activity. And because many don't know what they should be doing, they are not able to evaluate their work honestly.

The problem is that the churches and missions that send them don't know how to hold missionaries accountable to their calling. As a result, we face a genuine crisis in identifying the missionary task. The time has come when we must be honest with ourselves, asking what exactly has gone wrong and what we can do to correct the error.

Jesus Christ could not have made the Great Commission clearer than He did in Matthew 28:19–20: "Go ye therefore, and teach all nations, baptizing them in the name of the Father, and of the Son, and of the Holy Ghost: teaching them to observe all things whatsoever I have commanded you."

In this passage, the job description of the missionary is clear. In four other places in the New Testament we find the same mission statement elaborated. The task of the missionary is simply to *teach, convert and disciple nations to Christ.*

Too many of our missions have substituted their own human genius for obedience. "That can't be how Jesus would say it today" is their interpretation. "He knows that villages need wells, babies need milk powder and unjust economic orders must be overturned. So instead of preaching, dig wells in the name of Jesus."

The gospel these modern missionaries preach is usually not articulated in words, because their theology often avoids clearly proclaiming any kind of message. Digging the well and supplying humanitarian aid is considered a witness that speaks for itself. They vaguely hope that through such activity people will somehow come to understand their message, which often goes something like this: "God loves you, and we do too." Although the children of this world surely need to hear and know that God loves them, such a statement is a distortion of truth without the rest of the Gospel. God has called His Church not only to serve people but also to preach "all the counsel of God" (Acts 20:27).

Unfortunately, social programs are often the only "gospel" left behind by those who have control of mission agencies and programs from the West. Unlike those missionaries dedicated to preaching the whole Gospel, social programs alone do nothing to restore people to a right relationship with God. No wonder these "change society" mission strategies have made little impact on lives after nearly 150 years on almost every mission field. Hundreds of millions of dollars are being spent annually on this "half gospel," which is only a Band-Aid on the gaping wounds of sin and rebellion.

This substitute for the Great Commission is a deception cooked up by the god of this world. Satan's half-truths often cause guilt and even compassion. Yet this lie has caused millions to believe that meeting physical needs is somehow equated with preaching the Gospel of Christ.

Regrettably, many missions today are doing just about everything to help the human race *except* preaching and making disciples.

FIVE TASKS OF A MISSIONARY

During His earthly ministry, Jesus set an example for the disciples of five specific missionary tasks. By looking at them separately, we get a much clearer idea of what Jesus really meant missionary work to be all about.

PREACH THE GOSPEL OF THE KINGDOM.

Matthew 10:7; Mark 3:14, 16:15; Luke 9:2, 60; Acts 5:42, 16:10, 17:3; Romans 15:20; 1 Corinthians 1:23; 2 Corinthians 4:5; Galatians 1:9

The emphasis is always on announcing the arrival of Jesus as the messianic Savior. By the end of each Gospel, there is no longer any doubt that the Gospel of Christ refers to a spiritual, heavenly kingdom rather than an earthly one. In fact, whenever the disciples pushed Jesus to inaugurate an earthly kingdom, He put them off. The priority of the Lord was elsewhere. In Christ's Gospel, the invisible world is recognized as superior and separate from the material kingdoms of this earth, and the good news is that He invited mankind to be part of it. So the Gospel we preach first must seek to reconcile men and women to God rather than create a new world order. It looks toward a kingdom coming in eternity.

BAPTIZE.

Matthew 3:11, 28:19; Luke 3:16; John 1:33; Acts 2:38–41; Acts 8:38, 10: 47–48, 16:33

By including the instruction to baptize in the Great Commission, Jesus made sure the disciples would clearly be calling people to repentance and conversion. In the waters of baptism, we publicly make a definite and conscious break with past religion and lifestyle, declaring allegiance to Jesus. Acting out the drama of salvation in the waters of baptism is an unforgettable way to declare explicitly our death to past sin and the new beginning of life in Christ.

TEACH AND DISCIPLE.

Matthew 4:23, 26:55, 28:20; Mark 6:34; Luke 13:22; Acts 5:42, 15:35; 1 Corinthians 4:17; Colossians 1:28, 3:16; 2 Timothy 2:2

The emphasis here is on training and instilling a new way of life into kingdom converts. No wonder, then, that Jesus spent three years living this lifestyle before the disciples. As they lived with Him and imitated His life, they were unconsciously learning how to model their new lifestyle to other converts. And it worked. People knew by the way the disciples acted and talked that they had been with the Nazarene.

CAST OUT DEMONS.

Matthew 8:16, 10:1–8; Mark 1:27, 3:11; Luke 4:36, 9:1, 10:17

Missionary work is spiritual warfare against the powers of darkness that hold men and women captive to sin. Missionaries are expected to use the authority Christ has given them in "casting down imaginations, and every high thing that exalteth itself against the knowledge of God" (2 Cor. 10:5). Jesus was routinely acknowledged as Lord by evil spirits, and He taught His disciples to take authority over them as He did.

HEAL THE SICK.

Matthew 4:24, 9:6, 10:8, 14:14; Mark 2:3–11, 6:56, 16:18; Acts 5:15–16; James 5:14–15

Obviously, Jesus wasn't talking about modern medicine here. He didn't tell His missionaries to open clinics and operate hospitals. Instead, He gave them the Holy Spirit so that they would share His power and authority to heal the sick. Of course, this doesn't mean medical ministry is wrong, but it does reveal that Jesus is making His healing power available to all His followers as they minister in His name.

This brief look at the work of these New Testament missionaries shows us that they were nothing less than agents of divine reconciliation and redemption. They followed in the steps of Christ. They walked as He walked, talked as He talked, and carried on the work He came to do. Anything more or less than previously described cannot qualify as authentic New Testament missionary work. At best it might be argued that other kinds of modern-day mission activities might *assist* evangelists and indigenous churches to reach their nations. But the Lord obviously expected a lot more out of the disciples He commissioned. And the actual New Testament record, as well as the history of the Church since, shows that great church growth is accomplished when missionaries move with New Testament power and authority.

The superficial add-ons of most modern mission movements actually have hindered rather than helped the spread of the Gospel and the Church, no matter how wonderful they sound in fundraising appeals. Nowhere do we see this more clearly than in the history of Chinese missions. Most historians estimate that in prerevolutionary China (that is, in 1949), the size of the Chinese church was from 3 million to 5 million souls. But, despite the small size of the church in relation to the total population, Christian missions in China then operated a large network of mission schools and hospitals, perhaps more extensive there than on any other mission field. In addition, there were Christian newspapers, publishing houses and a large infrastructure of influential parachurch organizations.

After the communist revolution, these institutions were confiscated, and the foreign missionaries who operated them were deported. Under communist persecution, the Chinese church was forced to worship underground and become indigenous. It was purged of all ability to offer materialistic ministries and thus was forced to return to the basic task of preaching and teaching the Gospel in small-group settings.

The results have stunned the missions world. Today, despite bloody persecution, the church in China is considered to be at least 10 times the size it was before the revolution. Most estimates vary from 30 million to 70 million, with responsible authorities believing it to be around 50 million. Even the communist-dominated Three-Self Patriotic Movement churches have grown dramatically. By rediscovering the correct emphasis on New Testament priorities rather than becoming preoccupied with institutions and social services, the church has actually grown faster and stronger than it did under foreign missionary control.

The lesson is obvious. True missionaries concentrate on doing the work of Mark 16:15 rather than operating social-welfare programs. True missionaries serve the message of Christ, not the institutions of the church.

THE MESSAGE OF THE MISSIONARY

Four elements characterize this Gospel message, and in His Great Commission, as recorded in Luke 24:44–49, Jesus touched on them all.

IT IS CENTERED ON THE MESSIANIC PERSON OF CHRIST.

Christ's coming with the Gospel was foreshadowed and predicted in the Law and the Prophets, Jesus says (Luke 24:44). The missionary message is the good news that God loves lost humanity and is establishing a new order under the leadership and direction of His Son.

The first missionaries were caught up with the person of Christ. They had discovered not just the Gospel but the Lord of the Gospel. This was Emmanuel—God with us. "Thou art the Son of God," exclaims Nathanael as he confesses Christ as Messiah (John 1:49). "We have found the Messiah," shouts an excited Andrew to Peter in John 1:41. From the beginning it was impossible to separate Christ Himself from His message. He personified the Gospel of God's love. The whole of Old Testament history looks forward to Christ, and the whole of the New Testament centers on Him.

THE GOSPEL ALWAYS DEALS WITH THE FORGIVENESS OF SIN.

Jesus says in Luke 24:46–47 that He had to suffer, die and rise from the dead for the "remission of sins." The real Gospel is a Gospel of atonement.

Jesus knew that injustice, crime, sickness and poverty were merely the symptoms of our iniquity, not the central problems of it. Jesus never taught that our behavior was the by-product of environment. Jesus understood that iniquity is genetically within our fallen race. The Bible says He knew the inherent sinful heart of man and did not trust it (Matthew 15:19; John 2:24–25).

Jesus came to deal with the root cause of sin by going to the cross. By offering Himself as a blood sacrifice to redeem and reconcile us to God, He made it possible for us to overcome sin and enter into the kingdom of God.

THE GOSPEL MESSAGE ALWAYS DEALS WITH A CALL TO REPENTANCE.

Jesus says that "repentance . . . should be preached in his name among all nations, beginning at Jerusalem" (Luke 24:47).

There was never anything in the life of Christ, in the message of Christ or in the New Testament that cheapened the grace of God and made the Gospel easy to accept. Although salvation was a gift of God purchased for us with Jesus' own blood, He made it uncomfortably clear that those who desired to follow Him must do so with their entire lives.

As He dealt personally with would-be converts, Jesus put His finger on the idols in their lives. Nothing that stood between Jesus and His disciples was tolerated. He demanded that each believer take up his or her cross and follow Him, dying to self. Ego trips are not allowed in the kingdom of heaven. The Gospel message is a call to discipleship and obedience. It requires nothing less than a spiritual U-turn at the cross of Christ. Unless one repents and is born again as a follower of Christ, the spiritual transaction of the Gospel has not taken place.

THE GOSPEL MESSAGE IS PRESENTED WITH POWER AND AUTHORITY.

In Luke 24:49, Jesus commands His disciples to wait before preaching the Gospel until they have been "endued with power from on high."

The message of the missionary is not understood primarily on the intellectual level but is "the living word" to be proclaimed through God's power. The Lord has promised to back up this proclamation with miraculous signs, wonders and other evidences of His divine presence in the message and the messenger. When this power is in operation, it has the wondrous ability to change lives, restore families, heal broken hearts and free the oppressed from addiction and bondage.

NOTES |

1 | Dr. and Mrs. Howard Taylor, *J. Hudson Taylor: God's Man in China* (Chicago, IL: Moody Press, 1978), p. 272.

2 | Ralph D. Winter, "The Long Look: Eras of Missions History," *Perspectives on the World Christian Movement* (Pasadena, CA: William Carey Library, 1981), p. 172.

I n the book of Acts and throughout the rest of the New Testament, we can see that the first missionaries were preoccupied with obeying Christ's command to make disciples. They did this through starting local churches, usually made up of what we might today call a network of home Bible studies. They were "continuing daily with one accord in the temple, and breaking bread from house to house . . . praising God" (Acts 2:46–47a).

These simple house meetings were the first indigenous churches. They were the clear evidence of successful missionary work—house groups that served as spiritual incubators in which the Lord was able to form a living, separated, witnessing body within the larger secular community.

In a few mission agencies today, the need for this practice is being recognized, and there are calls for a return to church planting. However, the tragedy in many Western missions today is that church planting among unreached people groups is barely even mentioned in planning strategies. The latest statistics provide little evidence that there has been a change in the situation. According to the World Evangelization Research Center (Gem-werc), only 2.4 percent of all missionaries are working among the unevangelized.[1]

At great mission conferences, the subject is barely addressed. For example, in 1989, at the Lausanne II Congress on World Evangelization in Manila, not one plenary session was devoted to the planting of local churches. No wonder more than two-thirds of Western missionaries today can't make a direct link between what they do and a growing body of believers. But according to the Great Commission, any so-called missionary activity that does not contribute to the growth of the Church is unbiblical. Such outreach usually results in spiritual malnourishment and a lack of true unity among believers.

When we give birth to physical babies, we wouldn't think of leaving them in the street to survive by themselves, so why should we do this in the spiritual realm? Missions that do not give birth to a local church are ineffective; they do not go far enough in fulfilling the Great Commission, which instructs us to make disciples of the nations and teach them to observe all the Lord commands. Mission organizations that do not build local churches drain billions of dollars (and over two-thirds of all Western missionaries) away from effective disciple-making ministries that are building the Church.

NEW TESTAMENT CHURCH PLANTING

A simple reading of the New Testament will show that the Lord Jesus longs for missionaries to be primarily concerned with church start-ups. The whole New Testament, in fact, is practically a church planter's handbook.

In Acts 2, the Holy Spirit fell on the assembled believers at Jerusalem, and the apostles immediately moved out into the streets to obey the commands of the Great Commission. As a result of these open-air meetings, thousands turned to Christ. Within days, the Church began to form as they were meeting in the synagogue and from house to house.

In the years that followed, as the missionaries went from city to city calling on Jews and then Gentiles to recognize Jesus, we find the new converts gathered immediately into groups for teaching, communion and worship. The first local congregations exploded into existence in

THE KEY: INDIGENOUS CHURCH PLANTING | 109

city after city without church buildings, schools, hospitals or other institutional ministries. Later, because of persecution from the Jews and then the Romans, many of these house fellowships met almost as underground groups.

This first missionary work was so effective that within a few decades the Church had spread cross-culturally throughout the entire Roman Empire. Hundreds of local ethnic groups and languages heard the Gospel. It is fascinating to contemplate that this was done during a time when Christianity was an unregistered, illegal cult that did not enjoy the protection of the Roman government.

The books of the New Testament concern themselves almost entirely with the work undertaken to disciple the first groups of believers, define doctrines for them, establish codes of Christian conduct and prepare them as the Bride of Christ for His soon return. When we begin to understand the New Testament in these terms, it is difficult to comprehend how mission policies and strategy could have gotten so sidetracked.

Most Western missionaries who go overseas as social workers do so under a philosophy that says they intend to "minister both physically and spiritually." Unfortunately, without a clear goal of making converts and planting churches, many find themselves swamped by an ocean of physical need. Sadly, some have gone to extremes and adopted a theological system that encourages this separation of the spiritual from the material and enthrones physical needs above spiritual.

PLANTING WHAT KIND OF CHURCH?

Even when we have missions that place the priority on making converts and planting churches, we find that many still get tripped up by the next logical question: *What kind of church will it be?* Will we plant indigenous churches, or should they follow the free-form style of American religion, with strong, entrepreneurial lay leaders? Will they be Congregational, Episcopalian or Presbyterian in polity? Will they seek to be independent from government, as the church is in the United States, or will they seek to be protected by secular authority, like the historic state churches in Western Europe?

Besides structural questions, the sensitive Western missionary must decide if he will allow an indigenous theological system to develop or propagate one of the great systems of the West, such as Calvinism, Pentecostalism, Wesleyanism and the like.

These and many other questions about the churches we launch are also answered by looking to the examples of church planting by the first missionaries. Please note that this is not meant to advocate primitivism. Utopian attempts to re-create a church cast in New Testament cultural terms can no more lead to indigenous churches than any other polity that merely imitates past tradition. It is true, however, that the student of missions must look to the New Testament for basic principles.

We must begin our quest for an authentic indigenous church by asking: What were the characteristics of the first indigenous churches planted by New Testament missionaries?

THEY WERE CENTERED ON CHRIST AND THE GOSPEL.

One cannot imagine the New Testament apostles building the Church around anything but the Lord Himself: "Other foundation can no man lay than that is laid, which is Jesus Christ" (1 Corinthians 3:11). They did not build churches around "brand-name" denominations, creeds, statements of faith or doctrinal fads, as some missionaries do today. It is interesting that Paul and the New Testament writers simply refer to churches by location: "the church at Corinth," "the saints at Ephesus," for instance.

Nor did the apostles build the Church around particular leaders, human personalities or any other division, such as a particular system of ecclesiastical government, language, mode of baptism, method of celebrating communion, race or social class. In fact, the apostle Paul specifically condemned this kind of behavior in 1 Corinthians 3. All these divisions have been added through the years by accidents of history, prejudices and the teachings of various theologians—some half wrong and some half right.

Because of these traditions, much of today's missions activity is not church planting at all but rather the export of doctrinal divisions that have already split the churches of Europe and North America. In a very real sense, this missions work is not spreading *the* Gospel but exporting "another gospel" and "another Jesus," as Paul put it (Galatians 1:6–7; 2 Corinthians 11:4).

THEY TRIED TO BUILD A CULTURALLY NEUTRAL CHURCH.

The early missionaries debated long and hard about whether to require Gentile converts to adopt the Jewish customs and laws they loved and grew up with in their synagogues. Many sincerely believed new converts to Christianity should become culturally Jewish—and they had some powerful Old Testament arguments for their belief. Finally, however, the Holy Spirit had His way, and they chose to allow the new Gentile converts to remain as free as possible from the foreign influences of Judaism (Acts 15:1–29). We can only wish that all modern missionaries would follow this same New Testament wisdom and consciously avoid mixing their cultural norms with evangelism.

The apostolic decision to leave the Gentiles culturally free paved the way for the local churches to develop customs and standards relevant to their own cultures. Details concerning the correct mode of baptism, the order of service, the style of music, the type of building (or lack thereof) were not spelled out by Jesus or the apostles. This principle should help us form policies that leave mission field congregations free to evolve their own interpretations and practices on nonessentials. No matter how much the missionary loves the familiar songs, symbols and creeds under which he was raised, they must be detached from the essential Gospel he presents on the field.

Bruce Britten shares an African viewpoint of this truth:

Today many Africans in central and southern Africa are saying, "We see that God planned for us to receive faith in Christ, but must we also follow the foreign customs which the missionaries brought?"

Professor B. Makhathini of the University of Swaziland gave the following excellent answer:

"Before the bread of life (the Christian faith) came to our part of Africa, it stayed in Europe for over a thousand years. There the Europeans added a plastic bag (their own customs) to the bread. And when they came to southern Africa, they fed us the plastic bag along with the bread. Now the plastic is making us sick! The plastic is theirs. But the bread belongs to everyone. We know that God planned for us to receive the bread just as He planned for them to receive it. We can remove the plastic and enjoy the bread."[2]

Too often missionaries unconsciously train new converts to follow imported policies and practices without considering local customs. No missionary activity should ever impose a foreign system of church government, liturgy, vestments or even technologies upon new converts. These cultural and historical attachments to the Christian faith are almost always of a fleshly or worldly nature. While they might have had some logical justification when first developed in Canterbury, Philadelphia, Nashville, Rome or Springfield, that doesn't mean they should be exported to the mission field.

Outside their original place and time in history, most foreign church laws and policies don't transfer to the mission field. Overseas, they only serve to build greater barriers between the local Christians and their neighbors. Through the use of these foreign policies by missionaries and denominational leaders, the local church gains a reputation of being more alien than it is, and her witness to the larger community becomes increasingly difficult.

Paul's principle of cultural accommodation is stated in 1 Corinthians 9:19–22: "Though I be free from all men, yet have I made myself servant unto all, that I might gain the more. And unto the Jews I became as a Jew, that I might gain the Jews; to them that are under the law, as under the law, that I might gain them that are under the law; to them that are without law, as without law, (being not without law to God, but under the law to Christ,) that I might gain them that are without law. To the weak became I as weak, that I might gain the weak: I am made all things to all men, that I might by all means save some."

NEW TESTAMENT MISSIONARIES BUILT A MORALLY SEPARATED CHURCH.

Paul rarely wrote an epistle without making practical applications of the Gospel to everyday living. Romans 12–15, Galatians 5–6, Ephesians 4–6, Philippians 4 and Colossians 3–4 are chapters that reveal the heart of the Lord for a pure and spotless bride. Christians are clearly to be different, but not in superficial cultural terms. The distinguishing mark of any true believer is holiness.

The New Testament word *ecclesia*, translated "church," means "a calling out" and implies separation from the world. True missionaries are preparing the Church described in Revelation 21, a holy bride adorned for her husband.

THE NEW TESTAMENT CHURCH WAS SELF-SUPPORTING, SELF-PROPAGATING AND SELF-GOVERNING.

Indigenous churches didn't begin with the "three-self" movement of the mid-1850s. The first missionaries planted "three-self" churches as naturally as breathing.

The apostles never "colonized" their converts or built an imperial system that taxed local congregations or linked them formally to a distant headquarters. These political-power issues seldom appear in the New Testament record. In fact, the first missionaries often made a point of offering the Gospel without charge (Acts 3:6, 18:3; 1 Corinthians 4: 12, 9:18; 1 Thessalonians 2:9; 2 Thessalonians 3:8). They were either supported by the believers who had sent them or worked with their own hands at trades in order to give the Gospel without charge.

Paul and the apostles, like Jesus before them, authenticated their missionary authority over the churches they founded on the basis of their sacrifice and suffering for the believers. By the moral weight of their proven servant spirits, they had already earned their leadership.

THE COST OF PLANTING INDIGENOUS CHURCHES

How are indigenous churches planted? The example of Paul and the apostles gives us the answer. Churches are planted by genuine missionar-

114 | COME, LET'S REACH THE WORLD

ies who lead by example, who live a consistent Christian life and who incarnate Christ's servanthood to the Church.

"Christ . . . loved the church, and gave himself for it," Paul wrote in Ephesians 5:25. True missionary work demands that the disciple care for the church as Jesus does. The missionary follows the example of Christ, whose love for the Church Paul likened to that of a husband in marriage.

The missionary call is not a career or vocation as such, but a lifestyle based on displaying the genuine concern of Christ for the welfare of His Church. The decision to live and walk in this reality cannot be made without total commitment. There is no such thing as a part-time missionary, even if one is temporarily doing tentmaking in a bivocational situation.

Every minute of every day, the missionary is modeling the life of Christ to his followers. He should be able to say, as Paul did to the Corinthians, "Be ye followers of me, even as I also am of Christ" (1 Corinthians 11:1).

The missionary's ethics, habits, finances, personal life and family life are a living object lesson for all to see. Paul, Silvanus and Timothy, a three-member missionary band to Thessalonica, were able to write back and tell the young Christians how to behave—using themselves as examples! In 2 Thessalonians 3:7, we find them saying, "For yourselves know how ye ought to follow us: for we behaved not ourselves disorderly among you."

Sri Lankan missions leader Ajith Fernando, in an exposition of Mark 10:35–45, put his finger on this need for servanthood:

God calls us to identify with our hearers, to become one with them—with their struggles, their aspirations and their experiences. Alas, this seems to be one of the blind spots of American missions. I regret to say this, but I think I need to say it: I believe Americans are possibly the most generous and open-hearted people in the world. They are blessed with a sense of fair play that is unusual in most parts of the world.

But I fear that there has not been sufficient serious thinking about incarnation, about lifestyle, about what it means to identify. Perhaps it is understandable considering the relative affluence here. Your poor people have much more than most of the people in our countries. So a sacrificial dropping of lifestyle which seems very drastic to an American missionary may still not be enough of an incarnation in poorer nations.

I fear this is happening a lot today. Not among everyone, but I think there are too many people with a warm heart, with genuine love, but with insufficient identification.[3]

Jesus said, "The Son of man came not to be ministered unto, but to minister" (Matthew 20:28). To minister in this way, the real missionary to the Two-Thirds World must represent Christ in at least four essential areas: obedience, suffering, sacrifice and commitment.

The beautiful story of Rajan and Deva Lal (not their real names) illustrates what it really means to represent the love of Christ. No family should be asked to pay the price they did to bring the Gospel to the lost, but I have never heard a murmur of complaint from them. And they never talk about the deep sacrifices they have made to pioneer their mission to the unreached tribal people of North India.

Brother Rajan sensed the call of God on his life to leave the rich, beautiful paddy fields of Kerala in southwest India. Friends and family couldn't believe he would leave his comfort and security for the sake of the animistic tribes of the north. The people there lived on freezing mountainsides, practiced slash-and-burn farming and were enslaved to alcohol and the worship of demon spirits.

Rajan shared this burden with the leaders of the nominal Christian church in his home village, but they had no money or vision to send a missionary. Even his own pastor advised him not to go and finally refused to help. But Rajan knew God was calling him to go. He didn't know of any missions agency or way to raise funds for such a mission, but he knew he had to go.

After praying for many months, Rajan and Deva decided to sell all they had and move to the cold and barren hills of the north. The move meant learning a new dialect, adapting to a new lifestyle and patiently working with an illiterate tribal group that was without a Christian community.

Rajan and Deva were compelled by a supernatural love they could not explain. When they finally arrived and saw the terrible poverty and ignorance that gripped the mountain people, they were more certain than ever that God had called them to bring Christ and the Gospel to these people who had lived in darkness for centuries.

The first few months and years were the hardest. They knew no one, and at first no congregation supported them. Rajan walked from village to village, learning the dialect and sharing Christ. As the months passed, their money began to run out. At first they skipped a meal each day. Then they would go without meals for a day or two, buying only milk for the children. But soon even that ran out.

As time went by, it became obvious their five-year-old was seriously affected by the lack of food. His weak little body was wasting away, and each cold or fever left him weaker than the last. They prayed and called out to God, but there just wasn't any money to provide the boy with the diet he needed to recover. One day Rajan came home to find Deva weeping beside the still form of their firstborn son. He had slipped quietly into eternity, his tiny body too weak to face the rigors of life on that barren mountainside.

Rajan and Deva knew that thousands of starving Indian children die daily from diseases brought on by malnutrition, but why their boy? Weren't they the servants of God? Undoubtedly, back on the rich plains of Kerala, with family and friends, the child would have lived—but they knew God had called them to the people of these mountains. Could God really have wanted their little boy as a price for evangelizing the tribes?

The question had no answer. So they prayed and buried the boy's little body—offering him back to the Lord. Rajan could only comfort his grieving wife with the words of Paul in Colossians 1:24 when he said he rejoiced in his sufferings because they "fill up that which is behind of the afflictions of Christ in my flesh for his body's sake, which is the church."

After years of sacrifice, the Lord used the Lals to build a wonderful ministry with a large evangelistic team of over 30 indigenous missionaries reaching many different tribes. Gospel for Asia took on their support with the help of sponsors in the United States—and every child in their mission was properly cared for. But without the Lals' faithfulness during those months and years of hunger, loneliness and sacrifice, there would be no work among the tribal people of that particular state today.

Rajan and Deva are not unusual. Throughout the Two-Thirds World today, there are thousands of unknown missionary couples and singles like them. They are dedicated men and women who have voluntarily chosen to risk hunger, stonings, persecution and rejection in order to bring Christ to people groups still without a Gospel witness. They are the ones the book of Hebrews identifies as heroes of the faith—the ones described as those "of whom the world was not worthy" (Hebrews 11: 38). As Paul wrote in Philippians 3:10, these indigenous missionaries have chosen to know "the fellowship of his sufferings, being made conformable unto his death."

How then does a true missionary start an indigenous church? For anyone in the Two-Thirds World today, it begins with a decision to identify totally with Christ. It means being willing to live with the suffering and poverty of unreached people—unselfishly surrendering comforts, security and privacy in order to reach them. Missionary life and work are an ongoing obedience to Christ, submitting to His will daily and incarnating what He would do to reach the thousands of people groups without a witness.

How many of us from the West today are able to fulfill this job description? That is one of the many questions some of our mission agencies and societies no longer want to talk or write about.

NOTES |

1 | "The Scandal of World A," World Evangelization Research Center (http://www. gem-werc.org/scandal/scandal04.htm).

2 | Bruce Britten, *We Don't Want Your White Religion* (Manzini, Swaziland: Britten, 1984), p. 26.

3 | Ajith Fernando, "Servanthood: Jesus' Model for Missions," *Mission Frontiers*, October 1987, p. 9.

11 | WHAT MISSIONARIES DON'T WANT TO TALK ABOUT

There is a marvelous excitement when your plane touches down in the United States after living and working overseas. Efficiency and effectiveness seem to crackle in the air Americans breathe. Phones work; clean water runs hot and cold; restrooms smell fresh; food is served appetizingly and hot.

Americans are a people on the go. Pragmatism and technology rule. If it's broken, they fix it immediately. If it can't be fixed, they replace it. Often a spare part is on the way from some computerized warehouse the same day, delivered the next morning by overnight courier.

Compared to their counterparts overseas, American business and even government institutions are wondrous in the way they realistically measure and evaluate results. Dishonesty is not tolerated for long—if something is unprofitable or inefficient, Americans won't stand in line long before speaking out in protest. Because they live in a market-driven economy, Americans eventually vote with their feet and pocketbooks, closing down redundant and ineffective organizations.

This efficiency based on sober reality seems almost universal—until we look at the way we are now dealing with the current crisis in Christian missions. Suddenly, on this one subject, we no longer measure productivity. Recent history, logic and current events go out the window.

It sometimes appears as if the past 50 years have not happened. Too often missionaries talk as if we're still back in the days of the British Empire.

When it comes to discussing indigenous missions, romantic paternalism often reigns supreme. The conversation loses all touch with reality and is cast in terms of "we" and "them"—and "we" (as in *we the sending church*) always know what's best for "them." Some believers, usually so fair-minded and just, still insist on dealing with indigenous church leaders and missionaries as if they were children. Only infrequently will the typical Western missions leader talk in terms of becoming a servant to the indigenous leadership.

THE NEED FOR CHANGE

There seems to be a century-old wall of sentimentality that stands guard around many mission programs in the United States, an attitude that Two-Thirds World leaders find hard to deal with. Mission leaders have difficulty parting with Western mission programs that are no longer functioning effectively. Especially puzzling is the attitude of former missionaries who have returned to the United States and sit on boards and committees that control the purse strings of support for indigenous missions and programs overseas.

When these Western mission leaders consistently vote down requests for support by needy indigenous missionaries, we must ask the question of 1 John 3:17: "Whoso hath this world's good, and seeth his brother hath need, and shutteth up his bowels of compassion from him, how dwelleth the love of God in him?"

When we quote John 3:16, we must also remember 1 John 3:16: "Hereby perceive we the love of God, because he laid down his life for us: *and we ought to lay down our lives for the brethren*" (emphasis mine). Next to the Great Commission, that is the greatest theme verse ever written for our global missions outreach. Note that I am deliberately speaking of "our missions" in this context. I have chosen that pronoun carefully.

These tears and cries from my heart for the state of missions come from one who loves the people and the churches of this wonderful country. I cry out for change in our mission policies as one who identifies as fully as I can with this, my land.

Nothing in this book will come as a particular surprise to knowledgeable mission leaders in the West. The facts of the situation are well known to key church and mission leaders, but they are too often unwilling to deal with the situation. This is especially true of my fellow mission leaders, association executives, editors, fundraising executives, professors and teachers. Privately, most agree that a reformation in missions support policy is long overdue—but they don't want to be the first to speak out.

Meanwhile, we are living in a day when 54 million people a year will die and slip into eternity. That's more than 1 million souls a week.[1]

Yet there is some hope that reformation might come, if we will faithfully fan the flames of change. At the 1989 Lausanne II Congress in Manila, knowledgeable observers who had attended international mission conferences for years reported that a major change had occurred. From the platform, indigenous leadership was spoken of in new terms. There was a growing realization that the initiative in world evangelization had slipped from the West into the hands of indigenous missionaries.

However, not everything at Lausanne II reflected the reality of the change. *Christianity Today* noted that "the majority (27 of 43) of the plenary speakers were white Westerners . . . despite two LCWE [Lausanne Committee for World Evangelization] consultations in the past two years for the purpose of identifying and encouraging a new generation of worldwide leadership."

Correspondent Lyn Cryderman commented on the dominance of missions by "the old guard," noting that "some questioned whether the [Lausanne] movement is ready or willing to welcome individuals from the Two-Thirds World or North American minority groups, and if it is serious about passing the torch to a new generation."

Yet while the leadership remained dominated by the West in 1989, it was obvious that younger Western leaders were more willing to yield the control of missions to indigenous leaders. In the workshops, which best represented the frontline activities of missions, indigenous missionary speakers were clearly setting the future agenda to reach the last of "the hidden peoples" and to "evangelize whole nations—with or without the assistance of the West."[2]

The trend seemed to continue at Amsterdam 2000, where more than 10,000 evangelists gathered from 209 nations. Although the United States sent five times more attendees than any other country (2,767), three-quarters of the evangelists came from the developing world. The other countries in the top five were India (495 attendees), Ghana (249), Kenya (204) and South Africa (182).[3]

But this shift to Two-Thirds World leadership is no surprise to observers who have been studying developments. Ralph Winter noted in an interview that "we in the West will have a strategic role, but missions in the remaining part of this century will clearly be dominated by the Two-Thirds World, not the West."

THE NEED TO BECOME SERVANTS

And what role does that leave Western churches and missions to play in these new movements? The sole available option is the one offered by Christ Himself—to assist and participate as a servant. Samuel Ling, in a 1996 article in *Evangelical Missions Quarterly*, agrees: "Gone are the days of 'randomly' sending our sons and daughters in the name of 'church planting.'" The question is, "Which sons and daughters will best *serve* [emphasis mine] the maturation of the Third World church?"[4]

This indispensable supporting role is really the important one left for Western mission agencies that want to be part of the Great Commission in the days ahead. To do so means, of course, a change in heart and attitude that must be deliberate and intentional. If Western Christian leaders will return to New Testament principles for assisting indigenous missionary movements overseas, it is likely we could see world evangelization completed in our generation.

This truth does not apply just to the North American missions community. The churches in Australia, Europe and many other developed nations also can play a valuable role in missions. Just as small nations like the Celts, the Irish, the Spanish and the Portuguese have profoundly impacted world evangelism in the past, there is no reason why mission movements cannot be born anew in nations and places other than North America.

Will Korea, India, Japan or the Philippines rise up with Holy Spirit–empowered vision for a reformation in missions? Perhaps, but they will be able to fulfill their role only if church and mission leaders change support policies toward indigenous missions.

But will this change happen in North America? It would be good to report that the necessary attitudes of humility, repentance and servanthood are prevailing. It would be good to report that Western agencies are using their support-raising networks to support indigenous missions. However, many mission leaders continue to turn a deaf ear to the truth about indigenous missions, inhibiting a release of funds for their support.

A friend of mine, a veteran of colonial-era missions, spent over 20 years of his life on the mission field. His comments about the lack of servanthood in our Western leaders shed new light for me on a problem that would be hard to believe were it not for the weight of his experience. He tells me of some leaders who will say almost anything in order to perpetuate personal power, often using a smoke screen of rumors and untruths to discredit the ministries of indigenous leaders seeking support in the West. Apparently, the ultimate motive for this is a determination to keep the flow of mission dollars and personnel in their own hands. Some have been known to malign the character of indigenous mission leaders. They may characterize attempts to support indigenous missions as a violation of "sound indigenous church policy."

THE INSTINCT FOR SELF-PRESERVATION

Many denominational mission agencies and independent mission boards employ public relations agents and fundraisers in the same way that secular businesses and corporations do. Research shows that "250 of the 300 largest international Christian organizations regularly mislead the Christian public by publishing demonstrably incorrect or falsified progress statistics."[5] Why would Christian organizations deceive the public? They know people will not continue to support policies and programs that are not accomplishing the task.

North American agencies and denominations publish 38,000 periodicals. Tens of thousands of newsletters and appeals for funds flood the mailboxes of Christian homes every month in the United States alone. In addition, news releases, films, videos and special newsletters cover local congregations and church leadership with the missions challenge. Daily mission broadcasts are also heard on virtually every Christian radio and TV station in the United States. According to David Barrett, "publicized self-congratulation is rampant in most churches, agencies and ministries."[6]

Of course, to raise prayer and support, it is necessary to have trained media staff. Unfortunately, a large part of these mission communication programs is focused on maintaining the status quo in missions—even though many of the programs they defend have continued for decades without honest evaluation. Again David Barrett minces no words when he claims that any secular enterprise "recording such a spectacular failure to achieve its own trumpeted goals would have been mercilessly exposed by the media and then closed down."[7]

Some mission leaders sincerely believe that indigenous missionaries cannot be trusted to do as good a job as white foreigners. The bottom line of their thinking is basically this: "Our way is better—and more important." Their refusal to share resources with indigenous missionaries is thus in direct disobedience to New Testament commands about sharing and serving and esteeming others better than oneself.

Most alert mission leaders today know better. They realize that the fastest-growing churches in the world are spearheaded by indigenous missionary movements. They realize that the leadership and initiative for global evangelism must now be transferred to indigenous leaders if the work is to be completed.

These leaders are well aware that they are perpetuating a system that desperately needs to change. The emergence of groups such as the Third World Mission Association and COSIM (Consultation on the Support of Indigenous Ministries) and the increasing flow of direct support to indigenous missionaries represent a threat to the establishments they serve.

The presence of visiting indigenous missionary speakers in the pulpits of American churches is startling new evidence of the maturing indigenous missions movement. It clearly reveals that the Western church is no longer the essential link to world evangelism.

When mission leaders speak against indigenous missions, too often they appear to be trying to convince themselves and their audience that God is not capable of completing the task of world evangelization without them in control of the missions enterprise.

PAINFUL QUESTIONS ABOUT THE FUTURE

The instinct for self-preservation and self-perpetuation is strong among the powerful advocates of conventional missions. Yet they are facing ever more painful questions about the long-established practices that have sustained their missions for decades. Here are some of them:

- Why are young people challenged to go overseas as missionaries even though most of the world's population lives in countries closed to them as true missionaries and almost all of the unreached people groups are deep in the interiors of these restricted-access countries?

- Although it is impossible to evangelize the unreached groups without sending indigenous missionaries, why do many mission leaders speak week after week in local churches without mentioning this critical situation?

- Why are funds raised, supposedly for spreading the Gospel, while they are largely spent on perpetuating organizations that are involved in maintaining existing churches rather than supporting frontline missions to reach the unreached peoples?

- Why do traditional mission promoters speak only of traditional mission activities at conferences, schools and seminars, while they usually ignore indigenous missions? The truth is that these events cost millions of dollars to stage, yet they net almost nothing for the needy indigenous workers who are most likely the ones actually doing the work of the Great Commission on the mission fields in question.

The Lausanne II conference, for example, totaled $10.5 million in direct costs, plus millions more in additional costs to participants. If you count the time lost by over 4,000 top leaders who attended, plus observers and staff, the actual cost probably was several times the official price tag. The Amsterdam 2000 evangelism conference cost a staggering $40 million.[8] *World Christian Trends* reports that Christian organizations spend $8 billion per year on conferences.[9]

If a fraction of that money had been spent directly on indigenous missionaries, it would have been enough to complete the work of world evangelism in any number of countries. This is not to say that Lausanne I, Lausanne II or Amsterdam conferences were a mistake, nor that we should cancel any of the 500 annual conferences on evangelism.[10] Only heaven knows what good will come from them. But the track record of these conferences in general gives us every reason to question their value. Have these hundreds of conferences and billions of dollars made a major difference in the total number of unreached people groups in the world? David Barrett's analysis is scathing: He calls the 1990s "a golden opportunity" that was "catastrophically squandered." He argues that the hundreds of broken promises to reach the world with the Gospel "appear to demand the replacement of [missions] leadership by a new generation."[11]

The sad truth is that after spending hundreds of millions of dollars to talk to themselves in these giant conferences, Western missions are little nearer meeting the challenge of the unreached or "hidden" peoples than they were before they started.

Phil Bogosian, director of church relations in the mobilization division of the U.S. Center for World Mission, says it well:

> In 1974 Lausanne I . . . a strong mandate was given by the Lord to His Church to complete the task of world evangelization. In response thousands of global church leaders entered into "a solemn covenant with God" stating their shame that so many had been neglected. They covenanted with God to "pray earnestly," "develop a simple lifestyle," and "sacrifice" so that "by all possible means and the earliest possible time" every people group could be reached.
>
> This has not even remotely been done—especially by the church in the West. In the course of my assignment at the U.S. Center . . . I have studied church involvement in missions for about seven years. In all candor and to our continuing shame, let us admit that the world's perishing unreached peoples are very seldom mentioned or thought about in almost all churches.[12]

In a later interview, Bogosian stated that he believed most mission leaders are ready and anxious to send out missionaries to unreached peoples if they can find responsiveness from denominational leadership and local churches.

We enjoy talking in general, nonspecific terms about building the "national church," but how often do we read a missionary newsletter that tells about the new congregation that was planted last week? Millions of dollars and thousands of people are engaged in studying unreached people groups, but when was the last time you read a report of a new church being formed among one of them? Our traditional missions structure is no longer doing the job. The talk is triumphant, but the facts fail to back it up.

NOTES |

1 | "World Vital Events," U.S. Census Bureau (http://blue.census.gov/cgi-bin/ipc/pcwe).

2 | Lyn Cryderman, "Global Camp Meeting," *Christianity Today,* August 18, 1989, pp. 39–41.

3 | "Amsterdam 2000 Called the Most Multinational Event Ever," *Christianity Today* (www.christianitytoday.com/ct/2000/131/32.0.html).

4 | Samuel Ling, "Asia: Past and Future Center of the World," *Evangelical Missions Quarterly,* July 1996, p. 357.

5 | David Barrett, "An AD 2001 Reality Check," World Evangelization Research Center (http://www.gem-werc.org/gd/findings.htm).

6 | *Ibid.*

7 | David B. Barrett and Todd M. Johnson, eds., *World Christian Trends, A.D. 30-A.D. 2200* (Pasadena, CA: William Carey Library, 2001), p. xiv.

8 | "Amsterdam 2000."

9 | Barrett and Johnson, *World Christian Trends,* p. 661.

10 | *Ibid.,* p. xiv.

11 | *Ibid.,* p. 71.

12 | Phil Bogosian, "Prophecy at Manila," *Mission Frontiers,* August-September 1989, p. 8.

12 | TIME FOR ACCOUNTABILITY

At a church missions conference where I spoke on the subject of this book, I encouraged the congregation to be sensitive to the changing times and to reprioritize their missions giving in light of the needs of indigenous missionaries in the Two-Thirds World. After my message, a young couple asked to speak with me—I'll call them John and Mary. As they spoke, I could sense a tremendous sadness in their hearts.

John had been an engineer and was bringing in a promising salary when the Lord first called him, his wife and their three children to the mission field. Convinced that the Lord was truly speaking to them, John left his secure job and went to Bible school, where he earned another degree. Then he and Mary took two years of special missionary training provided by their denomination before they were assigned to work in a South American country.

When they finally arrived at their destination, John and Mary had a great love and burden for the people they were coming to serve. As they settled into their new surroundings, they soon met the 14 other missionaries who were working in the same region. The house that was provided for them was beautiful. In fact, it made John feel a little uncomfortable. It was one thing to be living in the most luxurious house in the entire community; it was another to realize he was enjoying better living conditions on the field than he had at home.

John soon noticed that the lifestyle of the local people was very different from that of the missionaries. In fact, the indigenous evangelist who worked with him was really quite poor. His family's clothing looked worn out, and he had to work hard at a second job to provide for his family. Yet despite their poverty, this evangelist and the other families who had come to the Lord were loving and caring in their concern for the people to whom they ministered. They had gentle servant hearts and were willing to do anything to help.

In the months that followed, however, John and Mary became aware of a troubling attitude among their fellow missionaries that went beyond the external incongruities. At first it was hard to pin down, but as time went on, John discovered it pervaded every facet of the missionary lifestyle around them.

He saw it in the monthly missionary get-togethers, at which the conversation usually ended with criticism of the local people they were supposedly serving. The missionaries had complaints to air about these people. They would give each other advice on dealing with these "locals"—whom to watch, whom to avoid and how to treat them.

John and Mary became burdened about this situation, but they really didn't know what to do except pray. Then one day something happened that demanded action. They had gone to a fellow missionary's house for a visit. While the two couples were talking, a knock was heard at the door. The missionary's wife answered it and found one of the senior native pastors. She invited him into the living room with the other three missionaries. He stayed only a few minutes to discuss a matter with them, and then he left.

As soon as he left, the missionary's wife immediately brought out a can of Lysol and sprayed it on the chair where the native pastor had sat. As she wiped, she fussed, "They know they are not supposed to sit in these chairs. We have chairs outside on the porch where they can sit if they want to talk!" Then she told John and Mary how to keep the nationals at a distance. "Otherwise," she said, "they will have no respect."

This was more than enough for John and Mary. After going home and discussing it further, they sent a letter to their missions board. "Only if we are allowed to live on the standard of the local people we minister to and maintain their lifestyle, do we feel we can continue on the field," John wrote.

Word soon got back to the field of John and Mary's letter. The primary reaction of the missionaries to the couple's decision was shock. But within a year's time, they had completely ostracized John and Mary and their family. The mission board's response was simple: "Come home." So they left the mission field and the people they had come to minister to because they were not allowed to live among them.

When John and Mary finished their story, they were both weeping. "What you said tonight was so true," they said. "If only you would share what you said tonight with every church and every missions organization in this country!"

It's Time for Honest Reporting

Sending churches are being led to believe that traditional missions are growing and effective. Part of the reformation we need in missions includes stricter measures for accountability than have ever been demanded before. We desperately need to have honest reporting from the mission field. And we need to understand how keenly some truly devoted missionaries regret seeing the shabby treatment of worthy indigenous missionaries.

No objective agency polices overseas missions. The only reports most Western supporters receive are the self-serving ones generated by the mission leaders for fundraising purposes.

Today's generation of Western missionaries is too often like an army camped on the banks of a river. Every day they talk about crossing to the other side. Their commander has ordered them to cross. They have many methods available—building a bridge, ferrying over or even swimming. Now, suppose these soldiers put on river-crossing displays and conduct river-crossing conferences year after year—but never cross the river. Wouldn't you have every right to think there was something seriously wrong? Yet this is exactly the current status of much of Western missions.

The topics no one wants to talk about fall into five basic categories:

- Prejudice against indigenous missionaries
- Our spiritual powerlessness
- Missionary lifestyles
- Stewardship of funds
- Our lack of authenticity in staff appointments

Because we can't or won't talk about them, our healing has been postponed again and again.

IT'S TIME FOR ACCURATE STATISTICS

Why can't we acknowledge the contribution of indigenous groups to modern missions? In my first book, *Revolution in World Missions,* I called them "God's third wave." Nationals are now completing what colonial missions began. The indigenous missionary movement is already the cornerstone of world evangelism today, but you'd never know it from missions coverage in the West. European and American Christians have no idea of the importance of indigenous missions because reports in the Western media chronically ignore the presence of indigenous missionaries.

The Association of Church Missions Committees (ACMC) was at one time a powerful missions group in the United States, with 800 member churches. On the front page of one of their newsletters, some interesting statistics appeared, supplied by scholars at the Midwest Center for World Mission, one of the many regional centers inspired by the U.S. Center for World Mission in Pasadena, California.[1] The editor reported that the Midwest Center relied on MARC and Global Mapping for its information—two fine research organizations considered authoritative by mission scholars in the United States.

The chart listed 26 countries that are top priority for North American "tentmaking missionaries." To build its case, the chart purports to reveal how many "missionaries" and "churches" are in each country.

The two most unreached countries were China and India, with a total of 5,025 unreached people groups. According to the chart, China had only 26 missionaries, and India had 834—all from the United States and Britain. India had only 2,198 churches, and China's number of churches was listed as "not available." Because the Midwest Center did not recognize the contribution of indigenous missions and indigenous churches not controlled by Anglo-American mission boards, it had misinformed the ACMC membership about the true nature of the task before us in China and India.

Here are a few facts not mentioned:

- The 860 North American missionaries reported in these countries were actually social workers and technical-support people, not missionaries involved in evangelism or church planting. Virtually the only evangelism and church planting being done in China and India were being done by indigenous missions!

- In India, I conservatively estimate, there were at that time at least 10,000 indigenous missionaries engaged in full-time, New Testament witness. China probably had at least the same amount or more. The report ignored these numbers.

- The number of churches in India was probably a lot closer to 200,000 than to the mere 2,198 listed. There were probably that many Bible-believing churches in the tiny state of Nagaland alone. Based on an estimate of 70 million Christians in China, meeting in house churches averaging 30 members each, there would have to be about 2 million churches in China.

Even Bishop H.K. Ting of the official Three-Self church movement admits that at that time there were two Protestant churches opening in China every three days—and, of course, that doesn't even count the unofficial house churches![2]

Why didn't ACMC and the Midwest Center report on the number of indigenous churches and missions on these two fields closed to American missionaries? When we asked the editor the reason for the obvious distortion, he said he expects all his readers to take statistics like these with "a grain of salt," knowing they aren't accurate! "Why print them then?" we asked.

The reason, he said, was to give the compilers of the chart a chance to show the need for tentmakers to go from the United States—and the native church and mission figures don't contribute to making the point.

"Does that mean," we asked, "that it is all right to lie to make a point?"

"No," he replied, "but I see our newsletter as a forum for thought, and the Midwest Center was trying to build a case for tentmakers."

That such distortions occur when Western mission boards report only their North American missionary activity is regrettable. What is tragic is that millions of souls for whom Christ died may remain unreached because funds are withheld from the thousands of indigenous missionaries eager to be about their Lord's business.

IT'S TIME TO ACKNOWLEDGE RACISM

Selective reporting and nonreporting are a tragic sign of prejudice against indigenous missionaries, but so also is the attitude of some missionaries on the field against their national coworkers. Actually, the problem John and Mary struggled with goes beyond prejudice. There is a much stronger word to describe the sinful attitude that is still prevalent in the hearts of many colonial-era missionaries and mission leaders. We need to recognize this underlying mind-set and call it by its true name—*racism*.

During my years of ministry in Asia, I've traveled through many Two-Thirds World countries where some Western missionaries still live in established centers. It is unfortunate that even in this modern age some missionaries still treat the most educated, enlightened, godly, capable indigenous leaders as servants or less than equal—simply because the color of their skin and their culture are different.

NOTES |

1 | Mike Pollard, "Jumping on the Bandwagon," *ACMC Newsletter,* Spring 1989, p. 1.
2 | "China Opens Wider Door for Nora," *China Today Newspaper,* Spring 1990, p. 1.

13 | OUR SPIRITUAL POWERLESSNESS

As missions have grown increasingly ineffective, a strange phenomenon has occurred: The social sciences appear to have altered missions strategy. Western missionaries have introduced education and communication theory as a complement to preaching the Gospel. Such an alteration is understandable. The lure of human knowledge and wisdom is powerful. Many missionaries today are accommodating the Gospel to the religion and philosophy of the culture when they try intellectually to defeat animism, Buddhism, Islam or Hinduism.

Paul's experience with education and religious philosophy suggests another approach. In 1 Corinthians 2:1–2 he wrote: "I, brethren, when I came to you, came not with excellency of speech or of wisdom, declaring unto you the testimony of God. For I determined not to know any thing among you, save Jesus Christ, and him crucified."

ARGUING VERSUS PREACHING

In my early years as a street-preaching evangelist in North India, I had to learn this lesson the hard way. I read everything I could to defeat Hindu and Muslim philosophy, including the Bhagavad-Gita, the Ramayana, the Qur'an and other non-Christian scriptures. The better my apologetics skills became, the more I relied on my own logic and knowledge. Time and again, I found myself winning arguments—but not converts.

Then early one morning in my quiet time, I read Hebrews 4:12: "The word of God is quick, and powerful, and sharper than any two-edged sword, piercing even to the dividing asunder of soul and spirit, and of the joints and marrow, and is a discerner of the thoughts and intents of the heart." Later that morning, as I climbed onto the tailgate of our Gospel van to preach, I determined that I would preach "as a blind man to voiceless people." At that moment I threw out my communication theory. I laid aside my sophistry, my anti-Hindu arguments and my knowledge of local religious philosophy and culture. Instead, I expounded the simple Gospel to my Hindu audience. I talked about sin, salvation, faith and repentance.

To my surprise, a non-Christian teenager came forward, weeping in repentance to accept Jesus Christ—the living God of whom he had never heard before that sermon.

The lesson was heaven-sent. I learned that we must not rely on our knowledge and education to win the nations to Christ. As I led the youth to Christ, it was obvious to me that if I had argued against his religious prejudice that morning, he never would have come to find the Savior.

Education is not wrong in itself. The desire to understand and communicate with heathen cultures is often sincere and well-intentioned, but it short-circuits the power of the Gospel. Efforts to communicate to the natural mind of man do not bring radical conversion. The Gospel goes straight to the heart of man. It converts the spirit, not just the mind.

So much of modern missions theory relies on man-made principles, including what is passing itself off today as church-growth and people-movement strategy. Many of these sociology-based notions rely on merely arguing against social sins such as the Hindu caste system, racial segregation and economic class differences. Along with applied psychology, many of these principles are the same ones used as a basis for secular mass-marketing technology in the West. As a result, the power of the

Holy Spirit is frequently ignored.

After missiologists have presented their doctoral theses and shown their overhead transparencies, mission committees should ask some of these questions before they send a check:

- Where in the Bible is this approach to missions taught? What, especially, did Jesus and Paul say about your particular theory of church growth?

- On which fields have you successfully implemented the strategy or theory being proposed?

- Is there any historical precedent for using this method? If so, was the methodology central to what happened or incidental to a larger movement of the Holy Spirit? What role did simple preaching by indigenous missionary evangelists and pastors play in the church-growth movement used as an example?

- Will the implementation of this theory cause the indigenous church to be dependent on foreign missionaries for direction and leadership, for special funding and for equipment and supplies unavailable in the local economy? Must other materials be imported from the West?

Extravagant versus Christlike Lifestyles

My good friend David Mains, radio host of "The Chapel of the Air," presented an unforgettable challenge to attendees at a late-1980s convention of the National Religious Broadcasters (NRB) in Washington, D.C. He based his message on the best-selling book *The Accidental Tourist* by Anne Tyler. David began his talk by passing out an ugly, wrought-iron nail to everyone in the audience. At first the mysterious nail was not explained.

The story line in *The Accidental Tourist* revolves around a jaded writer named Macon who turns out travel guides for American businesspeople going overseas. Tyler describes Macon and his work this way: "He covered only the cities in these guides, for people taking business trips flew into cities and out again and didn't see the countryside at all. They didn't see the cities for that matter. Their concern was how to pretend they had never left home."[1]

The message of *The Accidental Tourist* for the convention delegates, said David, was not to be like that fictional writer and the businessmen. Instead, he challenged them to attend the NRB convention as they imagined Jesus would have attended. He gave four rules for really being present at the convention.

1. Don't be thinking constantly about yourself and your agenda.

2. Show genuine interest in what others are doing, viewing them as better than yourself.

3. Make your bottom line the advancement of the common cause.

4. Pray daily that you and your fellow workers will be drawn together in Christ's love.

Then the nail began to make sense. We cannot relate to people effectively until we, like Christ, are willing to open our palm and receive the nail as Jesus received the nails in His palms. We must die to ourselves in order to bring life to the lost. David challenged the delegates to carry that nail throughout the convention as a reminder to work at being Christlike.

These same four rules must apply to our missionary outreach. How I wish every missionary would carry a nail at all times! Foreign missionaries need to be reminded that they will be effective only to the degree that they are willing to surrender their own interests and culture and adopt those of the people to be reached. Donald Smith expressed this well in a 1999 article in *Evangelical Missions Quarterly*: "We must not retain our own lifestyle simply because it is our own. Such ethnocentrism cripples involvement with people, and thus cripples our efforts to build the church."[2]

The greatest cultural barrier between Western missionaries and the local population is still their alien, extravagant lifestyles. A visit to the average missionary home is the ultimate turn-off for the nationals on most mission fields, especially in Hindu, Muslim or Buddhist cultures. Missionaries simply cannot set a Christlike example and make disciples if they are trying to live with one foot in each culture. Native Christians must be able to see that missionaries cope with the same struggles they do, and in the same way, in order to see the power of the living God at work in their culture.

Missionaries who retreat to family and a Western lifestyle are setting up obstacles the nationals cannot overlook.

LIFESTYLE QUESTIONS

In light of the barriers that alien, high standards of living tend to raise, we need to ask some critical lifestyle questions of every missionary we support. For example:

- Do they live in a home far above the normal standard of the people they are trying to reach? Are their homes air-conditioned or heated when those of the average nationals are not?

- Do they take vacation-furloughs to the homeland, leaving the work behind for extended periods of time?

- Do they use separate medical facilities, schools and institutional environments that separate the missionary psychologically from the local people?

- Do they maintain a circle of friends, have separate worship services and live segregated lives from the rest of the population?

- Do they have cooks, drivers, maids and other servants that are abnormal in the society of those to whom they minister?

- Do they wear different clothes and shoes, use modern appliances and own other luxury goods that are beyond the reach of those around them?

- Do their church halls and institutions have a foreign appearance or are they furnished in a way that creates culture shock for native visitors?

- Do the liturgy, music and worship styles on the mission field tend to be similar to those in the homeland of the missionary? Are the art and even the musical instruments of worship imported from the West?

Perhaps in a few cases these are superficial matters, but every missionary needs to pray through these questions in the light of his or her particular assignment. In most cases it is arrogance that separates them from the unreached people they came to serve and win to Christ. The reason traditional Western missionaries prefer to live as foreigners often is their dislike for the ways of those among whom they work or their unwillingness to give up Western comforts.

Am I saying I believe effective missionaries must "go native" and sacrifice their culture and way of life to reach the lost? Absolutely yes. Do I think it is ever possible to lose your identity in the culture? Probably not in most cases—but even if it isn't possible, I think every missionary must try. Adopting local customs, dress, food and language may seem merely symbolic, but it is the first and essential step in identifying with the local people.

Ultimately, only to the degree that missionaries neutralize their own alien cultural barriers will they successfully plant indigenous churches. This is one reason Jesus chose to be born a Jew and be raised in a Jewish home. How could He ever fully identify with the Jews and become their Savior if He didn't forsake His heavenly kingdom, language and lifestyle to become one with mankind and the Jews?

What about adopting a bicultural lifestyle? There may be a few situations on university campuses, in large urban centers, in "base towns" around foreign military bases or ministries to servicemen or other specialists where a so-called bicultural ministry might work. But in most cases the use of this term is merely semantics—an excuse Western missionaries use to keep double standards. What is a bicultural person in any real indigenous culture? Is it not just another word for being a foreigner?

The real unreached people groups are almost always rural, tight-knit, closed cultures. Successful disciple making and church planting require maximum identification with the local people and death to the culture of the incoming missionary. If missionaries are not willing to forsake their culture and live like the people they desire to reach, how can they expect to be able to transfer spiritual life to their disciples?

Foreign missionaries will give a hundred reasons why they can't try to identify with the people. Many of these reasons are ones involving children, family and government restrictions. However, in the end they start to sound like better reasons for not going overseas than for attempting to live a life in the cultural schizophrenia imposed by colonial-style missions practice.

QUESTIONING OUR MINISTRY

Every missionary must be willing to answer some painful questions:

- How long have you been on the field, and how many disciples have you made?
- How many churches have you planted?
- What spiritual impact have you made on the people among whom you minister?

If the answers are unacceptable, perhaps part of the reason is an unwillingness to sacrifice the comfort, culture, freedom, position, power, riches and rights of being a foreigner in Two-Thirds World society. If we can't give up our culture, we must consider honestly whether God has called us to be a "sender" rather than a "goer."

Frankly, the problem with many of us is our unwillingness to face the fact that Jesus called us all to be servants, not masters. I cringe when I hear Western leaders talk of "using the nationals." We're not to use anyone in the kingdom. An authentic, New Testament missionary must give up the idea of being superior or having the right to use anyone else.

The personal lifestyles we choose for ourselves and our families reflect the heart of our management and ministry styles more than anything else we do. Westerners on the mission field are likely to instinctively choose a lifestyle they feel comfortable with—that of a detached overseer. Instead, we need missionaries who are forever feeling those nails in the palms of their hands, surrendering their ways to Christ's. We need missionaries who are like Paul, becoming all things to all men in order that they might win some.

Too few foreign missionaries from the West demonstrate the art of living as Jesus did, and their sending churches do little to prepare them for this kind of commitment. The cause of Christ would be better served without them. Western Christianity and society are not presently producing many Christians of this caliber—the kind of person willing to live that lifestyle of sacrifice and selflessness required on the mission fields of the Two-Thirds World.

NOTES |

1 | David Mains, "Working at Being Christlike," *Reveille Magazine,* June 1989, p. 6.

2 | Donald K. Smith, "Reviewing the Place of Western Missionaries for the Third Millennium," *Evangelical Missions Quarterly,* January 1999, p. 59.

14 | OUR STEWARDSHIP OF FUNDS

A missionary who spent years in Sri Lanka and India, where he successfully discipled a number of indigenous missionary workers, later invested his life in raising sponsorships for them in the United States and Canada. Even though he was more effective on the field than most foreigners, he felt his time was better spent representing the indigenous missionaries in the West.

"Right now," he said, "we know beyond a shadow of a doubt that we're having a more effective impact on Asia than we did when we were there. I believe that because of the hundreds of sponsors I've helped raise up for indigenous missionaries here, I have multiplied my missionary effectiveness thousands of times."

George Otis Jr. is among the small band of thoughtful mission leaders who are wondering out loud if we can still afford to keep sending traditional missionaries overseas.

The cost of maintaining a missionary family in Kenya or Zambia today runs in the vicinity of $45,000. Placing a missionary family in Japan, however, is an even greater fiscal adventure. First-year expenses there can easily top $100,000, with subsequent maintenance costs in the neighborhood of $55,000 to $65,000 (annually). In Brazil, the nation with the greatest number of North American missionaries, hyperinflation (currently running at an annual rate of 1,000 percent) threatens to push support costs through the roof. On balance, the cost of supporting a conventional American missionary abroad has risen 75 percent over the last five years.[1]

In Asia, more than anywhere else, the difference is amazing. In China, the per capita annual income is only $911; in Vietnam, $1,430; in India, $444. It is still possible to support indigenous missionaries working in village evangelistic bands for as little as $30 to $90 monthly. In cities and other countries, of course, the cost can multiply, but the average indigenous missionary supported by Gospel for Asia is still living on $90 to $150 a month.

John Maxwell, former pastor of Skyline Wesleyan Church, the largest Wesleyan church in the world, says we need to ask ourselves this bottom-line question: What is the return on investment for all the missions money that we give every year? Maxwell illustrates his point: "You can have one American missionary on the field for 15 years, costing the church $585,000—over half a million dollars—or a Filipino missionary, trained and on the field for 15 years at a cost to the church of $17,000.

"For the same amount of money that it takes to train and supply one American missionary to the Philippines, we could support 35 national missionaries. *Look at the difference.*"[2]

Can missions still afford this long, costly investment, especially when it is no longer necessary on most mission fields? Indigenous missionaries can routinely be organizing their first church in six months to two years of arriving at their assignment. Recruiting time for indigenous missionaries is usually only weeks or months because most indigenous missionaries are already involved in Christian service and need only be moved to an area that is unevangelized. Even when they have to learn a new language, it is frequently similar to their own. Thought patterns, food and dress can be readily adapted by a culturally near indigenous missionary. All this results in reduced costs.

True Mission Fields

Whether we should support indigenous and/or Western missionaries is not the only consideration. We must also prayerfully consider *where* our missionaries are working. There is enough evangelism taking place today to reach the world dozens of times. Unfortunately, most of it is happening among people who have already heard the Gospel.

In fact, so few resources are being devoted to reaching the unreached that the World Evangelization Research Center calls it a "scandal." Its 2002 update reports that 99.9 percent of Christian resources are spent in countries that are already over 60 percent Christian (World C), 0.09 percent are spent in countries where over half the people are evangelized but less than 60 percent are Christian (World B) and only 0.01 percent is spent in countries where less than half the people have heard the Gospel (World A).[3] That means that only $1 out of every $10,000 spent on ministry goes to reach those in countries where most of the people have never heard the Gospel. This is reflected in the following table:

	To the Unreached	To those who have already heard
Scripture Distribution	20 million (0.4%)	4.6 billion (99.6%)
Christian Books	4 million (0.1%)	3.5 billion (99.9%)
Christian Broadcasting	$6 million (0.1%)	$5.8 billion (99.9%)
Full-time Workers	20,500 (0.4%)	5.5 million (99.6%)
Tract Distribution	10 million (0.2%)	5 billion (99.8%)[4]

No one would claim that we should stop preaching the Gospel to the lost in countries that have already heard. However, any reasonable person must admit that spending 99.9 percent among the reached and 0.1 percent among the unreached is a grossly unfair distribution of resources. Why should some people get to hear the Gospel over and over again while more than 1 billion people are still waiting to hear it for the first time?

The apostle Paul in 1 Corinthians 11:1 encouraged others to "be ye followers of me, even as I also am of Christ." As Paul followed Christ, he stated his desire in Romans 15:20: "to preach the gospel, not where Christ was named, lest I should build upon another man's foundation." A cursory look at the distribution of mission resources will reveal that our desire is apparently not the same as Paul's.

David Barrett, in his amazingly detailed research published in *World Christian Trends*, calculates the number of times the Gospel is presented each year. In the year 2000, that figure was a staggering 938 billion times. Unfortunately, only 2 percent of this evangelism was done where Christ was not named.[5]

Several denominational and independent mission agencies today have annual budgets of over $100 million. I praise God for the good work that they do, but it cannot be said that they are concentrating on the unreached. Only 2 percent of Assembly of God missionaries work in World A; Campus Crusade has 2.5 percent; International Mission Board, SBC, has 3 percent; and Youth With A Mission has just 1.2 percent working where less than half of the population has heard the Gospel.[6] There is clearly an unbalanced proportion of missions personnel going to areas where a majority of the people have already heard the Gospel.

There is also a great disparity concerning the availability of literature for the reached and the unreached. Although Gospel for Asia is producing approximately 50 million pieces of Gospel literature each year, it is still not enough to keep up with the demand from our own missionaries and requests that we get from other organizations. Missionaries working among the unreached are crying out for literature that we are unable to supply. Imagine what could be done if mission organizations targeting the unreached had even 5 percent of the resources used by organizations ministering to those who have already heard.

In the United States, we have one full-time Christian worker for every 181 people, while in parts of Bihar State in India, there is not one missionary for 9 million people. In North America, there is one full-time Christian worker for every 185 people, while in Asia it is one for every 5,405.[7]

Barrett estimates the cost per baptism in the United States at an unbelievable $1.5 million.[8] Obviously each soul is worth much more than $1.5 million, but when you consider that the cost per baptism in India is only $9,803, it raises some serious questions. Is the soul of an American worth 153 times more than that of an Indian? Should we take some of the hundreds of millions of dollars that are being spent to preach to those who have rejected Christ over and over again and use it to tell over 1 billion people who have never heard of Jesus even once? Barrett estimates the average American is exposed to the Gospel 368 times a year.[9] How much is enough?

TRUE COST ACCOUNTING

Mission leaders and sending churches must start asking the tough questions about their financial stewardship. For example:

- How much did it cost to present the Gospel to each hearer last year as a mission overall? As a field? As an individual missionary?
- How much would it have cost to support an indigenous missionary to do the same evangelistic work? Would it be more efficient and effective for us to support indigenous missionaries?
- How much was the average cost to start a new church last year as a mission overall? As a field? As an individual missionary?
- How much would it have cost to support an indigenous missionary to do the same church-planting work?
- In terms of pure proclamation, how much would it cost per thousand to blanket an unreached people group with Gospel radio, literature, newspaper, poster and tract evangelism?
- What would it cost to assist indigenous workers with other simple tools, such as Bibles, cassettes, flip charts and audiovisuals?
- In your missions program, how are both foreign and indigenous missionaries accountable for the funds entrusted to them? Are

results measured in terms of return on investment, or does financial accountability end with only a financial audit in the U.S. offices?

- What about overhead costs on the field and in the United States? How much of each donation is used for direct ministry and how much for overhead?

- What about conference attendance, missionary consultations and other strategy sessions? How does your missions program attach numbers and measure results from these meetings in terms of converts, new churches planted and missions launched to unreached people groups? Are we getting benefit out of these meetings equal to their cost?

- As we look toward completing the missionary task, how much is it going to cost to complete a church start-up in each of the 10,000 unreached people groups still without a witness? How much is it going to cost using Western personnel and methods? How much is it going to cost using indigenous personnel and methods?

Measuring the results of missionary investment by ratios and forcing ourselves to answer the hard financial questions is a painful process, especially for mission leaders who have never really made themselves accountable before. If, however, we view the self-evaluation process as an adventure rather than a way to judge one another and fix blame, it can be wonderfully constructive and liberating. We must never forget, though, that not all fields are alike. In fact, not all situations are alike even in the same country. Sometimes we are sowing seed spiritually and breaking up fallow ground; sometimes we are blessed to be in harvest time.

Naturally it is going to cost far more in terms of finances and people to penetrate resistant unreached people groups than the more open ones. Costs of living in cities are more than in rural areas, but you can often reach more people faster in cities. These and many other factors need to be considered prayerfully when we evaluate missionary finances.

Just because it is sometimes difficult to be a good steward doesn't mean missions or missionaries should be left unaccountable! Even though some ministries are by definition more expensive than others, we will be truly foolish if we continue to finance missions without counting the costs and finding ways to do the work more effectively and efficiently.

An article in *Evangelical Missions Quarterly* titled "Confessions of a Sender" addresses the need for an open line of communication and accountability between "goers" and "senders." "I believe," the writer says, "that stewardship is the issue. Stewardship on my part demands that I pay attention to how the funds that I give are spent. . . . When missionaries are not serving responsibly . . . should not their senders know about this? We are not a partnership until we do."[10]

TRUE WITNESSING

I'll never forget the fascinating talk I once had with a so-called village development missionary in Nepal. This man had been in the country for 22 years. We talked about his work and the Gospel, and I learned that during that time he had not won a single soul to Christ, let alone planted a church.

Incredulous, I questioned him about the nature of his work. He had learned the language and obviously had a lot of contact with local people of all kinds because he was digging tube wells. His work took him out to remote villages, and it was hard to imagine that the subject of his faith could be avoided.

Indeed, it was hard to believe he wouldn't have some kind of opportunity to witness and that his life wouldn't attract somebody to Christ. But he was adamant. He truly believed with all his heart that God had called him to dig wells and that this was his ministry. He didn't preach or witness because he honestly didn't believe that was part of his job description.

Although I'm sure the directors of his mission in New York City probably felt he was doing a great job, I couldn't help but wonder what the
folks in his church back home would think if they could hear his explanation. I dare say a good many of them gave to their mission because
they assumed this man would be extending the kingdom of God, even if
he was digging wells as a vocation.

Although this well-digging missionary had his theological rationaliza-
tion down pat, I'm certain his work would not be considered authentic
missionary ministry by most laypeople in the denomination that sent
him out.

Does that mean we don't need social workers, pastors and support
people? Of course not. There is a legitimate need for these people in
many local church situations on the field. But in most cases they should
rightfully be getting their support from the local congregations on the
field, not from mission funds. And certainly not while we still have
approximately 2 billion people without a Christian witness.

A California congregation invited me to present the challenge for
indigenous missionaries. When the pastor gave the final challenge to his
people on the last night, 160 people pledged to each support a full-time
indigenous missionary. The congregation was already supporting 40, so
their total came to 200 indigenous missionaries sponsored. And these
missionaries were working in pioneer situations on the front lines of the
Gospel.

The cost for sending out 200 of these indigenous missionaries is
about $216,000 a year. If the congregation were contributing to tradi-
tional American missionaries with that same money, how many could
they send? It may come as a shock to you: only 3 missionaries to Japan;
7 or 8 missionaries to the Philippines; and 10 or 11 missionaries to rural
Two-Thirds World countries.

The decision is obvious. Unless there is some compelling reason, it
makes overwhelming sense to support indigenous missionaries rather
than foreign missionaries.

TRUE REPENTANCE

Plainly, we must talk openly about this serious problem and study the alternatives. We would do so in a minute if we treated missions as seriously as we do our business transactions.

It seems as if God is saying to us, "My child, it is time for a radical change. Put your house in order." I have had to do this in my own life, and I believe God is now calling on Western church leaders to take this kind of action concerning our current mission programs. We must be honest with ourselves and make changes. The only way we as the Body of Christ can begin walking in the light is by opening up and admitting our weaknesses.

The beautiful thing is, when we confess our sins and turn the control back over to Him, the Holy Spirit rushes in with cleansing and power. What wonderful things the Lord will do in our lives if we only surrender our "hidden corners" to His light of truth.

Homer Firestone and David Miller, missionaries to Bolivia, agree. Writing in *Evangelical Missions Quarterly*, they say, "Self-examination, although painful, can be tremendously beneficial. Repentance is a great way to make new beginnings. Healing and reconciliation are central themes of the gospel. Everyone in the missions enterprise—board members, administrators, missionaries and church leaders—ought to include these elements in their working agendas."[11]

NOTES |

1 | George Otis Jr., "We Could Learn Some Lessons from the Business World," *ACMC Newsletter*, Spring 1989, pp. 6–7.

2 | Sermon by John Maxwell at Skyline Wesleyan Church, La Mesa, CA, May 6, 1990.

3 | "The Scandal of World A," World Evangelization Research Center (http://www.gem-werc.org/scandal/scandal04.htm).

4 | David B. Barrett and Todd M. Johnson, eds., *World Christian Trends, A.D. 30-A.D. 2200* (Pasadena, CA: William Carey Library, 2001), p. 55.

5 | *Ibid.*, p. 49.

6 | *Ibid.*, p. 57.

7 | *Ibid.,* pp. 418–419.

8 | *Ibid.,* p. 419.

9 | *Ibid.,* p. 425.

10 | "Confessions of a Sender," *Evangelical Missions Quarterly,* October 1990, pp. 445–446.

11 | Homer L. Firestone and David Miller, "Mission Boards: The Self-Critical Alternative," *Evangelical Missions Quarterly,* October 1990, p. 414.

15 | THE REWARDS OF SPONSORING INDIGENOUS MISSIONARIES

The tiny congregation of the Church of the Blue Ridge near Waynesboro, Virginia, numbers only 30 adults. But one thing they do possess is a missionary vision—and their board of elders is serious about frontline evangelism. For some time they have wanted to make a significant impact in evangelizing an unreached people group.

So the elders contacted a missions society that specializes in helping indigenous missions. "Could our church help sponsor the evangelization of one of the 12,000 unreached people groups still without an established Christian witness?" they asked.

Within minutes a missions executive was checking his files of indigenous missionary groups in the Philippines. Using his Unreached Peoples Data Base from Global Mapping International in Pasadena, California, he matched the church with a Gospel team. This team had targeted the unreached Waray Waray tribe in Leyte, Philippines, for its next evangelistic thrust. He discovered that a nearby indigenous missions board would be able to send a team of three Filipino missionaries to the Waray Waray people for only $550 a month. This would cover their transportation, housing, support, government-required taxes and supplies.

The elders of the tiny Virginia church were astonished at the huge impact their tiny missions budget could have overseas. By investing their limited resources in indigenous missionaries, they could help one of the thousands of remaining unreached people groups to hear the Gospel. In June the elders presented their vision to the whole congregation. They used maps and slides from the Philippines, in addition to information one of the elders had discovered from looking up the Waray Waray people in the *Ethnologue* from Wycliffe Bible Translators.

There were 2 million Waray Waray in the northern and eastern parts of Leyte. One of the largest unreached people groups in the world, they are a hostile and difficult group to reach. Except for nominal Roman Catholics and some cults, no Christian group had yet established a viable work among them—this in spite of the fact that revival and spectacular church growth continue in many other parts of the Philippines.

That Sunday morning the congregation prayed and pledged to send the nearby indigenous Gospel team to help reach the Waray Waray. To recruit, train and send three American families would have taken years. The Blue Ridge church wouldn't have been able to afford such support, because the annual cost would have been at least $84,360 for three American missionaries.

THE LOWER COST OF INDIGENOUS PERSONNEL

According to a study by a conservative missions board in the Philippines, an American couple needed an annual budget of $2,400 for language training, $720 for support-raising "prayer letters," $1,200 for contingencies, $2,100 for insurance and Social Security and $1,500 for furlough fund, making a total of $7,920. None of this is needed by the indigenous missionaries.

Other comparisons are equally revealing. The American couple would need $6,000 for field work expenses; the Filipinos, only $132. Miscellaneous costs for the Americans would total $1,200; for the Filipinos, $67. A car for the Americans would cost $3,000 annually, amortized over five years; for the Filipinos, only $67 would be needed for jeepney fares. Housing costs for the American couple would total $4,800; for the Filipinos, $267. Personal family needs for the Americans would be $7,200, as opposed to $667 for the Filipino missionaries.[1]

This study was based on the average costs of supporting an American missionary family in the Philippines in 1987. It might vary somewhat for work among the remote Waray Waray tribe, but the cost differential is amazing no matter where you make the comparison. Many missionary couples in Manila and remote assignments in the Philippines are having to raise even more funds than this. It is not unusual to see individual family budgets ranging from $40,000 to $50,000.

What a challenge it will be for this little group of Americans in Virginia to pray for their Filipino witness band and share in this pioneer work among one of the world's most lost and forgotten peoples!

Yet isn't this a direct fulfillment of the promise the Lord Jesus gave the Church, as recorded in Acts 1:8? "Ye shall be witnesses unto me both in Jerusalem, and in all Judea, and in Samaria, and unto the uttermost part of the earth." This local church is enjoying the excitement of seeing that prophecy fulfilled through its global and local outreach.

BEING INVOLVED IN A WORLDWIDE ENTERPRISE

What an awesome and comprehensive command the Great Commission is! It not only sends us out to cover the geography of the world, but it makes us part of seeing the Gospel supernaturally cross barriers of culture as well. In the Great Commission, the Lord Jesus intended us to miss no one with the Gospel.

The implications of fulfilling such a worldwide commission are staggering. How could Christ have actually expected us to be involved simultaneously in multicultural ministries locally and to the uttermost part of the earth?

That means translating the Gospel into 13,500 world languages with thousands of additional variations of these languages, including 30,000 dialects. It means accommodating it to 12,600 major ethnolinguistic groups, further subdivided into 60,000 minicultures or tribes and even further subdivided into 250,000 clans—what anthropologists call culture complexes. It means identifying with five major world races further divided into about 70 miniraces. And it means crossing 238 national and political frontiers that have taken millennia to construct.

In addition, in today's world, we also now have 402 megacities that are becoming cultures unto themselves.[2] Urban evangelism, because it addresses so many cultures and needs simultaneously, is one of the greatest challenges facing the Church today.

Yet it is obvious that Christ literally meant for us to reach out to this whole world—apparently in something almost like concentric circles, according to the Acts 1:8 rendering of the Great Commission.

Does that command mean that everyone in the Body of Christ must literally and personally be responsible to go into the whole world? Does it mean each local church must literally send members from its own congregation to the whole world? I do not think so. There is no other logical way to fulfill this assignment but to help support many different missions that will reach not only our own cities, states and nations but the rest of the world as well.

Today many people believe the Great Commission means they should go into all the world to increase their denominations—to make more people like themselves, with labels like Anglican, Baptist, Catholic, evangelical or Pentecostal. At other times the labels are related to special ministries, outreaches, issues or causes. We must remember that the Great Commission is not given to one individual, to one local church or even to one race or denomination or nation. Otherwise, churches and mission organizations will waste valuable resources by constantly reinventing the wheel and embarking on overlapping projects.

AN ENTERPRISE FOR THE MEEK

It seems to me that many in our church today cling to a false belief that they and their group are the only ones who can reach the world for Christ. This kind of thinking reflects a paternalistic attitude in its basest form.

Rudy Barlaan, a linguist and lecturer with Wycliffe Bible Translators and a native Filipino, describes some signs of a paternalistic mind-set: *One,* there is a feeling of indispensability—"they can't do it without us"; *two,* there is an attitude of excessive pity—"those poor people need our help"; *three,* an attitude of overprotection—"they can't make decisions for themselves"; *four,* an excessive feeling of responsibility—"we have to meet their needs"; *five,* a feeling of sovereignty—"we're in control."[3]

The late Charles Troutman, former general director of InterVarsity Christian Fellowship, warned, "Paternalism is not just a harmless attitude but a despicable curse. It is a denial of the integrity of the individual as a responsible person. It denies that the Holy Spirit is capable of transforming and developing anyone.

"Paternalism robs us of the confidence that God can do what we cannot, and gives us built-in arrogance that we cannot hide."[4]

But Western missions are slow to give up this paternalism. Many organizations remain rooted in doctrinal pride and superior attitudes. And because of this, most of the grand designs that come from the Western church are either stillborn or headed for an early grave. Missions that attempt to impose alien organizations, programs or talents are doomed. Oh, that we would pray as David did: "Keep back thy servant also from presumptuous sins" (Psalm 19:13).

Meanwhile, the mission fields of the world are still waiting for those truly called of God—those who will give up their efforts to impress others and abandon their own agendas, plans and pet doctrines.

Where are the meek who will joyfully demonstrate that they are indeed slaves of Christ? Where are those who will take up the towel, as Jesus did, and become servants to His servants? That kind of missionary leader is irresistible, though you seldom see him at the podium or covered by the media. He is too busy, out doing the work.

THE MOST GIFTED WORKERS ARE ALREADY THERE

Such missionary leaders already exist on most of the world's mission fields. Often, as well as having a burden for the lost and unreached, they are faithfully serving the Lord in existing churches as lay leaders. Few of them are ordained by men. They usually lack degrees from Western seminaries or from Bible schools. Yet they are compelled by the love of God to witness and gather converts into the Church. They usually are known only by their fruits.

These lay leaders don't wear the robes and collars of clergy. They have no special rank or status. Though frequently considered the offscouring of the earth, these "barefoot missionaries" are often the best qualified and most gifted for the work. These are the hidden missionaries—ready to be called, commissioned and sent forth to carry the Gospel to the unreached villages, peoples and nations. On almost every mission field, thousands of dedicated servants wait only to be identified and sent into the harvest field.

Does this mean we should put a premium on sending out ignorant and uneducated missionaries? No, education is important. But not the kind so many Western missionaries and churches refer to when they glibly declare, "We must train the nationals." The training they receive will be based in their home countries—thousands of small Bible schools found in the far-flung corners of their native lands. These local training centers educate 15 to 100 students at a time, in their mother tongue, with hands-on experience and solid Bible teaching. After two to three years of intensive study and labor, they are deeply rooted in God's Word, well-equipped by godly leaders and ready to go into the unreached areas.

Does this mean we should put a premium on recruiting the simple and unsophisticated? No, on the contrary, the best missionaries are those who are well aware of worldly planning methods yet have chosen to renounce human wisdom and rely on God for divine wisdom. They are not stupid but have chosen to trust God rather than man for their success. But because they haven't yet learned Madison Avenue marketing and fundraising techniques, they are invisible to the West and its missionary machinery. So they go unsupported and unreported.

The best news for world evangelism is this: *The workers are already there!* While mission leaders in the West are wringing their hands at the lack of new missionaries from traditional Western sources, thousands of spiritually qualified missionary candidates are waiting on the field to be sent to the hidden peoples.

There is no shortage of missionaries in our world today. All the staff needed to complete the harvest is already out there—often gleaning in a nearby field because they don't have the means to get to the untouched harvest. Today an almost unlimited source of missionary labor waits to be commissioned and sent into the ripened fields.

A CHANGED PERSPECTIVE

We will never finish world evangelization in our generation until we reverse our thinking. We must stop viewing the missionary problem as a need to get more white missionaries from here to go there. Instead, we must adopt a field perspective. *We must discover the power of sending the nearest indigenous missionary.* We'll know the task has reached completion stages when the primary talk of sending churches is not about transferring missionaries from "here to there" but from "there to there."

When we sponsor indigenous missionaries, our perspective changes. We learn to examine each mission field opportunity from the perspective of the unreached people groups still without an evangelical witness. Take, for example, Bihar State in North India. There are about 12 million unreached Muslims in that state. From this new perspective, we must ask ourselves where in India we can recruit missionaries to go to these people.

Our first place to look should be the nearest Christian churches. If we cannot find enough volunteers among the existing churches in Bihar, then we can go next door to West Bengal State and look there. If they are not there, we must go north and south and east and west until we find the nearest church willing to send a missionary team.

Somewhere among India's nearly 100 million believers there are Gospel teams who will be able to go among the Bihari Muslims.[5] But at present, is any missions agency from the West actively helping the church in India to mobilize indigenous witness teams to Bihari Muslims? As I write this, there is only one—and their teams have been mobilized at the request of Indian leaders, not by the initiative of the international agency that is helping with support.

See how this perspective differs from the solutions offered by traditional, colonial-era mission agencies? If they want to evangelize unreached people groups, such as the Muslims of Bihar, they usually have three responses.

The first response is, *Let's send one of our own from the West.* But for India, this is now impossible, because India will not issue visas to evangelistic missionaries. And the problem is compounded by the fact that Western missionaries are hard to recruit for Muslim work and even harder to support financially.

If that fails, Western missions will next try to send *a missionary social worker, teacher or medical worker to maintain a witness of presence.* India might allow a token teacher or well digger into Bihar (but no one to witness), and not because the government really needs the outside help. At present there are supposedly 1,310 such missionaries in India to reach the whole nation of over 1 billion souls.[6] Missionary social workers are outnumbered nearly a million to one. No surprise then that their impact on the nation has been minimal, to say the least.

The latest solution being offered to meet such requests is to *send in a foreign tentmaker who will be a part-time witness while holding a secular job.* This has not yet worked in India, since there is little demand for foreign English teachers or outside workers. The government remains opposed to giving work permits to Westerners, whom they view as taking jobs away from local citizens.

All three of these solutions attempt to solve the missionary staff problem from a Western perspective and are based on the unspoken assumption that a Western missionary is always the first and best choice. By this kind of thinking, it is considered better to send even a part-time English teacher from the West than to support an Indian citizen who would preach and plant the church by working 16 hours a day for $60 to $120 a month.

A UNITED EFFORT

As we have seen, Jesus gave the Great Commission to the whole Church, not just to a single individual or even to the 12 apostles alone. As persecution came, the entire body of believers joined in the evangelization of Judea and Samaria in fulfillment of Jesus' commission as recorded in Acts 1:8. This is an order given to the universal Body of Christ. Jesus was telling the *whole* Church to take the Gospel to the world.

Before we send anyone overseas, let's get out our maps and see where the nearest local church is. Let's check with the leadership there and see if we can unite our hearts with them to reach their own Judea or Samaria rather than trying to send in a foreigner from the outside. Why not help fund indigenous missionaries when senders from the indigenous church have used up their resources to support their people going from Jerusalem to Samaria or to the uttermost parts? In fact, there are many situations in which the local church needs help just to support missionaries to reach millions of local "hidden people" living almost on their doorsteps.

This sending and going relationship is made clear in Romans 10: 14–15, where Paul explains that some are called to preach and others are called to send them. While we still send Western missionaries overseas now, most pastors in the West recognize that we are in the "goer" role at home in our own Jerusalem, Judea or Samaria. And we are at the same time "senders" of other missionaries to the uttermost parts. Let's be partners with the whole Church and send not only white missionaries but black, brown and yellow missionaries as well.

SEEING THROUGH THE EYES OF JESUS

Intellectually, sending churches and the Western missions establishment have begun to acknowledge indigenous missions. But by and large, Western mission publications, posters, bulletin boards and photography still train the spotlight on the foreign missionary. The emphasis is on *our* going, on the needs of *our* missionaries. The stories are always on *our* hardships, risks, health and welfare.

How different would our missions program look if we saw the mission field through the eyes of Jesus? Would we see the pictures of people who are fabulously rich in comparison to the indigenous missionaries in those distant lands? Or would we see instead the faces of local citizens who are suffering and dying to pioneer the Gospel in the remote villages, hospitals, prisons and slums of Asia and Africa?

If we saw missions outreach through His eyes instead of our own, yes, we would see some white faces on our mission maps, but we would see many more faces of brown, black and yellow missionaries. We would discover that God already has many harvesters ready and waiting to go into the mission fields. As a result, we wouldn't send Americans who can't speak Spanish to Mexico for $50,000 a year, while hundreds of Mexican soldiers of the cross don't have the $1,000 a year they need to be effective preachers of the Gospel.

THE SOLUTION TO THE PERSONNEL CRISIS

What would happen if we were to assign missionaries from the nearest, existing indigenous missions and local churches? I believe the entire crisis in missionary staff shortages would be solved almost overnight.

- We would multiply the impact of our funds. In many cases, we could deploy 30 to 75 indigenous missionaries where we now have only one Western missionary family assigned.

- We could start to make a real impact on the 10,000 unreached people groups, including those in China, India and the former Soviet Union.

- We could redeploy some Western missionaries to other assignments on the field where their skills and talents are more needed or to areas where the door is open to foreigners and where they could serve most effectively.

- We could reassign other Western missionaries to the homeland. Here they could use their overseas experience to become expert advocates of indigenous missionaries and the unreached people groups they have encountered on the foreign fields. One of the biggest needs in the days ahead will be for an army of itinerant missionary leaders to reeducate and interpret what is happening on the field to Western churches, prayer bands and donors.

- We could also reassign these Western missionaries to expand campus, refugee and other ministries to foreign populations in Western nations. The knowledge of culture and language and the people skills that they have developed on the field could be used to make an even greater impact on foreign visitors and guests in the West.

- We could save millions of dollars annually in funds and personnel that are now involved in missionary recruiting, administration and fundraising. These funds instead could be sent overseas to support indigenous missionaries and be used to raise up more sponsors for them in the Western churches.

NOTES |

1 | "A New Day in Missions," *Christian Mission,* 1987, p. 12.

2 | David B. Barrett and Todd M. Johnson, eds., *World Christian Trends, A.D. 30-A.D. 2200* (Pasadena, CA: William Carey Library, 2001), p. 38.

3 | Rudy Barlaan, lecture notes (Dallas, TX: International Linguistics Center, 1985).

4 | Charles Troutman, *Everything You Want to Know about the Mission Field, but Are Afraid You Won't Learn until You Get There* (Downers Grove, IL: InterVarsity Press, 1977), pp. 72–76.

5 | Although the official government census reflects a figure much smaller than this, a number of key Christian leaders who understand the situation believe the number of Indian believers is actually much greater than reported. This figure comes from David B. Barrett and Todd M. Johnson, eds., *World Christian Trends, A.D. 30-A.D. 2200* (Pasadena, CA: William Carey Library, 2001), p. 428.

6 | Patrick Johnstone and Jason Mandryk, eds., *Operation World,* 21st century ed. (Carlisle, Cumbria, U.K.: OM Publishing, 2001), p. 749.

B y now you are probably asking, if indigenous missionaries are so effective, why don't more mission agencies and boards change their policies and start to include them in support programs? That is perhaps the most puzzling question in missions planning and strategy today—the one every informed Christian leader should be asking at every opportunity.

THE TIMES ARE CHANGING

One answer relates to our attitude toward change. An interesting leaflet I read recently does such a good job of getting to the heart of the matter that this book would not be complete without a few paragraphs from it.

During the decade 1910–1920, many people who had been riding horses began to drive cars. Some became so enthusiastic that they said it was silly to trot along on a horse when you could be riding in a car. Others said the day had come when horses were no longer needed.

Horse lovers were shocked. What kind of talk was that? Think of all the faithful horses that had carried their masters through heat, cold, rain and snow over the centuries. Are we going to say that their labors were futile?

Who would dare imply a lack of appreciation for all the horse had done for humanity? It was like throwing out the baby with the bath water. Those who loved traditional things became very critical of the "new fangled machines" with youthful drivers. They wanted things to stay as they had always been, with horses and carriages.

Blacksmiths and harness makers were especially hostile. Buggy manufacturers were too, at first, but most soon switched to making car bodies. Slowest of all to change were the military men. At the start of World War I some generals shouted, "Shut off those infernal machines; they scare the horses. Wars have always been fought on horseback and they always will be."

If all this sounds ridiculous, I wish you could see some of the stacks of letters I have received in the past 20 years. I have been saying that a new era has begun in the history of foreign missions. The only way to do it 100 years ago seemed to be to send representatives of American denominations and mission boards to preach the Gospel in foreign countries. But today the situation has entirely changed.

Now there are hundreds of mission groups in Asia, Africa and Latin America made up of the citizens of those countries. Why try to perpetuate the horse and buggy? A new day is here. I challenge Christians everywhere to stop spending millions of dollars of God's money unnecessarily to send North Americans overseas. Let's send it instead to some of the excellent indigenous missionary movements that God has raised up among the Christian citizens of Asia, Africa and Latin America.[1]

It must be said, however, that an increasing number of Western mission agencies are struggling with ways to include indigenous missionaries as equals. But after generations of discrimination, biased policy rulings and outmoded practices, the changes are coming at a sluggish pace. When the independence and national liberation movements began overseas, almost every foreign missions board had an established policy of racial segregation.

To give up power and prominence when one has held them for decades, as established mission leaders have done, is difficult. To accept that one's way of life is changing is painful.

Until recently, few traditional mission agencies were willing to recognize that the post–World War II years were the dawn of a new age in missions. But beginning in the mid-1980s, an increasing number of American-based independent foreign mission groups started to support indigenous missions. Many denominations have also experimented on a limited scale with occasional grants to indigenous mission boards and groups, although most funds are still funneled through the traditional channels.

One would hope that all traditional mission agencies will choose to use their vast resources, networks of contacts and good relations with churches to support indigenous missions. If they would share with needy, indigenous missions, the face of missions would be altered overnight. Indigenous missions should be viewed as an answer to four centuries of prayer rather than as a competitor for the missions support dollar.

WHAT PREVENTS SHARING?

Despite the signs of increased support for indigenous missions, the overall picture remains grim. Of the over 600 U.S. Protestant agencies listed in the 2000 edition of the *Mission Handbook,* only half report any non-USA-supported staff. Of this 50 percent, many have a nominal representation of national workers. One organization has one non-USA laborer among its 157 missionaries; another has two out of a total of 226.

Traditional mission leaders have put forward seven main reasons why indigenous missionaries should not be supported by the Western church:

- It would cause Christians in the West to think that their Great Commission obligation is fulfilled by merely sending money overseas. Thus, it would weaken or even destroy overseas missions, because American Christians would lose interest and stop supporting missions work if they were not supporting missionaries from their own denomination or race.

- Supporting indigenous missionaries weakens the indigenous church. To send support from overseas violates the concept of planting indigenous churches.

- Indigenous missionaries are not accountable to the sending church.

- Indigenous missionaries cannot be trusted. They are not accountable in the same way traditional missionaries are.

- Indigenous missionaries present a communication barrier. That is, they will not be able to let the sending churches in the West know how their work is going.

- Indigenous missionary leaders will be corrupted by Western affluence and luxury when they raise support in the West.

- Indigenous missionaries are not true missionaries because they seldom cross cultural lines.

These charges are serious indeed. They must be considered carefully. Too much is at risk if funds given for missions are misused, either for traditional mission programs or for indigenous missions.

But the reverse side must be considered as well. For example, the first charge states that *supporting indigenous missionaries will weaken the overall emphasis on missions in the church.* The thinking is that Westerners will stop supporting missions when they are less involved in sending members of their own race and church.

This position has been most effectively argued by Wade Coggins, former general director of Evangelical Foreign Missions Association (EFMA). His widely quoted and reprinted article from *Evangelical Missions Quarterly* is titled "The Risk of Sending Our Dollars Only." "If our churches give only their money, and not their sons and daughters, our missionary vision will be dead in a generation or less," insists Coggins.[2]

It is true that itinerating missionaries, while home on furlough, have historically been powerful advocates for overseas missions. However, there is no indication that interest in missions declines among churches and individuals who start to sponsor indigenous missionaries. In fact, just the opposite is true, as Gospel for Asia has discovered. Believers seem to have a greater interest in missions after sponsoring nationals.

No responsible indigenous mission advocates ever call for sending dollars only. The need for prayer, communication, information and other kinds of involvement is just as great for indigenous missions as it is for traditional missions. So, far from spelling the death of missionary vision, a well-run program to support indigenous missionaries will actually increase the awareness and participation of Western Christians in the Great Commission.

To investigate this claim further, our organization surveyed churches that had taken on indigenous missionary sponsorships through Gospel for Asia. The goal? To see if their overall support for missions had increased or decreased since the decision to support indigenous missions. The churches were asked to list mission societies they support. The replies showed that most churches involved gave to a wide range of denominational and independent missions. Of the 245 churches that responded, the poll showed that 86.9 percent had found their experience of supporting indigenous missionaries to be rewarding—and they were still supporting indigenous missions.

When asked if the congregation's interest in the Great Commission had increased, decreased or stayed the same, 65 percent said it had increased, 1.3 percent said it had decreased, and 33.6 percent said it had stayed the same.

When asked if the church missions budget had increased, decreased or stayed the same, 65 percent said it had increased, 3.2 percent said it had decreased, and 31 percent said it had stayed the same.

The only conclusion that can be drawn from this survey is that there is no indication whatsoever that supporting indigenous missionaries significantly decreases giving to missions or the interest of the local church in missions. The majority of churches reported both an increase in missions interest and missions giving as a result.

The second charge states that *supporting indigenous missionaries weakens the indigenous church overseas.* The history of this argument revolves around the concept of planting indigenous local churches, a theory that had to be introduced about 150 years ago because of the abuses by Western colonial missions that were then dominating the churches they had planted. Western missions created the problem and then came up with an inflexible "solution" that today has become one of the main hindrances to fulfilling the Great Commission.

Although it is not necessarily a biblical concept, the notion of self-supporting, self-governing and self-propagating churches has been raised by colonial-era Protestant missions to a theological tradition considered almost as important as the Bible. Therefore, financial aid is rarely if ever given to local indigenous churches or pastors today because it is feared this will spoil the pastors by making them dependent on Western aid.

"What these traditional mission leaders fail to see," says one indigenous missions supporting agency, "is that there is no such thing as a self-supporting missions board or Bible school.

"Hudson Taylor started the China Inland Mission in England, but he also received support from Europe and America. Years later Andrew Gih started the Evangelize China Fellowship in Shanghai; why should he not also receive support from abroad?"

Let's carry this example one step further. Hudson Taylor not only received financial assistance from outside sources, but he received prayer and moral support as well. His ministry was not weakened by outside support; rather, it was *strengthened.* In the same way, the relationships formed through Western support of indigenous missionaries can only serve to bolster and encourage them in the calling God has placed on their lives.

It is also believed that *indigenous missionaries are not accountable to the sending church.* In reality, rarely do we find *any* missionaries today being directly accountable to sending churches, whether they are indigenous missionaries or foreign missionaries.

Most missionaries today are primarily accountable to the mission boards and agencies that sponsor them. The majority of indigenous missionaries, like foreign missionaries, also report to formal and informal field councils or eldership boards that hold them accountable for their activities and personal Christian testimonies. These field-level committees usually report back to mission agencies in the West, who in turn report back to the sending churches and donors. This may seem to be a cumbersome process indeed, but it is one that I personally see working effectively on a daily basis.

Therefore, the practical relationship of trust and accountability between the sponsoring group and the missionary actually hinges on *indirect* accountability through committees and boards. It really depends mostly on how much trust the donors have in the home office of the missions agency in the sending country. Few church leaders or mission donors ever travel abroad to inspect the work of the missionary on the field. So they must rely on the network of intermediaries between them and the missionary.

In the homeland or among sending churches, financial accountability is quite easy to establish, because most reputable missions offer audited annual reports. Plus, many belong to watchdog agencies such as the Evangelical Council for Financial Accountability or the Better Business Bureau or are audited by denominational authorities.

On the mission field, many similar organizations, both formal and informal, are in place and operating. Most mission boards and agencies that adhere to high standards in the United States are working just as hard on the field to ensure accountability from indigenous missionaries. However, accountability standards need to be watched constantly both in the homeland and on the mission field.

Wise donors and sponsoring churches need to exercise vigilance and ask questions, just as they would in any stewardship decision. But there is no reason whatsoever to believe that indigenous missionaries are any less accountable than traditional missionaries.

Another charge is that *indigenous missionaries cannot be trusted.* The truth is that we entrust indigenous missionaries with only a fraction of the funds we put into the hands of Western missionaries. Yet we are looking for controls and audits we wouldn't dare ask of traditional missionaries. Meanwhile, there are ample controls and checks and balances on all legitimate native missions work equal to or better than what are in place for foreign missionaries.

Sending churches have an obligation and a right to be good stewards. They should expect a sound statement of faith, regular reports from the field (including financial reports) and a system of accountability that is consistent with New Testament principles.

This is available if supporting churches and individual donors will establish several policies:

- Do not send support directly to missionaries on the field.

- Do not start supporting indigenous missionaries on your own, but work with a team of other believers.

- Plug into existing mission agencies, especially those that sponsor indigenous missionaries.

- Recognize local leadership on the field and never bypass their authority.

- Assist existing leaders in extending their vision for their nation rather than funding and financing your own vision.

- Examine the fruit of the ministries you support in terms of the personal holiness of leaders, souls saved and churches planted.

- Minister to native-born citizens of the country you're interested in who are temporarily living in North America, such as students, tourists and businessmen. Become personally involved as a church with immigrants from that mission field who still have relatives back in their homeland.

The Holy Spirit leads us into all truth, and He will guide any sincere individual or church that wants to get involved in assisting indigenous missionaries overseas.

The fifth charge states that *it is difficult for indigenous missionaries to report back on their work to sending churches and donors.* Bonds to the home church and family ties have traditionally been an important part of initial support raising and communication in general. This custom was an important factor in many mainline sending churches and denominations during colonial days. From there it spread to many of the older evangelical churches.

Mission societies that sponsor indigenous missionaries realize they must overcome the lack of expected personal contact and look for new ways to bond sponsors and the missionaries they support. They have discovered that it is possible to develop a deep prayer and support relationship between the missionary and his or her senders in the West. Most of these methods involve strong communication programs. Supporters of indigenous missionaries can receive photographs, testimonies and reports from the field. In addition, mass media tools, such as newspapers and videos, bring the missionary and the field much closer to sponsors and help compensate for the lack of face-to-face visits.

We need not be enslaved to the old methods of raising support based on visits from itinerating missionaries, although a growing number of indigenous missionary advocates are traveling in North America. These visitors help put the sending churches in closer touch with the field.

Thus, the missions movement does not need to be dependent on visits home from supported missionaries, as cherished as this tradition has become. In fact, mission agencies who want to add indigenous missionary support programs to their ministry can easily do so. It may mean adding different kinds of support-raising programs than have been used in the past, but it can be done.

It is also believed that *Western support will corrupt indigenous missionaries by exposing them to the affluence and luxury of Western lifestyles.* Although it is necessary for a few older indigenous missionary leaders to travel in the West to report on the work and help raise support, I have consistently opposed the coming of indigenous missionaries to Western nations and their itinerating for support. There are two reasons for my opposition.

First, I believe there is a real danger they will grow accustomed to Western mores and become less effective when they return to the field.

Many indigenous missionaries become filled with pride after visits to the West, and they pick up bad habits that hinder their ministries on the mission field.

Western methods and culture are intoxicating and deceptive to the visitor. Many methods that work well in the West will not transfer into another culture. Many a Western-educated church leader has found rejection and failure when he first returned to his native country and tried to implement the new lifestyles and technologies he acquired abroad.

Second, from personal experience, I have found that cross-cultural communication is just as difficult for indigenous missionaries visiting the West as it is for Western missionaries going to Two-Thirds World nations. Most indigenous missionaries find it difficult to communicate and present their ministries to Western sponsors and congregations. Many go home bitter and confused by the lack of hospitality they experience in Europe and North America. They cannot understand why their ministries and projects are rejected by Western believers. Ironically, most Westerners are not even aware they have offended the visiting indigenous missionary.

In this case, therefore, the argument against indigenous missionaries working in the West is a valid one. However, in future years it may be necessary for more indigenous missionaries to itinerate in the West just as traditional missionaries have done. The Western churches need to see the fire and zeal of indigenous leaders firsthand. Also, indigenous missionaries frequently have a message from God for churches in the West. As this trend develops, it will be necessary to trust the Holy Spirit to protect and guide these indigenous missionaries just as we have prayed for the protection of traditional missionaries over the years.

Another question must be asked at this point. How much of this concern for the indigenous missionary is genuine? It could be that much of the fatherly concern expressed for indigenous missionaries traveling in the United States is really a selfish attempt to protect donor bases. Why isn't this same concern expressed for American missionaries whose salaries are 40 to 45 times higher than those of indigenous missionaries?

Aren't they also exposed to materialism and endangered by the lures and temptations of luxury in the West? All of us, in fact, stand in the same danger.

The final charge states that *indigenous missionaries are not really missionaries at all because often they are not cross-cultural; therefore, they should not be supported.* Most indigenous missionaries are, in fact, working cross culturally according to the strict definitions of anthropologists and sociologists. When a Tamil from South India goes to work among Punjabis in North India, it is a completely valid cross-cultural witness (according to the popular concept of cross-cultural evangelism championed as essential by many Western missiologists).

However, there is not a shred of biblical evidence to elevate cross-cultural evangelism to the place it holds today in popular missiology. Certainly, to require that missionaries work cross-culturally is unbiblical and contrary to common sense.

Consider these facts:

- The apostle Paul, a Jew, born and raised in a Hellenistic Roman colony, spent his entire missionary career going to other Greco-Roman colonies where he was a natural part of the culture. He spoke the languages and moved freely as a native-born member of both societies.

- From the day of Pentecost, it was foreign visitors to Jerusalem who carried the Gospel back to their homes throughout the Roman Empire. In reality, the Gospel was spread by immigration and tourism more than intentional cross-cultural witness.

HOW ARE WE TO SHARE?

"So what is left?" asks the traditional missionary. "How should the Western church most effectively involve itself in the Great Commission today?"

Rediscover the real meaning of the Great Commission. Beginning in our own prayer and devotional lives, we must begin to feel the compassion of the Lord for a lost and dying world. As we have already seen, the Great Commission is not something that was given to a tiny group of specially trained and educated envoys. It was given to all Christians—to the whole Church. It is something that we are all to be engaged in naturally every day.

Reach out to the lost world around you, including international students, visitors, refugees and immigrants in your community. Through the aliens in your community who are submitting themselves to your culture, the Lord will open a witness for you and your congregation to reach out to the globe. And don't forget to witness to your peers and others in your own ethnic community. Establish a balanced witness to your "Jerusalem" and "Judea," as well as looking to "Samaria" and the uttermost parts of the world.

Become a sender. Personally and as a congregation, become involved in sponsoring indigenous missionaries and adopting an unreached people group. Pray for those who can effectively take the Gospel to places where you cannot go.

Go as God calls you. But realize first of all that there is no biblical basis for most of the colonial-style missions activity in operation today. That fact, however, does not preclude your going overseas for the sake of the Gospel. Although much colonial-style missions activity often appears ineffective, we have many examples in Scripture and in history of God's sending out prophets like Jonah. When God makes such a call on a person's life, it is the obligation of the rest of the body to rally around and send that one into the harvest.

The challenge to the Western church and to missions leadership today is to move with the Holy Spirit. We must support the men and women whom the Lord of the harvest is sending into the mission fields of the 21st century.

NOTES |

1 | *Those Who Drove Cars Were Against Horses, Right?* (Charlottesville, VA: Christian Aid Mission, n.d.).

2 | Wade Coggins, "The Risk of Sending Our Dollars Only," *Evangelical Missions Quarterly,* July 1988, pp. 204–206.

Brother Mathew looked out over the crowd and felt his heart would burst with love for the people before him. It seemed a long time ago that he had first encountered these primitive people located in the interior jungles of India's Maharashtra State. Actually, it had been only a few years, but the Lord had moved so mightily among them that thousands had turned from animism to serve the living God. Today many of them gathered to hear Mathew share from the Word.

He spoke simply, yet his voice carried the weight of authority. The words were few, but the villagers listened intently as they sat under a makeshift shade covering of poles and branches.

Suddenly a distant cry was heard. Mathew stopped his preaching and squinted to see a small group of people hurrying toward the meeting place. What was that they were carrying? It looked like a small child. *Perhaps he is sick and they want prayer,* thought Mathew.

As the group drew closer, a cry went up: "The child is dead!"

The sobbing parents related the tragedy quickly. The boy had gone to wash in a pond near his home, and he had slipped and fallen in. Four hours went by before anyone noticed he was missing. That's when someone saw his body floating facedown in the water.

The stunned parents, who were believers, prayed desperately for their son. But nothing happened. Then they remembered the meetings going on in the nearby village, where Brother Mathew was preaching. "Let us go," the boy's father said simply. "They will pray, and our child will live."

Now the group climbed to the platform where Mathew was standing and placed the lifeless body in his arms. The crowd waited expectantly. "Pastor, pray for the child. The Lord will raise him up."

Mathew looked down at the body he was holding. There was no sign of life. The normally golden-brown skin was a pasty yellow; the body was damp and cold. He called some of the villagers together whom he knew to be strong in their faith. "Come and lay hands on this child, and we will pray."

As they gathered around the still body, Mathew prayed, "Lord! In this situation, let the faith of these people be established by Your miracle. Let Your name be glorified."

Minutes went by as the group prayed for life to return to the little child. Then Mathew felt something, a slight stirring. Could it be? He dared not open his eyes as the group continued to pray. But the movement was unmistakable. He looked down as the boy in his arms started to cry!

"Glory to God!" shouted Mathew. "The child is alive!" The crowd erupted with joy, and the parents were reunited with their son.

The rest of the day became a spontaneous praise service to the living God. Those simple villagers had seen a mighty act of God performed before their very eyes. This miracle was related again and again in that area, and wherever it was shared, people believed and turned from their idol worship and pagan ways.

WHY THE SILENCE?

This incident is only one of thousands of such miracles that are occurring on the mission field daily. In these countries, whenever the Gospel of the kingdom is preached along with signs and wonders, people are repenting of their sins and turning to Christ. Is there a secret to these success stories? Simply this: Mathew and the thousands like him are following the example of Jesus and His believers in the New Testament.

Jesus' ministry was characterized by the miraculous. Matthew 9:35 says, "Jesus went about all the cities and villages, teaching in their synagogues, and preaching the gospel of the kingdom, and healing every sickness and every disease among the people." Wherever Jesus went, He healed the sick and cast out demons.

In Matthew 10:8, when Jesus commissioned His disciples to go and preach, He told them to "heal the sick, cleanse the lepers, raise the dead, cast out devils: freely ye have received, freely give." These signs were evidence of the Gospel of the kingdom.

All five renderings of the Great Commission in the New Testament make a clear reference to the promised divine authority and supernatural power that will accompany the preaching of the Gospel. In fact, the Lord Jesus specifically forbade His disciples to undertake the Great Commission until they had received the promised power from the Holy Spirit (Acts 1:4–8). With the Spirit's descent came the authority to proclaim the Gospel with compelling conviction as first demonstrated at Pentecost.

After Jesus ascended to heaven and His followers received the promised Holy Spirit, they went everywhere preaching the kingdom of God, casting out demons and healing the sick in His name. The book of Acts continues the exciting story of how the Great Commission was carried out in the first century.

Yet when these same wondrous endorsements of Gospel preaching occur on the mission field today, a strange silence descends over Western mission gatherings. Dan Whitby of Bible Translations on Tape asserts that most Western missionaries are actually afraid to acknowledge them publicly. When they come home on furlough, they often are careful not to discuss or report the miracles that are regularly occurring on the mission field.

In his article "Discovering the Living God," he writes:

It is a shame that so many missionaries feel stifled and unable to share the wonders they see the living God performing overseas. In most mission

184 | COME, LET'S REACH THE WORLD

publications and at conferences, there is a studied effort to downplay the supernatural.

Why is this? Many missionaries fear their reports won't be believed or even that prayer and financial support will be lost if they share miracle stories. Many fear they will become labeled as fanatics.

What specifically am I talking about? Actually, nothing more extraordinary than the supernatural events that were a normal part of the New Testament. God's people through the ages have routinely seen miracles, healing, casting out of demons, resurrections, dreams and visions. Angelic visitations and supernatural supply are commonplace in Scripture.

You see, God is doing mighty things around the world today. As His people invade enemy territory, simple believers often see answers to prayer as in the Gospels and Acts. The living God is supporting His servants as they establish the kingdom of God in the hearts of lost millions.

But the philosophies of scientific rationalism have captured the hearts and minds of Western societies. Like a cancer, this unbelief has even spread into the churches of North America.[1]

Yet the promise of power and authority and the enabling of the Holy Spirit are an integral part of the Great Commission. Jesus promised that His missionaries would have such a supernatural endorsement on their ministry.

WHY ARE WE AFRAID TO ADMIT OUR NEED OF GOD'S POWER?

Could it be that most Western missionaries, educated into unbelief and powerlessness, are afraid to acknowledge miracles because it reveals their own spiritual weakness? Is the sin of spiritual pride keeping some of God's choice servants defeated and impoverished in their spiritual warfare?

Why would anyone not want the miracle power that Jesus promised to missionary witnesses? Without it, how else could one ever come against the spiritual forces that hold the harvest fields in bondage? How else does one handle spiritual ignorance and fear built up over centuries? And how would one handle the inevitable encounters with demons?

Missions is not applied anthropology, comparative religion or sociology. It is storming the gates of hell. It is a power confrontation—hand-to-hand combat with Satan and his demons. Consider, for example, this true account of a missionary experience in Sri Lanka. How else could it have been faced unless the Lord Himself intervened along New Testament lines?

This situation occurred in the life of an indigenous missionary. He is now a church-planting evangelist supported by Gospel for Asia. Before turning his life over to the Lord Jesus, Harath Bandula was a prominent member of a prosperous Buddhist business family. He, along with 12 other members of his immediate family, operated several successful firms based in the village of Teldeniya near Kandy. But their wealth provoked envy and jealousy from others in the community.

Spiteful neighbors and distant relatives hired a local Kattadiya witch doctor to cast a spell over the family. As a result, two members of the family were plagued with visits from strange, evil powers. In order to free themselves from the black magic, the family retained their own Kattadiya medium. Like millions of other Sri Lankans, they daily consulted astrologers to help search for a charm that would successfully break the curse.

But their efforts to fight witchcraft with witchcraft failed. After spending the family savings on the most famous astrologers and sorcerers in the nation, they were told that nothing could be done. In fact, a leading astrologer predicted that the strange series of misfortunes would eventually take the lives of all 12 family members!

Signs of demonic activity in the family homestead became more frequent. Their once comfortable and peaceful lifestyle turned into a nightmare. Strange sounds and voices could be heard when no one was present. Unidentifiable and vaporous figures would appear walking in the house and garden. Physical objects moved. Glass and pottery shattered. The garden would be littered immediately after being swept clean.

Money disappeared from inside locked boxes. Family members were living on the verge of hysteria and madness. And townsfolk began to believe that their house was haunted.

Then the demonic attacks became violent and threatening. The demons would possess various members of the family in turn, causing them to attempt suicide. Terrible faces and forms would appear in windows and throughout the house—spirit manifestations with unkempt hair, bared teeth and tongues dripping blood.

Another sympathetic Kattadiya made an attempt to cut the knot of the curse, and his wife immediately died. Disillusioned and overcome by the evil powers he could no longer manipulate, he gave up witchcraft. Now the family was left completely on its own to fight the spiritual attacks in any way it could.

They pilgrimaged to nearby temples, appealing to Buddha. But to no avail. They wrote for advice to a leading astrological newspaper and received a confirmation that the spell was irrevocable. The newspaper's advice column said the omens and signs were very negative. The entire family was "doomed for destruction" on July 10, the medium asserted.

GOD ANSWERS A PLEA FOR DELIVERANCE

Finally, the eldest son determined to offer his body to a benevolent spirit for possession, hoping that the malevolent forces would flee. This plan failed as well. Then he remembered a correspondence course he had taken from a Bible school in the capital. In desperation he wrote and asked for help from the Christian God, because everything else had failed.

Touched by the plea, a student from the Bible school and a local pastor came to visit the family on July 7, three days before the deadline predicted by the fortune-tellers. No sooner had they knocked on the door than a demon in one of the women of the family screamed out in recognition and horror at the presence of Jesus in the missionaries. The woman fled to a nearby cemetery, where she was found later, hiding among the tombs like the Gadarene demoniac in Luke 8:26–39. She was so violent that it took several men to restrain her and bring her back to the house.

But the indigenous missionaries prayed and took the authority that was theirs in Jesus Christ. The powers of darkness were overcome by a power greater than they and were cast out in the name of Jesus Christ. The grip of fear and death over the family was broken through the prayers of two of God's faithful servants. Not only was the woman delivered from the demons, but the rest of the clan members were set free as well.

Eventually every member of the family became a born-again Christian, and many in that area have come to believe in Christ. There have been no more demonic manifestations in the house. When the haunting began, there were no Christians in the village. Today there are 40 converts from Buddhism in Teldeniya. Weekly worship services are now held in what was once a haunted house, and the Christian witness as a result of this deliverance is known for miles around.

Young Harath was converted and answered the call for full-time Christian service. He went on to Bible school and became a powerful preacher and witness throughout the large Buddhist community in Sri Lanka.

WARFARE IN THE HEAVENLIES

No veteran missionary would be surprised to hear this kind of report. Yet Ken Baker, missionary to Africa with SIM International, explains what it is like to serve on the mission field armed only with a rational, Western education:

One time in Monrovia, Liberia, a young fellow in my discipleship group came to see me. He wanted to return to his village to see his mother, but he had learned that his uncle had placed a curse on him because he had become a Christian and would no longer participate in the bush (Poro) society. In view of his fear and nervousness, we prayed briefly, and I told him that he did not need to worry about the curse because he was a believer in Jesus. (My response still haunts me.) However, my answer did not satisfy him.

I did not see him again for more than three months. When he came back, he told me that he had become extremely ill and almost died. All along, he had feared that he would never leave the village alive. Well, I thought, he must have drunk some contaminated water or something. With my Western scientific worldview, I interpreted the events the only way I knew how, by rational deduction. But this incident, and many others like it, forced me to conclude that my teaching and counseling were totally inadequate.

My experiences in West Africa forced me out of my naiveté, because I had to reckon with the obvious presence of demonic power and the fear it generated. . . . I came to realize how much Western rationalism had clouded my understanding of the spirit world.[2]

Encounters with supernatural powers of evil are routine on the mission fields of the Two-Thirds World. The Gospel for Asia offices receive reports nearly every day that sound exactly like pages from the book of Acts. And these are not emotional experiences whipped up in the frenzy of a mass meeting. Such miracles are performed by the Lord quietly through indigenous missionaries who know how to exercise their God-given authority over the powers of Satan as explained throughout the Gospels and the New Testament.

When Christ commissioned the 70 disciples, He told them, "Heal the sick that are therein, and say unto them, The kingdom of God is come nigh unto you" (Luke 10:9). When a healing took place, it was visible evidence of the kingdom of God entering into that village. Today, in the remote, unreached corners of the world, when a miracle is performed, it is still a dramatic testimony to the power of God conquering the forces of darkness.

Over the years, respected indigenous missionary leaders have witnessed many such supernatural victories by the forces of light over the forces of darkness. We have found that such miraculous manifestations of the Holy Spirit almost always occur in conjunction with large movements of whole families and villages toward salvation in Christ.

Jesus told His disciples that the only way to capture enemy territory for the kingdom of God is to bind the strong man (Luke 11:20–22). The only way to gain victory over the powers of darkness—and thus fulfill the Great Commission—is to conquer each stronghold through demonstration of the power of God.

This kind of authoritative witness is essential on most mission fields, lands where evil manifestations of demon power are routine. Billions of people are still held captive to idol and spirit worship, beginning and ending their days with ritual offerings. They burn incense and sacrifice the living to propitiate the horrible spirits that animate their idols.

Even the most benevolent of demon spirits require ceremonial worship and offerings on a regular basis. So it should not surprise us to discover that Satan will not loosen his grip of terror unless the Gospel is preached powerfully in word and deed. For millions of people enslaved in spiritual darkness, they must see evidence of something better and stronger than their idol gods and shrines. Only this will give them courage to cast off their chains of bondage to folk religion.

MISSIONS' RESPONSE TO THE SUPERNATURAL

One of the saddest legacies of Western-style colonialism on the mission field today is the rationalism of many missionaries, accompanied by unbelief in the power of the supernatural. As a result, most traditional missionaries and their converts are powerless to deal with common demonic attacks.

Colonial missionaries, whether sent by liberal denominations or evangelical faith missions, were deeply affected by 19th- and 20th-century worship of science and technology. Humanistic beliefs in the ultimate goodness and supremacy of man left the church and missions with a bankrupt theology. This philosophy left no theological foundation for the living God of the Bible, who is an active partner in the enterprise of outreach and Christian witness.

It is no surprise, then, to find that modern missions seek to duplicate the healing miracles of Jesus and the apostles by opening hospitals. This attempt to imitate the liberating light of the Gospel by starting schools and hospitals can bring only limited benefits. Because this gospel is not the true good news of Jesus Christ, it lacks power to change people and societies.

Too often evangelical missionaries rule out the possibility of divine intervention in the everyday challenges of the mission field. Such missionaries are going out to proclaim salvation. But if they do not demonstrate their message of hope when they face the inevitable victims of demon possession and illness that characterize heathen lands, their message is weak and often futile. According to their teaching, the living God became inactive in human affairs following the last chapter of Acts.

Brad Hill, an Evangelical Covenant missionary to Zaire, shares his experience of this truth:

> Something else I learned from the African people is the reality of the spirit world. There is a whole demonic spirit world that I didn't learn about at seminary. . . . I didn't learn about exorcisms and healing and casting out demons. I haven't learned a lot of that yet, but I am very aware of the whole different realm of life. I want to talk to my students about the authorship of Hebrews, but my students want to know how Paul cast out demons. These people are teaching me what the Scripture means when it says that "the Kingdom of God is upon you." It certainly refers to more than I have experienced. These people know something about the battle between the kingdom of darkness and the kingdom of light. They know what it is like to have Christ present and to see people healed and demons cast out.[3]

With the exception of a handful of missionaries who first appeared in the 1920s, few colonial-era missionaries expected to preach a Gospel that would be backed up by the Holy Spirit with the signs and wonders referred to in Acts 5:12. For the most part, they succeeded in branding the few Pentecostals who appeared as "divisive" and "fanatical," thus avoiding a painful confrontation with the fact that their own ministries were powerless and ineffective.

NOTES |

1 | Dan Whitby, "Discovering the Living God," *The Vision 1*, no. 2 (Fall 1989), p. 7.
2 | Ken Baker, "Power Encounter and Church Planting," *Evangelical Missions Quarterly*, July 1990, pp. 308–311.
3 | "Door Interview: Brad Hill," *The Wittenburg Door*, February-March 1987, pp. 22–27.

18 | WHEN GOD PERFORMS MIRACLES, PEOPLE BELIEVE

The God of the Bible is a living God who invades the present and demonstrates His character and His power through His servants. But the Jesus preached and worshiped by many Western missionaries is too often presented as a god in a neatly sealed-up package.

The god of the modern, Western church is functional, easy to understand and unobtrusive. He is always there when you feel like using him for a little comfort, but otherwise he stays politely out of the way. Once, long ago, in the days of the prophets or during apostolic times, this god was alive and active in the affairs of men. But now he has retired and left the Church without his ongoing presence and power.

This inadequate concept presents us with a false image of God. He saves souls from hell but then leaves us to our own wits and skills to live the Christian life on this earth. This god is in reality a man-made idol. Such an innocuous concept of God is found nowhere in Scripture. And certainly such a powerless god is not the God of kingdom authority who promised us we would receive power from the Holy Spirit to fulfill the Great Commission.

Why is it so important for Western seminary professors, theologians and churchmen to fight the miraculous? Instead of denying the supernatural or substituting Western technology, theology and doctrines, the Western church must submit to the power of the living God.

The missions world today is bulging with statistics of all kinds. One can pick and choose mission and church-planting theories like the varieties of soda pop in a vending machine. There are enough available courses and seminars on "Reaching the Unreached" to make your head swim. The Western mind-set is the measurement of individuals, events and even spiritual matters by scientific rationalism. Education, logic and mental ability have become interwoven with everything we are and everything we do. And so we encourage prospective missionaries to educate themselves as fully as possible, assuring them that then they will be fully equipped.

We can study maps, expound theories and juggle statistics all we want, but until we experience the power of God in our ministries, there is little chance for eternal fruit.

In his classic book *Paths to Power*, A.W. Tozer puts an accusing finger on one of the most vexing problems in the world of missions today. "No one with a knowledge of the facts can deny the need for supernatural aid in the work of world evangelization. We are so hopelessly outclassed by the world's superior strength that for us it means either God's help or sure defeat. The Christian who goes out without faith in 'wonders' will return without fruit. No one dare be so rash as to seek to do impossible things unless he has first been empowered by the God of the impossible. 'The power of the Lord was there' is our guarantee of victory."[1]

EVIL FORCES ARE OVERCOME

Effective missionary work occurs when we renounce our own wisdom and methodology and go out to witness for Jesus with the anointing and power of the Holy Spirit. Only then can we experience what Elijah experienced when he confronted the prophets of Baal on Mount Carmel. God comes down to earth and vindicates His true servants, sending consuming fire onto the altar.

Brother Mathew shares one of the many "Mount Carmel experiences" he has confronted:

When I went to one village for the first time, preaching that Jesus Christ is the one true God, a group of men came up to me, followed by a bullock cart. A man was lying in the cart, and I could see that he was very ill, perhaps on the point of death. His friends had heard of my preaching, and they thought I was bringing another god to be added to the ones they already had in their tribal villages.

They told me, "This man has been bedridden for three weeks, and he is dying. We have brought him ten miles on this bullock cart. If your God is the true God, then this man should be healed. You stop your preaching and you pray to this new God for our friend."

Then the ultimatum came: "Either he will stand up, completely well, right now—and we will take you to our village and hear about this God—or, if he dies tonight, we will drive you out. You cannot escape from our hands."

Quickly I prayed: "Lord, You are the living God. Let Your power be displayed so that these people may believe."

Before I could even open my eyes, this man threw the blanket that had been covering him out of the cart. He asked for his walking stick and began to stand up shakily. The Lord gave me great boldness, and I shouted, "Throw away your stick and jump from the cart!" He tossed his cane away, jumped out of the cart and walked to the platform where I was standing.

The next morning our team was taken to his village and received like kings! The people believed the Word of God, and a great number were saved. This is how a large chain of churches was started in that area— through the healing of this one man.

In the interior villages of North India, in the jungles of Africa, in the tribal areas of Indonesia, in the villages of Latin America, people are not going to be won to Christ through ideological or philosophical arguments. The kingdom of darkness is ruling the lives of millions of people today who live in places like these. All of our abilities, arguments and theories will never set these people free. There has to be a demonstration of the power of God—a direct confrontation with the forces of darkness.

The people who live in our generation are just like those who lived in Jesus' day. If those people were given signs, wonders and miracles by the Lord Jesus Christ as proof of His deity, I believe that those lost and dying millions who live with unbelief in our generation also need to see and experience the power of God in their own lives. Only in this way will they be drawn to Jesus and have eternal life.

A well-known evangelist and missionary has said, "I am fully convinced that on the mission field today, one mighty miracle in the name of the Lord Jesus Christ among Hindus, Muslims, Buddhists or animists is worth more than a lifetime of preaching theory and philosophy."

I have experienced this principle in my own life, I've seen it applied in Brother Mathew's ministry, and I've seen it repeated time and time again in thousands of brothers we serve on the mission fields of Asia. Throwing ourselves upon God and believing in Him to endorse our witness in this manner has a powerful effect on lost souls. It often opens doors long closed to the Gospel and is the first step in winning families, tribes and even whole villages to Christ.

A DAUGHTER'S HEALING OPENS A CLOSED VILLAGE

The power of God often breaks open villages that have been closed to any kind of Christian witness for centuries.

Han Vithal Shinde was born and raised in a small Hindu village in Maharashtra, India. Until he attended a Gospel meeting in a nearby village, he sacrificed to spirits and worshiped the village idols just as his family and friends did and just as their ancestors had for countless generations.

But after hearing the plan of salvation, Han turned from his life of rebellion and followed Christ. The decision terrified his family, who begged him to keep his new faith a secret. However, he kept on witnessing and threw all the family idols out of the house in a dramatic demonstration of his faith.

This act enraged the villagers, and Han was driven out of town by the angry elders. For over a year he was not allowed to come back. During that time, he went from village to village throughout the surrounding district sharing the good news of salvation with anyone who would listen. His life of holiness and sacrifice became well known in the meantime, even to those in his home village who had forced him to wander homeless for Jesus.

But then the daughter of the village leader became deathly ill. The doctors gave up all hope, and the same elder who had cursed Han now sent a messenger asking him to come back and pray for the girl.

"When I prayed," recalls Han, "God healed that little girl completely, and this opened the way for me to come back to my village. The leader told me I could preach my Jesus, and 11 people came to the Lord."

Since then, many others in the village and surrounding areas have shown interest in Jesus. Han has dedicated the rest of his life to establishing local churches throughout that part of India.

FIVE HUNDRED COME TO JESUS AFTER A HEALING

James Sangma, an indigenous missionary in Bangladesh, grew up in a Hindu village of that predominantly Muslim nation. He tells the remarkable story of a healing miracle in his home village that resulted in the conversion and public baptism of more than 500 people.

His family and village worshiped a terrifying Hindu god that they had carved from bamboo.

One day an itinerant evangelist came to a village where Sangma was working. "As the evangelist was preaching," he recalls, "I realized that this was the most wonderful message I had ever heard in my life. The love of Jesus touched me deeply, and that night I gave up all my idols and accepted Jesus as the true God and my Savior. My life was completely changed. I was publicly baptized, and I worshiped the Lord along with other believers. I found the peace and joy I had longed for over many years."

But Sangma feared to return to his home village, knowing that his new faith in Jesus would make him the object of hatred and scorn.

198 | COME, LET'S REACH THE WORLD

Finally, however, he made a trip home. There he announced to parents, relatives and friends his decision to follow Christ. An angry mob formed and tried to force him to worship the village god at a sacred tree in the center of the village. But Sangma refused and was finally forced to leave the village and seek work elsewhere.

During this period, he sensed the call of God on his life and began to feel a burden to go back to his own people to establish a church. After attending Bible school for two years, he returned home, but again the village shunned him. He became an outcast, and even his own family refused to accept him back. Then a young boy in the village became seriously ill. The family of the boy hired Hindu priests to pray and call publicly upon the idol to save their son. Each day the boy grew worse as the family begged and pleaded for healing at the sacred tree. But the idol was deaf to the sacrifices and cries of the family.

One day, as they entreated favor from their demon god, Sangma asked the grieving family to give him a chance to pray to the living God. They agreed. "I prayed over the boy," says Sangma, "and commanded him in the name of Jesus to get up."

The boy stood up, started talking and asked for something to eat. He was completely well. "The people standing around immediately believed on Jesus Christ, having just seen His wonderful love and power," says Sangma.

Today a strong church exists in that village, and Sangma has gone on to witness and establish more churches in the tribal areas of India's Assam State.

RAIN SHOWERS AND DELIVERANCE START THAI CHURCHES

Lun Poobuanak, a hardworking indigenous missionary working with Buddhists and animists in Kalasin province, Thailand, saw an entire village of 134 families turn to Christ after God answered his prayers for rain.

The confrontation came one Sunday morning while he was holding services for a tiny group of Christians in one village. Although it was the rainy season, the monsoon had not yet come, and the crops were only days away from ruin. The village was in despair, and during the service, village leaders came in and interrupted the prayers with a strange offer.

"If you ask your God to give us rain this month, all 134 households in our clan will worship your God and become Christians," said the *mooban,* or head man.

"At first," says Lun, "I rebuked them for trying to play games with the living God, but they insisted that they were serious."

"We vow to become Christians," said the *mooban.* "If we do not, your God can send judgment on us."

So Lun and the Christians gathered together for three days of prayer and fasting, asking God to send rain. On the fourth day, a cloudburst came that flooded all the *klongs* (canals) and rice fields. "The rain was so intense," says Lun, "that the villagers humbly admitted that Jesus is the only true and living God in the universe."

Word of the miracle storm spread to many surrounding districts, so that not only the 134 households converted to Christ, but others did as well. "This is a living testimony that still helps us win souls easily in this area," says Lun.

In another incident related by indigenous missionary Soontawn Rawang in Buriram province near the Khmer border of Thailand, a demon-possessed girl pointed her village toward salvation. In this region, the people were pure spirit worshipers, believing that both good and evil demons possessed certain trees, rocks, mountains, rivers and even people.

In one area an evil spirit was strong and much respected by the villagers. It was so feared that everyone believed those who refused to sacrifice to it would get sick and die. There were many stories of local people who became ill after mocking or joking about this particular spirit.

The indigenous missionaries prayed and fasted before going to the village for an evangelistic crusade, because they knew the grip this demon had on the hearts of the local people. What they didn't realize was that the landlord and his daughter who rented them their meeting hall were mediums for the spirit.

During the meeting, the demon spoke out through the landlord's daughter, saying that he didn't like the Christians visiting the area. The demon went on to insist that the Christians be forbidden to preach Jesus in the village.

Before the crowd could act against the missionaries, however, Soontawn and the Gospel team rebuked the demon, using Mark 16:17–20 as their authority. They cast the demon out of the girl as the awestruck villagers watched in fear and trembling. In the following days, the missionaries went from house to house without harm in the area. Soon many others in the village came forward, asking that demons be cast out.

Within a month there were nine church groups formed in the district, all as a result of deliverance from demon spirits in the area.

THE HEART OF TRUE MISSIONARY WORK

Whole volumes could be filled with stories from our files of how individuals, families and entire villages have been converted as a result of one healing or a miraculous answer to prayer. Often such inexplicable signs and wonders are the spark that sets off a whole chain of conversions.

The witness of simple believers relying on the power of God is at the heart of all successful missionary work. As you witness these miracles and hear stories from indigenous missionaries around the world, you cannot help but be struck by how similar their accounts are to the stories in the Gospels and the book of Acts. This is probably because new expectations and faith levels are actually being created by reading the Word of God.

"Faith cometh by hearing," says Paul, "and hearing by the word of God" (Romans 10:17).

The exploding church and mission movements of Africa, Asia and Latin America are discovering the Bible and taking it at face value. Jesus exercised authority over devils, and so do they. Nobody has told them anything different—or yet explained these miracles away—and so thousands of simple indigenous missionaries are moving across the map with apostolic power.

Indigenous missionaries often come from cultures in which territorial spirits, powers and demon authorities are taken for granted. While Western theologians write books and articles against the idea that there are spiritual powers that need to be bound, Asian missionaries with simple faith are claiming territory for God and planting churches deeper and deeper in enemy territory.

When will we learn this lesson? Why is the power of God still a taboo subject in many of our modern mission programs? Could it be that we've allowed our fear of extremism, emotionalism and abuse of these gifts to prevent us from exercising one of our most powerful tools in evangelism?

If we are going to see the Great Commission fulfilled in our generation, we must rediscover the simple fact that signs and wonders followed the New Testament disciples and were part and parcel of their everyday witness for Christ. Hebrews 13:8 says, "Jesus Christ [is] the same yesterday, and today, and for ever." All that Jesus ever was, He still is now. He still lives, and He is calling people to Himself, proving who He is through miracles, just as He did in the New Testament. Until we realize how sidetracked much of the missions world has become in this area of thinking and return to the original pattern Jesus set for us, we will never get the job done.

Let us repent of our unbelief and allow the Holy Spirit to move in our ministries just as He is doing for thousands of indigenous missionaries in the Two-Thirds World.

We should remind ourselves of what happened when Uzzah reached out to steady the ark. It can be fatal to substitute our wisdom and planning for obedience to the simple plans and power of God.

NOTES |

1 | A.W. Tozer, *Paths to Power* (Camp Hill, PA: Christian Publications, n.d.), pp. 12–13.

19 | CHANGING PERSPECTIVES ABOUT FUNDING

When we begin asking the wrong questions about missions strategy, we almost always get the wrong answers. Nowhere in the Christian world is this more true than in the matter of funding missionary causes. Correctly financing the Great Commission should not be nearly the problem it has become. Once a pastor, a missions committee or even a prayerful individual begins asking the correct questions, correct solutions follow rapidly.

Christians have the common sense to make these right decisions about mission priorities, provided they are given the truth about current conditions on the mission field. "For years I knew there was something fundamentally wrong with our approach to missions," confessed a leading pastor in one evangelical denomination, "but I just couldn't put my finger on it." His church is nationally known. It has been giving generously to traditional mission programs for decades. In his heart, however, the pastor knew the task of world evangelism simply wasn't getting done. In fact, after a lifetime of faithfully supporting traditional missions, all he could see was that his denomination's missionaries were falling steadily behind in reaching the world.

Although most denominational boards and mission agencies are faced privately with mounting evidence of the ineffectiveness of their cross-cultural missions, few local pastors have any way of knowing the true extent of this ongoing problem in world evangelism.

But this pastor is one of the privileged few who has traveled to a number of mission fields, so he was aware of the eroding respect Western missionaries have overseas. He stayed as a guest in a number of missionary homes and saw the radical gap in lifestyle between the local population and his missionaries. He realized that if he lived a similar extravagant lifestyle back home—one that separated him so far from his congregation—he would soon be without a pulpit.

He found that host governments, even those generally friendly to the West, continue to keep their doors closed to missionaries. Missionaries are unwanted despite the free social services they often provide. Meanwhile, populations are soaring. In terms of percentage, foreign missionaries are playing a smaller and smaller role in the overall effort.

Moreover, traditional, pagan religions seem unaffected by the presence of Western missionaries, and many actually grow stronger in reaction to the foreign presence. Saddest of all, the number of unreached people groups being touched by Western missionaries has remained almost unchanged for years.

THE RIGHT QUESTIONS CAN CHANGE PERSPECTIVE

Pastor Hoskins (not his real name) saw all this, so he began to look at the missionary personnel problem from other angles. Finally, after one particularly discouraging trip to the mission field, he approached his missions committee and posed a radically different question.

Instead of asking the classical question, "How are we going to evangelize the world?" he began to ask, "How are they going to hear the Gospel?"

What a change in perspective that question makes! It frees up mission sponsors to get behind the strategies, people and programs that are actually working. Instead of centering his missions outreach on how the church could continue sending more people from here to there, Pastor Hoskins was able to start looking at the challenge of world evangelism from the mission-field perspective.

Because the church already exists in some form in almost every country, the challenge facing the Western church is a simple one. The sending church needs only to identify who is best reaching out to pioneer areas with the resources they already have. Once this is done, the church needs to come alongside that board or mission and give them the help for which they ask.

The question that needs to be asked should sound like this: Who is winning souls on such and such a mission field right now—and what do they say we can do to help them? Phrased another way, we should ask, who is successfully planting churches, and what do they say they need in order to finish the task?

SOME SURPRISE ANSWERS ABOUT NEEDS

The answers to these questions were real shockers to Pastor Hoskins and his board. They were devout Christian leaders who had grown up in a typical evangelical church, and the colonial-style missions mind-set was the only one they'd known. They loved their missionaries and the comfortable routine of mission conferences and furlough visits from old friends. However, after studying the reality of the field, they discovered that they had to rethink their whole missionary support policy.

First, Pastor Hoskins found that *on most mission fields today, the only missionaries who are still winning souls and planting churches are indigenous missionaries.* In nations where there are great revivals and people movements, the leaders are inevitably men of the soil who are born and raised among the people they serve.

In fact, he couldn't find one field where a Western missionary was leading a major people movement or planting multiple congregations. As a pastor, it seemed to him that that should be a missionary's first order of business. But Western missionaries he talked to usually admitted they were unsuitable for this primary task and left it to the national church.

Second, he found that *the tools that indigenous missionaries really need and want are usually not even on the list of the average Western missionary*. They desperately need bicycles rather than Land Rovers, cassette tapes rather than floppy disks, rice for their children rather than private English schools.

The technologies still most requested are not medicine, rural development or computer services. These systems are being imposed on the Two-Thirds World without any help from the Western church. More needed are old-fashioned slide and film projectors, generators, flannelgraph lessons, World War II–era bullhorns, flip-chart teaching posters and basic Christian literature of all kinds.

These simple, inexpensive tools are what indigenous missionaries can use immediately with little or no training. What's more, they create no cultural shock waves when they are used by indigenous missionaries in the homes and rural villages of the Two-Thirds World. By chaining mission programs to the presence of Western personnel, Pastor Hoskins discovered that his church had actually blocked these needed resources from reaching frontline indigenous missionaries.

One of the tragedies of the current situation is that some of the biggest obstacles to completing the Great Commission are the people who should be helping the most. Too often they invest resources in personal comfort and pet programs rather than sharing the resources with indigenous leaders.

Again and again, thoughtful pastors and lay leaders like Pastor Hoskins are finding that their biggest challenge is discovering ways to get around the old mission bureaucracies! They want to transfer their aid to effective indigenous leaders, but it is painful to confront old classmates and friends with the facts they have learned.

As one of the leaders of his denomination, Pastor Hoskins also feels an obligation to support his foreign missions board and the independent missions that have cultivated support from his church. Several of the members on his missions committee are former missionaries themselves who are deeply committed to continuing to support their colleagues in traditional missions.

So today his church is operating a dual program. They are supporting a large number of effective indigenous missionaries as well as traditional missionaries. However, it is the indigenous missionaries, says Pastor Hoskins, who are leading the way to unreached people groups, winning souls and planting pioneer churches.

Learning to Fund the Critical Needs

As Christian leaders, our key question is simple: Are we going to continue placing the priority on sending our own people abroad, or are we going to fund the authentic needs of the hour? The eternal destiny of millions of souls depends on how we choose to answer that single question. By definition, the authentic needs in any given time and place will almost always be the critical ones—the ones that deserve priority in our funding, prayer and involvement.

We must pray for discernment to separate our plans from God's. Whose program is paramount—the one *we* work out or the one the Holy Spirit defines? Whose agenda will rule—God's or man's?

Many factors come into play when deciding how best to fund the truly critical needs.

We must learn how to deal with the urgent.

There is an urgency in missions that must be understood and moved upon, regardless of how painful it is to us. That is why missionaries must stay detached from this world and remain free to respond as God directs.

Many Gospel-preaching opportunities are tied to temporary current events. Depressions, famines, wars and other circumstances cause relocations of people groups and brief openings for the Gospel. The situation is often volatile and unstable, providing a brief ray of light that may disappear as quickly as it comes.

On the other hand, we need to keep a balance. The urgency of disaster, famine and war can also distort our perspective. Are we so caught up with the physical and worldly needs of the mission field that we forget the spiritual? In recent years, the majority of Western missions—especially those sent from older, established churches—has been so aware of the physical needs that they have almost missed the spiritual.

WE MUST BE SENSITIVE TO OPEN DOORS.

The freedom to preach the Gospel is often quite fragile. The truly missions-minded person must therefore be sensitive to changing opportunities—ready to redeem the time, for "the days are evil" (Ephesians 5:16).

According to Peter Deyneka Jr., his father, who founded the Slavic Gospel Association, used to speak fondly of a brief time during World War II when the Soviet Union allowed Bibles to be imported freely. It happened only once in Brother Deyneka's lifetime—a brief open door. At the time, the Christians in the Free World did not respond, and soon the door slammed shut. Miraculously the door opened again. This time Christians responded with great enthusiasm.

But unfortunately, too much of this response was in culturally inappropriate ways. As Russian pastor Evgeniy Nedzelshiy described the situation in a 1998 article, "The American protestants have now dashed in mounted on spirited steeds, brandishing their Stetson hats. And we Russian protestants adapted to and exist in a form that is not at all Russian. Is it any surprise that the Russian citizen looks on us as somewhat strange, sometimes amusing, or even dangerous and eccentric aliens. It's not so much that 99% of Russian citizens don't accept us; they can't even comprehend us."[1]

This cultural insensitivity has resulted in predictably disappointing results. Again I quote pastor Nedzelshiy:

After 10 years of full religious freedom accompanied by an incredibly high level of activity in every conceivable form of evangelism: crusades, festivals, marches, seminars, ministries: prophetic, healing and miraculous, various concerts, Bible Schools, seminaries, Bible studies, home groups, free Bible distribution in the millions of copies, not to mention Christian books . . . an unbelievable amount of energy, time and money has gone into all these efforts. But there is a Russian proverb that says, "As we traded and bartered we rejoiced, but then we settled our accounts and wept." Let's admit that we are struck to the depth of our souls and disillusioned by the miserly results we have attained in the last 10 years of persistent and often self-sacrificing labor.[2]

Other Russians have similar comments, "We do not want ready-made Western Christianity to be dumped on us." "We would love to have the tools, and then we will work it out for ourselves."[3] Alexei Melnichuk of Donetsk Bible College states, "We need Western missionaries in our country. However, we need a very small number who are experienced and well educated and who can help us prepare our own missionaries."[4]

New opportunities and strategies are always opening on some mission fields while doors are closing on others. Effective evangelism and church planting require mission boards to respond to immediate needs and opportunities. We cannot recruit and train Western personnel, hoping that political changes will come someday. Instead, we need to invest in staff and programs that will work right now.

In this sense, there are no closed doors. In nearly every nation where Western missionaries are now forbidden or restricted, there are indigenous missions in desperate need of support. And there are ways to get funds and supplies through even the tightest borders.

WE MUST LEARN TO RESPECT THE SOVEREIGN WORKING OF GOD.

There are mysterious movings of the Holy Spirit known only to God that cause certain people to be more open to Christian witness at particular times. We do not have to understand this phenomenon to move with it.

When God pours out His Spirit, be it through indigenous missions or in any other way, we need to be sensitive and follow. The mind-set that dares to say we will move with God only if He follows our bylaws, constitution or "the way we've always done it" is not just a mistake in strategy—it is sinful rebellion against the Lord.

Traditions or nationalism should not be allowed to prevent us from supporting a move of the Holy Spirit. Any such blockage should be openly exposed and rejected by sensitive leaders.

WE MUST CONSIDER PERSONALITY AND CALLING.

At times I find that God in His sovereignty has raised up an individual whose personality and ministry style are especially effective in reaching a certain area or people group. Again, it is important that we move with the Lord and provide special support as required by these individuals or Gospel teams. This is also a critical need that must be funded whether or not the individual happens to be from our denomination, race or nationality.

By these definitions, a *critical need* does not always have to be an *emergency need*. But it is a need that requires someone on the field to sense the mind of the Lord and respond as He directs, even if it is not according to our man-made rules, prejudices and programs.

That's why the best and most effective missions today are almost always the ones that concentrate on funding critical needs. The ineffective, dying missions are the ones that are not responding to current opportunities. They are, in effect, enslaved to history and tradition.

TODAY'S CRITICAL NEEDS

What are the critical needs of our day?

Because every mission field is different, we cannot make stiff recommendations that apply to all situations. But it is safe to say that the critical needs in *most* pioneer situations are still the needs for basic Gospel tools.

Key items are Bibles and New Testaments or literature such as tracts and booklets. Illiterates need simple audiocassettes, flip charts and other teaching aids. Open-air meetings require public-address systems and generators, slide projectors and video projectors. Simple transportation, such as bicycles, motorcycles and indigenous diesel vans, is vital. Jeeps are helpful in some places.

Almost always these vitally needed Gospel tools are manufactured and distributed by secular firms right on the mission field. It is rarely wise or necessary to import them, because local goods cost less, the spare parts or repairs are easier to obtain and they attract less attention. Imported witnessing tools associate the Gospel message with alien forces, sometimes former colonizers and invaders. It is far better to send funds to the field and let indigenous missionaries purchase local equipment and supplies.

Why are such simple tools critical needs? The fundamental fact is that most of the world's 2 billion unreached people are still living in rural villages. Although urbanization is occurring worldwide, the unevangelized remain in the most remote areas. India alone has over 500,000 villages, and most are still without a body of believers.

Most of the 10,000 unreached people groups are in Two-Thirds World nations—and among the poorest of the poor. The majority still live without running water, let alone electricity or television. To reach these last tribes and tongues, it is usually necessary to send men and women in on foot. The witnessing tools they carry must be inexpensive, portable and easy to use.

Because over 1.25 billion people are illiterate, and most of these are among the unreached, even printed literature is often useless. So the appropriate technology for use in many of these situations must by definition be both indigenous and back to basics.

But it would leave a false impression to say that all the critical needs in missions today are primitive. In many Two-Thirds World countries, radio and television are state-of-the-art mass media. In some situations, there is an urgent need for DVDs, full-color posters, sophisticated advertising and carefully prepared tracts, especially in large cities and on university campuses. I will address this in the next chapter.

NOTES |

1 | Evgeniy Nedzelshiy, "The Protestant Crisis in Russia," *Evangelical Missions Quarterly,* July 1998, pp. 296–297.

2 | *Ibid.,* pp. 293–294.

3 | Manfred Kohl, "Filling the Leadership Void in the Post-Communist Church," *Contact 23,* no 1 (Spring 1994), pp. 4–5.

4 | Alexei Melnichuk, "We Asked . . . ," *Pulse,* September 23, 1994, p. 3.

I n order to understand the critical needs on a mission field, it is important to listen to the leaders of indigenous missions. Before we fund programs, we need to find out from them what tools and technologies the Holy Spirit is currently using in their land.

This requires humility and sensitivity—virtues often in short supply when Western missions launch into the field thinking they already have all the answers. Western solutions, it seems, are more and more high-tech. Too often Western plans for world evangelization are simply too complicated to succeed in the Two-Thirds World. Their implementation requires infrastructures or resources that do not widely exist.

Although high-tech solutions are applicable in some situations, they are the exception rather than the rule. Any successful missions plan that succeeds in the Two-Thirds World today must be based first on assisting indigenous workers. It will usually then require only the most simple local tools with a view toward the end user. In many cases that will be peasants and villagers who lack not only education but often also electricity.

THE ILLUSION OF TELEVISION

Perhaps no better example of Western miscalculation on the mission field is the current attempt to export American televangelism around the world. The awesome power of this medium has done much to capture the hearts and minds of an entire generation in America and Europe. Therefore, it is a strong temptation to missions looking for a shortcut to reach the world with the Gospel of Jesus Christ.

A major American televangelist managed to purchase 13 weeks of half-hour programming time in Beijing on Central China Television. He thanked God publicly for what at first seemed to be a miracle breakthrough and proceeded to raise the $800,000 necessary to fund the project.

Regrettably, the project turned out to be less effective than anticipated. This misuse of resources reveals the problem faced by those who insist on exporting their TV shows rather than humbly financing indigenous programs by local preachers.

The programs were censored. The Chinese government owns all the broadcasting channels and does not allow freedom of speech. In China, communist censors permitted the evangelist to sing and play only Southern Gospel music in English.

The programs were culturally inappropriate. By keeping the English-language lyrics and a musical idiom alien to China, the government was able to continue portraying Christianity as a foreign import. This foreign image would, of course, be true of almost every religious program produced in the West. Only one in a hundred might be culturally transferable to an African or Asian audience.

There was no way for the program to generate leads or be followed up by the local churches. As an outside organization without a network of local believers with whom to share responses, the evangelistic association was not able to contribute to the growth of the Chinese church.

Two-Thirds World television has a limited audience. Although Chinese TV is among the most advanced in the Two-Thirds World, it still only effectively penetrates those parts of China that have electricity and are most modern. It reaches the educated urban dweller who has already been exposed to some form of Christian witness, and it rarely addresses the most needy audiences in rural, underdeveloped areas.

Christian television from the West is mostly entertainment and therefore does not offer a strong enough Gospel message. The content selected by the Chinese for showing was, of course, the most entertaining portions of the American televangelist's crusade ministry in the United States.

But even had the authorities run the content of the preaching and teaching shows, the material would have been irrelevant to most Chinese viewers. American Christian television presents programs mostly designed to inspire believers in their daily walk with the Lord. It is rarely evangelistic in nature because it depends almost solely on the donations of Christian viewers to keep it going.

When we measure ourselves by ourselves (2 Corinthians 10:12) and depend on our own logic rather than wait on the Lord, we cannot succeed. If television will ever be used as an effective missionary tool, it certainly won't be in the form we know it in the West today.

Not all broadcasting is ineffective, however. I know that in the future, television will become more of a common means of communication in Two-Thirds World countries. At this point, though, what is needed is much more radio broadcasting.

THE NEED FOR RADIO OUTREACH

Right now, radio is a perfect medium in many Two-Thirds World countries. It is an older technology understood by many indigenous evangelists. It is much cheaper both to produce and to purchase air time. It is often less censored, and often there are commercial stations available that sell time. Far more people have radio receivers than TV sets, and you can find battery-operated radios even in remote village areas that don't have electricity.

Radio can be directed at unreached people groups more easily than television. Local dialects can be recorded in simple studios for broadcast back into specific regions and communities. Radio is a perfect medium to carry the spoken word and the "foolishness of preaching" that Paul said God has chosen as the primary method for winning lost souls.

We can daily reach millions of people with the Gospel in some parts of Asia by using radio. For example, one program that Gospel for Asia sponsors goes to 5 million people on a daily basis. The cost for the whole year is less than a penny per person. Radio is a bargain indeed, especially when you consider that the average cost of each new baptized believer, according to David Barrett in *World Christian Trends*, is $330,000.[1]

SIMPLE PUBLIC-ADDRESS SYSTEMS

Radio is not the only way to magnify and multiply the impact of the spoken word. Indigenous missionaries desperately need simple public-address systems, handheld bullhorns or military-issue "half-mile" hailers. These loudspeakers turn street corners, markets and any public place into open-air Gospel meetings.

Voice amplifiers can easily be mounted on bicycles and vans to make mobile sound trucks for Gospel preaching. They also promote film showings, village crusades or meetings. Gospel teams can park a vehicle or bicycle almost anywhere in the Two-Thirds World and gather hundreds of people in just a few minutes with public-address systems. Even people who remain in their homes can hear the singing and Gospel preaching clearly.

A missionary can multiply the personal impact of his preaching ministry by hundreds of times using portable bullhorns—and again the cost is minimal. A typical small unit costs only $100 in Two-Thirds World Asian countries such as India. Large systems cost $400, and gasoline-powered generators cost another $1,500—a necessary cost when units are used in areas where no electricity is available.

CASSETTE BIBLES AND WITNESSING TAPES

For less than $1 each, cassette tapes are solving one of the most vexing problems facing missions today—how to reach the world's 1.25 billion illiterates.

Without cassette tapes and portable players, many nonreaders may never have a chance to hear the Gospel. A classic example is that of the Auca Indians of Ecuador. Massive world attention was focused on the Aucas when they killed five American missionaries in 1956—men who had dedicated their lives to help translate the Bible into the Auca language. In the following years, before Bibles were available, missionaries struggled to disciple new believers and establish congregations among the various Auca villages where there was an interest in the Gospel.

Cassettes were the solution. A technical missionary assistance ministry produced the Auca Scriptures on cassette tape in cooperation with missionary translators. They also provided the first of many hand-cranked cassette playback machines that operate without batteries, because the Auca villages had no electricity. The technology that runs the cassette player operates on a spring drive similar to the kind that runs clocks and music boxes, only much more powerful.

Cassettes allow indigenous missionaries to produce their own teaching messages and record whole books of the Bible for hundreds of playbacks. In oppressive societies where restrictions on printing Bibles and literature are in effect, it is often possible to obtain blank cassettes and record the Scriptures on tape.

Often the results of a cassette tape are astonishing. In Guatemala, an indigenous missionary to the Rabinal Achi people left a simple Gospel tape in a village. It was only the first eight chapters of Luke, but it was the "quick and powerful" Word of God. Somehow it was copied and fell into the hands of a 12-year-old boy. Awed by the power of the Scriptures, the enraptured child played it over and over again. He listened to it so often that he memorized every word.

But the story doesn't end there. The pastor of a struggling local mission church heard about the child and asked his parents if the boy could recite those eight chapters of Luke on Easter Sunday. Until then, according to missionaries, the mission church was one of the driest around and had never seen a moving of the Holy Spirit. But that morning, as the boy retold the story of God's love, using just the Bible itself, hearts melted. Stubborn wills were broken by the love of God—and more than half the congregation came forward to make first-time confessions of faith. Many older Christians rededicated their lives to Christ.

That life-changing tape cost less than a dollar. Gospel tools don't have to be expensive and complicated to change lives and bring nations to Christ.

THE VALUE OF GOSPEL FLIP CHARTS

There are other ways to reach those in the remote corners of our world, especially the most forgotten ones of all—illiterate farmers, the dying elderly, uneducated village women and children by the millions. One of the cheapest and most effective tools that every indigenous missionary needs are Gospel flip charts. Do they really work? Let me answer by telling just one story that is typical of thousands.

"Old Man Mohan" was a notorious drunkard in his North Indian village. His alcoholic rages made him one of the most feared men in the area. When he was drunk, everyone in the village knew to avoid him. That's why the crowd around the indigenous missionary Gospel team quickly cleared a path for Mohan when he stumbled forward one day to sit down in the front row of the crowd.

Mohan was attracted by the bright poster colors on the Gospel flip chart. He identified with the full-color sketches of a village man like himself. And the story intrigued him. He felt sorry for the villager pictured on the flip chart, who was in a difficult situation. He was running from a huge Bengal tiger, the kind that kills hundreds of Indians every year.

Grabbing a jungle vine, the man escaped by rappelling over the side of a cliff. But then below him he saw a huge crocodile waiting, snapping his hungry jaws. He couldn't go up, and he couldn't go down. He was trapped.

Then two rats began gnawing at the vine! Soon the poor Hindu man would fall into the jaws of death. *Yes, that's just the way life is,* thought Mohan as he recalled the hopeless doctrines of Hinduism that he had been taught since he was a little boy. Captivated by the story and the despair it portrayed, Mohan saw himself as that hopeless man.

The indigenous missionaries who were narrating the story as they flipped the poster sheets explained that the tiger represented our sins, the crocodile represented our coming judgment at death, and the two rats represented time—the passing days and nights of our lives.

Was there any hope at all?

A Gospel team member turned the laminated, plastic page to the closing scene. A ledge, shaped like a cross, appeared in the side of the cliff. "It represents the door of salvation provided by the Lord Jesus on Calvary," said the indigenous missionary.

The doomed man in the story was able to climb onto the ledge and be saved. "You can do the same," explained the missionary in the Hindi language. "God has provided a ledge of safety for your escape from the wages of sin. All you need to do is step out by faith and climb onto that ledge."

Tears came to Mohan's eyes. The Gospel flip chart had told the story of salvation in a modern parable that he could understand. In front of the crowd, he prayed with the indigenous missionaries, giving control of his life over to the Lord Jesus.

Mohan's story is repeated many times on the streets and in the villages of Two-Thirds World nations, where over 1.25 billion people still cannot read. Without wordless poster charts like these, it is hard for them to visualize the stories and truths of the Bible. That's why Gospel flip charts are such a critical tool. They don't need batteries or electricity to show them and comparatively speaking, they cost little—usually less than $10 each when they are produced in large quantities.

The picture stories are printed on large poster-sized, tear-resistant paper, in full color. Then they are laminated in plastic and bound with metal ring binders that allow them to be flipped easily during presentations. They are light and easy to carry by bicycle or on foot. They simply roll up, and missionaries can carry them slung over their backs. During the life of a flip chart, which can last for years, thousands of people can receive the Gospel. Most indigenous missionaries need three or four different flip charts in their inventory. Dollar for dollar, they find them a wonderful investment in souls.

One indigenous missionary in Thailand, Boonling Tong-Ngae, says he has seen more than 10,000 people pray the sinner's prayer after witnessing a Gospel flip chart adaptation of the famous "Four Spiritual Laws" (developed by Campus Crusade for Christ). Boonling gathers children and elderly villagers around him as many as 16 times a day to go over his beautiful but well-worn flip charts. He dialogues with the audience as he flips the pages, answering the questions Buddhists ask about Jesus.

At the invitation, it is not uncommon for three to four villagers to pray out loud and receive Christ while their neighbors watch with fascination and growing interest.

JESUS FILMS REACH MILLIONS

For preaching the good news of Jesus Christ to crowds, projectors and films rank at the top of the list.

There is a village in India—one of thousands like it—where most of the people can't read, no one has a TV and there was not a single believer until recently. Human existence was a cycle of suffering. People were born, plowed their fields, prepared and ate their food and reproduced themselves. This cycle went on year after unbroken year until death came and, according to Hinduism, the process began all over again.

But all that changed because everyone in this village went to a movie, and that movie brought many people freedom and a new way of life.

Cinema is by far the most popular form of entertainment in India. Village people will walk miles to see a film. In fact, India has the largest movie industry in the world. Bombay produces many times more feature films each year than Hollywood. So one day, when a van drove up to the village and strung a huge sheet between two coconut trees, everyone was intrigued. By the time the portable generator was cranked up that night, people from miles around had gathered to watch.

What they saw was not a 30-minute educational film. It was not a story set in an American town with the words in English or dubbed in their language. They sat captivated throughout a dramatic, feature-length, Indian-made, major studio picture called *Man of Mercy*. The 35mm film would have cost millions of dollars to produce in the West. But this one had Indian actors and was filmed on location in the Indian countryside, and the characters spoke the local dialect. It told the overpowering story of a man named Jesus who lived, died and rose again for their sins.

Was this film effective?

One of the Indian indigenous missionaries tells of the reaction.

The crowd of 2,000 was fascinated by Jesus' personality, the miracles He performed and the compassion He expressed.

They cheered when He drove the moneychangers from the temple. They wept when He was beaten. When He was crucified, I heard cries of anguish. And when He arose from the dead, the audience applauded, cheered and whistled.

With Asiatic features, wearing similar clothes, drawing water from a well and walking the dusty paths as they do, the One who "had no place to lay His head" was instantly loved by these villagers. They could identify with Him. He was not seen as a "white man's God" but as one of their own.

As a result of that one film showing, there is now a church of 85 baptized believers in that village. In fact, in the first year that this film was used in India, 40 new churches were formed in similar villages where there had been no previous church.

Although this film was originally produced by a Hindu, God is using it—and other similar films—to reach millions for Christ. Hundreds of copies have been made for use by indigenous missionary teams in India and other South Asian countries. Prints cost about $1,400 each and can be shown about 400 times before wearing out. Because the average audience is 1500, that means each film presents the Gospel to about 600,000 people at a cost of less than $0.0025 per person!

Because the local people in many of the Two-Thirds World countries are not exposed to thousands of other media impressions, for weeks after seeing the film they ponder and relive its dramatic message.

Films and even old-fashioned filmstrips and slides are still powerful teaching tools that can make a life-changing difference in the lives of millions. Although the video revolution has overwhelmed the West, these earlier methods of communication are still state-of-the-art in many Two-Thirds World countries.

The costs are remarkably low. In India, for example, it is possible to outfit a film van with a complete projector, screen and sound system for $14,250. To create a similar unit in the West would probably take $50,000. These relatively small investments in equipment can result in millions hearing the Gospel—and in a face-to-face way that effectively enables indigenous evangelists to lead people to Christ and start local churches.

BASIC TRANSPORTATION NEEDS

We may create romantic pictures of Jesus and His disciples walking from village to village in Galilee to preach the Gospel. The reality of their journeys, however, was far from romantic. And it is the same for indigenous evangelists who carry on the ministry today.

Travel in many mission fields is hot, dirty, sometimes dangerous and always woefully slow.

Yet there are thousands of such Gospel messengers who will walk miles under the scorching sun, as Jesus did, to reach yet another forgotten village with the message of God's love. In Africa, Latin America and Asia, pioneer work can require an awesome effort to reach even one new village a day.

Nilambar, an Indian indigenous missionary, rose every Sunday before dawn and walked nearly 11 miles to conduct morning services for the six families he had led to Christ in one village. After preaching, teaching and visiting in their homes, he walked back over the same 11 miles to a tiny room he used as his home base. During the week, he would walk similar distances to take the Gospel to other preaching points in his assigned district.

But he never complained about the lonely hours or the dangerous treks through the night. Suffering for the Gospel was a privilege for Nilambar. Born and raised in a staunch Hindu family, he is a Christian convert who has paid a heavy price to become an indigenous missionary. He was disowned by his family and cast out of his home village—losing security, status and any future he once had in this world. He is still hated and persecuted by his family and friends.

Because of his proven faithfulness, dedication and fruit-bearing ministry, Nilambar was chosen to receive a bicycle to help in his outreach ministry. Overnight his effectiveness increased almost 300 percent. With the added speed of his new bike, he is able to reach two or three villages each day instead of only one.

When Asians come to the West, they are surprised to discover that bikes are used mostly as children's toys or for sports and recreation. Asian bikes are heavy-duty, workhorse vehicles built for a long life of service on some of the roughest roads and trails in the world. A missionary on foot is greatly limited in what he can carry. But a heavy-duty bicycle allows him to carry up to 150 pounds of equipment and supplies—tracts, books, a megaphone and even a projector.

With a bike, an indigenous missionary extends his reach by at least 20 miles in every direction, and that makes a huge difference in the number of villages that can be reached. This is especially true in the more densely populated areas. Some indigenous missionaries can count up to 300 villages within a day's biking distance of their home base.

In China, Bangladesh, India, Pakistan and Vietnam, the bicycle is a primary method of transportation, both for people and for commercial deliveries. The same is true for many African and some European nations. Even in some of the Latin American countries, the bicycle remains the single most important method of transportation for soul-winning evangelists.

HOW SMOKING A GOSPEL TRACT BROUGHT SALVATION

Satish Sahu had never seen a tract or heard the story of God's love. He was a Hindu acolyte to the demon idols of a little village near Simdega, Bihar State, in North India. In order to find peace and forgiveness of sin, each year he would travel hundreds of miles to scoop water from the Ganges River. Then he would carry some back, traveling from one idol shrine to another with the village priest. There they would anoint the filthy stone idols, bowing before the images of demons.

One night all that changed when an indigenous missionary gave him his first Gospel tract. Like tens of millions around him, he had never before received the Word of God in any form.

When he first saw the indigenous missionary preaching in his all-Hindu village, Satish was enraged. Breaking up the street meeting, he argued that Hinduism had 333 million gods and goddesses to bring salvation, not just one God like Christianity.

He took the Gospel tract home, however, and began tearing the pages out to roll opium cigarettes in them. But that night he could not sleep. The Holy Spirit began to deal with him about the contents of the tract. In the darkness he lit a candle and read some of the pages he had torn apart. Then he found the words that changed his life: "The blood of Christ cleanses us from all sin."

The next morning Satish went to the quarters of the indigenous missionary with a broken and repentant heart. After some hours of questioning, he committed his life to Christ. "I felt a great burden removed from my back," testifies Satish today. He then started riding his bike 35 miles to find fellowship with the nearest Christians. He grew rapidly in the Lord because he was soon able to obtain his own copy of the Bible, a rare book in that part of the world.

Satish and his family were bitterly persecuted for his new faith. His own father, who had been a Hindu priest for 22 years, was beaten by fanatics for allowing his son to become a Christian. The whole village turned on them. But eventually Satish led his father and brother to Christ. Soon many others in the village listened to the witness of Satish and turned from idols as well.

Today Satish pastors a growing church among the Birhor tribal people and still regularly preaches to Hindus in the markets. All this because of the power of a simple Gospel tract.

There are millions of stories like this one—testimonies of people whose lives have been changed by a simple Gospel tract. In Two-Thirds World nations such as India, Gospel tracts are not thrown away on the streets as they are in the West. The printed word is treasured. Tracts are read and reread, passed from hand to hand until they wear out. Asians and Africans who can read are hungry for books, pamphlets and tracts of all kinds. Even simple Gospel tracts in some places can have the power of a book or magazine in the United States or Canada. For $50, it is still possible to print as many as 10,000 of these tracts.

Our mailboxes in the West are jammed with Christian magazines, newspapers and appeals for funds, but on the mission fields millions have not yet seen their first Gospel tract. Some Christians will receive three or four different devotional guides a month, while 2 billion have yet to receive a copy of John 3:16.

It is possible to change this pattern if we will change our priorities in printing and distributing Christian literature. I would like to propose a special literature tithe. If everyone who buys a Christian book, Bible or Christian music CD in the West would tithe 10 percent of the purchase price for overseas Gospel literature, hundreds of millions of dollars would become available to reach those who have never heard the Gospel—a wonderful step toward meeting the needs for Gospel literature in the Two-Thirds World.

THE WORD OF GOD IS STILL THE NUMBER-ONE NEED

In the coming years, we could face a real crisis in Bible printing and distribution, that is, unless Christians in the affluent West renew their commitment to sharing the Word of God. The open doors for Bible distribution in Asia are immense, and the need for Bibles and Scripture portions could soon run into billions of dollars.

The worldwide Bible shortage produces incredible stories of people who hand-copy the Bible page by page. Others have been known to photograph it, photocopy it and beg for it. Some believers weep when they receive their first Bible and kiss it joyfully. That's how precious the Word of God is to those who have not had it. Often Bibles are chained to the pulpits in churches so they won't be stolen.

The true story of T. Stephen is astonishing. Soon after he found Jesus, someone gave him a Bible, but he couldn't understand a word of it because it was printed in the language of the next state. But he was so hungry to read anything about the living God that he spent the next six months teaching himself the new language so he could read the wonderful words of life. That's how precious the Word of God is in India, a land in which hundreds of millions of people still have never even seen a copy of the Bible.

Asia is a vast continent starved for the Word of God. Most of the world's 10,000 unreached people groups are located there, almost all without the Bible translated into their mother tongues. Imagine—2 billion people without the Bible, a Gospel of John, a church or Christ!

By printing Bibles in large quantities, it is possible to get especially low prices. In India, for example, Bibles can be produced for around $2 apiece. When we compare this to study Bibles and special editions, some of which can cost between $40 and $150 in the West, it would appear that we should alter our priorities.

Bible counters in religious bookstores of the United States are rich with the smell of beautiful leather Bibles. Ironically, some of these luxury Bibles are printed on Indian paper, bound with Australian cowhide, manufactured in England, financed by Dutch banks and imported to the United States. Bookshelves in many homes in the West are lined with numerous versions of the Bible, while millions overseas are starving for a single copy of the Word of God.

This is dangerous spiritual gluttony. Where are the Christian leaders, pastors and mission advocates who will have the courage to stand up and hold the Western church accountable for hoarding the wonderful words of life?

Our mission dollars will go further and make a New Testament impact if we concentrate on supporting critically needed evangelism rather than putting such a large percentage of funds into pre-evangelism witness programs. Such a strategy will produce immediate, measurable results in terms of more evangelism, numbers of converts and numbers of churches planted.

Millions are not hearing the plan of salvation clearly articulated because indigenous missionaries and Gospel teams lack simple witnessing tools. If affluent Christians in the West would sacrifice to supply these tools, completing the task of world evangelism could be rapidly accelerated.

Pastors, mission committee chairpersons, mission leaders and donors in the West can insist on these changes in missions policy. And unless leadership redirects funds to these critical needs, the Great Commission may not be completed in our lifetime.

NOTES |

1 | David B. Barrett and Todd M. Johnson, eds., *World Christian Trends, A.D. 30-A.D. 2200* (Pasadena, CA: William Carey Library, 2001), p. 3.

21 | SEND AUTHENTIC MISSIONARIES

Missions is much more than just meeting the critical needs for soul-winning tools. It is being ready to obey, as the church in Antioch did when the Lord said, "Separate me Barnabas and Saul for the work whereunto I have called them" (Acts 13:2).

The most critical part of the missionary enterprise is identifying and sending out God's servants.

HAS GOD CALLED?

When it comes to sending out missionaries, the supreme issue is really not how we will determine our current staffing policies concerning indigenous missionaries. Far more important is whether or not the missionary candidate has truly received a call from God and is responding to it. In other words, whom are we sending out? Are we commissioning the real thing or a counterfeit? Is this missionary called to the work—and gifted by God supernaturally for service?

Just going across the street or across the ocean does not make a person a missionary. Only God can do that. At best, the sending church or missions board must determine whether God has sovereignly set aside a person for missionary service. Hence, the proper commissioning procedure waits on the Holy Spirit to set aside certain individuals for missionary service. That's why the Antioch believers prayed and fasted before setting aside the first missionaries; they waited for the Lord to guide them.

THE EXAMPLE OF WILLIAM CAREY

William Carey is often called the father of modern missions. It is a well-earned epitaph. He demonstrated an authentic missionary lifestyle. He had *both* the calling and the gifts of the Holy Spirit that characterize a genuine envoy of the Lord. That doesn't mean that he never made a mistake. Even the best missionary fails at some point. William Carey at times miscalculated or misjudged situations, pursuing practices and policies that are debatable today. Yet God intervened and "saved him out of all his troubles," as promised in Psalm 34:6.

He manifested the missionary motivational gifts of Ephesians 4:11. Carey was already a proven apostle, evangelist and prophet before he went to India. He arrived there with a New Testament definition of his work already in mind. His goal, he said, was "to build an indigenous church 'by means of native preachers.' "[1] His translation work and his educational efforts were simply necessary steps toward the goal, never an end in themselves.

Carey was uncompromising in his obedience to the missionary call. In fact, when asked to reveal the secret of his success, he replied simply, "I can plod. I can persevere in any definite pursuit. To this I owe everything."[2] He was the first to go to North India on a one-way ticket, never returning to England even for a furlough during his 40 years of service. He lived and died at the place of his calling, the mouth of the mighty Ganges River.

The thought of security, retirement, safety or his own future was never an issue. For the sake of India's lost millions, Carey gave up everything. He lived and died in poverty, never considering opportunities to enrich himself from the treasures of the East India Company trade that flourished around him.

In England, Carey fought a church and theological establishment that ridiculed his qualifications, his doctrines and his basic understanding of the Great Commission. Once on the field, Carey faced a pioneer situation that is unimaginable to most of us today. Misunderstood by fellow Christians and eventually betrayed by the board that sent him to Calcutta, he fought for most of his life against a solid wall of hostility. Hated by the white traders of the British East India Company, he discovered that he was shunned in Calcutta by both the British colonialists and the Hindus he had come to reach.

His first wife, Dorothy, refused to support Carey in his vision of overseas missionary work. She would not join him in the mission until he was practically on board ship for India. Once in India, she continued to resist and finally became "wholly deranged" after the tragic death of their five-year-old son in 1794.[3] Carey cared for his sickly children and mentally ill wife for 13 more years, unwilling to return to England or to slow down with his witnessing and translation work.

When the promised support from Christians in London failed to arrive, he worked in an indigo mill to support himself and still refused to consider returning home. He faced spiritual and other barriers that can only be compared to what believers today might face in anti-Christian lands such as China, Libya, Cuba or North Korea. Besides this, he had no missionary role model or teacher to disciple him, only the Bible to guide him in his new work.

THE SERAMPORE COVENANT

Despite the lack of a senior missionary mentor, Carey discovered and wrote out 11 amazing principles that have since become known as the Serampore Covenant. He required all his staff to affirm publicly the terms of the covenant three times a year:

- To set an infinite value on the souls of men.
- To acquaint ourselves with the snares that hold the minds of the people in bondage.

- To abstain from whatever deepens India's prejudice against the Gospel.

- To watch for every chance of doing the people good.

- To preach Christ crucified as the grand means of conversion.

- To esteem and treat Indians always as our equals.

- To guard and build up the flock that has been gathered.

- To cultivate their spiritual gifts, ever pressing upon them their missionary obligation, because only Indians can win India for Christ.

- To labor unceasingly in biblical translation.

- To be instant in the nurture of personal religion.

- To give ourselves without reserve to the cause, not counting even the clothes that we wear as our own.[4]

In these principles, Carey showed that he had grasped the essentials of authentic missionary work: love and respect for the people, a commitment to winning souls and making disciples, a willingness to sacrifice, a commitment to indigenous missionaries and a dedication to consistent personal holiness. The fruit of Carey's ministry is amazing by today's standards.

Most of all, Carey won many to Christ and established pioneer congregations in numerous unreached people groups, including all the major ethnic groups of the Ganges River Valley.

Today the biblical principles and lifestyle he embraced are being reapplied by hundreds of indigenous missionary societies in India and throughout the Two-Thirds World.

The principles of successful missionary work were taught by Jesus and the apostles from the beginning. The first challenge facing any missions committee, pastor or sending church today is finding true missionaries, like Carey, who are living and working according to the New Testament pattern. The second challenge is to reform our sending policies and transfer critical assistance to these brethren so that they can continue to move into new territories for the Lord.

NOTES |

1 | Ruth A. Tucker, *From Jerusalem to Irian Jaya* (Grand Rapids, MI: Zondervan, 1983), p. 121.

2 | Mary Drewery, *William Carey: A Biography* (Grand Rapids, MI: Zondervan, 1979), p. 25.

3 | Tucker, *From Jerusalem to Irian Jaya,* p. 117.

4 | Abraham Philip, "Third World Missions: Interfacing with Western Missions" (unpublished study paper, Manila, Philippines: Lausanne II Congress on World Evangelization, July 1989), pp. 2–3.

T housands of indigenous missionaries are following in the footsteps of William Carey. As a result, hundreds of new churches are being formed every day worldwide. David Barrett reports that, each day, an average of 122,000 new believers are baptized.[1] It is estimated that from 20,000 to 30,000 people a day are coming to Christ in China.[2] Similar astonishing growth is occurring through indigenous movements today in Brazil, India, Korea, Nigeria, Thailand and Indonesia.

Pius Wakatama, author of *Independence for the Third World Church,* comments on these changes taking place in Africa: "It is time to realize that, although the Western missionary movement has had a glorious past in Africa and has accomplished much, we have reached the end of an era and are seeing the dawn of a new one. There is much Africans can learn from the experiences of their Western missionary forebears. However, our situation is drastically different from the days of the pioneer missionaries, and we cannot just ape what they did. We need to listen to what God is telling us in our own age and in our own situation."[3]

As we have seen throughout this book, times are different, and the main work of the harvest is now in the hands of indigenous workers. But our missionary sending and funding policies have been slow to catch up with what has happened on the field. The frontline work of missions today has already shifted into the hands of indigenous mission boards. Missiologist Larry Pate, author of *From Every People,* reported in 1989 that indigenous missions were growing five times faster than traditional missions.[4] The 21st-century edition of *Operation World* reports that indigenous missionaries now outnumber traditional ones.[5]

Many indigenous missionary leaders believe the tempo of change will quicken. This will mean even *more* nationals offering themselves for service in the coming decade. David Cho, chairman of the Third World Missions Association, has sounded a call for 1 million indigenous missionaries to be sent into the harvest.

Thus, while Western mission societies struggle to recruit and train hundreds of staff, indigenous missionaries by the thousands are waiting for sponsors to send them into the fields. As a result, reports of a missionary staff shortage are actually inaccurate. Except for some neglected Muslim fields and in some Marxist-controlled regions, there are large numbers of native Christians who are ready to be challenged and sent forth into the harvest.

TIME TO CHANGE OUR SENDING POLICIES

To repeat, most of our evangelical churches are decades behind the reality on the mission fields today. All too often our mission programs are still prisoners of outdated policies based on the realities of the harvest fields just after World War II.

Many of the oldest and most important "missions churches" in the United States and Canada have adopted mission policies that limit their ability to fund effective, New Testament missionaries. In many cases, these old rules and traditions are being applied in a way that was never intended by their authors. Sometimes these very rules are now hindering rather than fulfilling the Great Commission.

Some mission agencies and important "missions churches" have adopted bylaws that actually forbid them from supporting indigenous missions. Whatever the logic was for the policy when it was adopted 40 or 50 years ago, it is now time to amend the constitution. Others have adopted rules that forbid missionary support going to anyone other than those of their particular denomination or theological conviction. Thus, when an effective indigenous missionary movement emerges that is not controlled by their denominational leadership, the rules forbid support, no matter how excellent the ministry may be.

It is important to note that this aid is not denied to indigenous missions because of a conflict over essential doctrines. Aid is almost always denied because of a particular sectarian slant on Bible teaching that disagrees with that of the sending church.

Finally, some well-meaning churches have long-standing commitments to certain mission fields, mission agencies and individuals. Often these loyalties are to people and organizations who have completed their pioneer work and are no longer on the front lines of world evangelism. In these cases also, painful decisions must be made to step out and obey the Holy Spirit, responding to the greater needs of pioneer indigenous missionaries who are now working with unreached people groups on the frontiers.

I realize that just because the change to an indigenous policy is logical and wise in theory, that doesn't mean it will be easy to make when the time comes to vote for a change in the budget. Old connections, relationships and networks are hard to sacrifice. But we need to ask whether God is asking us to make new ones in light of current conditions. Human pride is hurt when asked to give up the feeling of direct control that old-fashioned, traditional missionary structures have provided over the years. But were these desires to dominate others of the Lord in the first place?

TIME FOR REPENTANCE AND REVIVAL

In order to shift our policies from a "going" mode to a "sending" mode, we need to experience repentance and a revival of our overall burden for the purpose of missions. Many churches and individuals who have lost the vision for the unreached world need to renew their basic commitment to the Great Commission and world evangelism.

Great Commission Christians don't care who gets the glory or who is on the front lines. Instead, they are willing to be goers or senders as the Lord leads. If our hearts are in the right place, we will want to be involved in the battle wherever the Commander-in-Chief puts us. We know from Acts 1:8 that it takes the whole Church working together to reach Jerusalem, Judea, Samaria and the uttermost parts of the earth.

Ultimately, it will take prayer and reeducation for us to be involved in the lives of indigenous missionaries. They are rarely able to travel to the West to inspire us as Western missionaries have done from the older, colonial-style missions. It takes a little more work not only to communicate with indigenous missionaries but also to understand them and learn about their needs.

Becoming partners with indigenous missions requires more faith in God and a willingness to trust in our brothers and sisters in the Two-Thirds World. This is a challenge to our comfortable prejudices and notions about other nationalities and people.

NOTES |

1 | David B. Barrett and Todd M. Johnson, eds., *World Christian Trends, A.D. 30-A.D. 2200* (Pasadena, CA: William Carey Library, 2001), p. 762.

2 | Assemblies of God (http://www.aogwm.org.au/default.asp?ID143).

3 | Pius Wakatama, "The Role of Africans in the Third World Mission of the Church," *Evangelical Missions Quarterly,* April 1990, p. 130.

4 | Larry Pate, *From Every People* (Monrovia, CA: MARC Publications, 1989).

5 | Patrick Johnstone and Jason Mandryk, eds., *Operation World,* 21st century ed. (Carlisle, Cumbria, U.K.: OM Publishing, 2001), p. 747.

23 | SUPPORTING INDIGENOUS MISSIONS

Missions in the 21st century have entered a new and exciting era. They still depend on the presence of godly missionaries whom God has called and prepared to labor in His harvest field. But today these missionaries are far more likely to have black, brown or yellow skin.

The challenge of Romans 10:13–15 still speaks to us, demanding that we stay invested in this people process till Christ returns. Mass media and other modern technologies are important, but they cannot replace the frontline missionary church planter. Missionaries are still the foot soldiers in the army of the Lord.

So Western mission agencies and churches are facing a painful challenge. We must base our mission policies on supporting whoever is doing the work of the Gospel, not on who is going overseas from our circle of friends.

We must start promoting "their" plans and stop talking about "our" plans. We must give money to "their" budgets by taking it from "our" budgets. We must decide we're going to send "their" people and stop planning to send "our" people. We must find new ways to be informed about and involved in world missions emotionally, mentally and spiritually without depending on having "our" people resident on the foreign fields.

We must pray and work to amend bylaws and constitutions that chain us to colonial mission policies and practices. Any program or policy that doesn't put the priority on funding indigenous missionaries and programs needs to be reevaluated. Prejudice and nationalism must not be allowed to determine church or missions policy.

THE TRUE STORY OF M. THOMAS

Tens of thousands of indigenous missionaries today are exhibiting the authentic lifestyles still demanded to win souls and plant churches. Yet many live their whole ministries without the support they need to effectively reach the lost on their field. M. Thomas, a pioneer missionary to Rajasthan, is typical. He grew up in a nominally Christian home in Kerala, the most Christianized state in South India.

As a teenager, Thomas was miraculously saved from drowning in a swimming accident. Though he was never particularly missions-minded before that day, the closeness of death had a profound effect on his adolescent mind. Realizing God must have saved his life for a purpose, he dedicated himself to the most radical kind of service he could imagine—becoming a missionary in North India.

Ministry in North India is an enormous sacrifice for believers in the South. They must give up the comforts they have grown up with, moving from lush jungles to scorching-hot plains, from beautiful coasts and rain forests to a world of dust and deserts. Food, dress, language, culture and religion change. They go from being surrounded by a comfortable, relatively Christian atmosphere in the South to areas where Hindus, Sikhs and Muslims have resisted Christ for centuries.

But, to an Indian, the most painful sacrifice of all is giving up career and family ties with all the security they promise. For Thomas, the decision to serve Christ was viewed as insane by most of his family and friends. It meant giving up a fine future as an engineer. A professor from his school was so distraught at hearing of his decision that he visited the family in their home, begging his parents to prevent Thomas from going.

But his parents had dedicated him to the Lord before he was born and could not stand in the way of their son's apparently suicidal desire to start a ministry in Rajasthan, then known as the graveyard of Christian missions in India. So without the backing of a church, missions board or any other visible means of support, Thomas used everything he had to go to the North.

When he arrived in Rajasthan, Thomas had two rupees, or about 20 cents, in his pocket. That was in 1962. Today he has helped plant hundreds of congregations and has a staff of hundreds of missionaries. He has a Bible school and evangelistic teams that range over several Indian states. Between then and now, there were many sleepless nights on the street, days without food, beatings, fire bombings and the martyrdom of several who came to Christ through his ministry.

THE FINANCIAL COST

At one of the lowest points during his early ministry, Thomas fell three months behind in the rent on his single room. Although the rent was only 15 rupees (or about $1.50) a month, he was so poor that he didn't have money for food, let alone the rent. Without food for days, he was slowly starving and almost discouraged enough to quit. His angry Hindu landlord came demanding the rent of 45 rupees ($4.50). When Thomas didn't have it, he threatened to come back the next day and throw him out.

As yet there were no Christian converts in the area. Like most pioneer missionaries, Thomas had no one on earth to turn to for help in a hostile community that hated the presence of a missionary in their midst. He had prayed and fasted for days. Now he was in such despair that all he could do was huddle under his blanket like a child and cry out to God.

The next morning he heard a loud knock at the door. Fearing that it was the landlord, he didn't answer. But the stubborn caller wouldn't quit. Finally he got up.

"Go away!" he shouted. "I'm leaving today!"

"Open up," said the voice on the other side. "I have a registered letter for you."

When he opened the letter, Thomas found a postal money order for 50 rupees, or about $5. It was enough to pay the back rent and buy food for a week.

For those who know M. Thomas today as one of the boldest and most courageous missionary leaders of North India, it is hard to imagine a time when he was so destitute. But this is a true story that Thomas often recounts today. His story can be repeated thousands of times not only in India but in almost every Two-Thirds World nation. The few dollars that cannot even buy a meal in an American restaurant are enough to keep a soldier of the cross alive for days on the mission fields of the Two-Thirds World.

There are other true stories of missionaries whose children have died for want of food and medical care; others who have slept in the street for months as homeless persons; and others who go hungry and without simple Gospel-witnessing tools because there is no one to support them in the ministry to which God has called them.

Are these foolish men and women who went out without planning? Are they lazy and shiftless? Are these missionaries without the spiritual covering of elders and mission boards? No, they are simply devoted missionaries who have chosen to obey the Lord no matter what the cost. They are missionaries who counted the cost, knew the risks and still went out to fulfill the Great Commission on faith. In fact, it is these indigenous missionaries who are now writing the final chapters of the book of Acts.

Should they be penalized for their trust in the Lord and simple obedience because rich Christians in the affluent nations of the world have no "easy way" to support them? Our budgets can be changed to support indigenous mission agencies and supply the needs of indigenous missionaries. Why don't we make these changes now?

This is the question every concerned Christian in the West should be asking. It is the question that church leaders at every level should be answering. It is already too late to wait any longer.

The year was 1916. The young man looked strangely out of place among his impeccably dressed, English-looking Indian colleagues. Wearing typical Indian clothing, he sat on the platform and waited for his turn to speak.

It had been over a year since he had returned to his native land from South Africa. The past 12 months had given him a chance to observe his country. He had listened to grievances aired by the poor and downtrodden and had heard brave plans for India's future from those who wanted Britain to "quit India."

He had heard enough. Now Mohandas K. Gandhi was ready to speak. He stood and faced his audience. Most of them were India's elite, dependent upon the British to perpetuate their comfortable lifestyles. Not one was prepared to hear Gandhi's bold plan of civil disobedience to free India from British rule. And certainly they were not ready for his method of attack, which was to identify with his own people instead of living above them. But this was exactly what Gandhi proceeded to tell them.

"Foreign rule would be replaced, he said, when Indian leaders begin to serve the needs of the villagers better than the British. Thus, to the keen discomfort of the educated and the well-to-do, did Gandhi begin his ministry in India."[1]

Gandhi had made a commitment to become one with his people, to stand beside them and not above them. He wore Indian-made clothing instead of British-made, and he traveled in the third-class train compartment rather than in first-class comfort. He had seen the peril into which these wealthy, educated men had fallen. They were calling for home rule, yet all the while they had slowly become just like those they were fighting to escape. They longed to be free of colonialism but had taken on the mannerisms of the people who were over them.

In the Two-Thirds World today, some national missionary leaders are living and working just as these educated Indians were—separated from their own people. They continue to live above the lifestyles of their lost countrymen, and their ability to reach out with the Gospel of Jesus Christ is seriously hindered. Many of these leaders have traveled abroad, pleading their cause to the churches in the West. Well-meaning Christians have given out of love and compassion for the lost, not knowing that sometimes these funds went to perpetuate comfortable lifestyles rather than further the Gospel.

As believers longing to reach the Two-Thirds World's unreached, what can we do to give wisely and with discernment? The answer is not to give up supporting nationals. Instead, we must be as discerning with them as we are with any other opportunity to invest the money God has entrusted to us for the sake of His kingdom. This discernment will require asking appropriate questions and looking to God for guidance.

Being indigenous doesn't guarantee genuineness, purity, consistency or effectiveness any more than being North American does. But when measured by appropriate standards, *if qualities of value are equal,* indigenous missionaries generally yield a far greater harvest for the investment.

GIVING WITH DISCERNMENT

It is often said that failure is the best teacher. How true this is! In our beginning days, we at Gospel for Asia often had to learn these lessons through our own mistakes.

The lessons we have learned over the years from our experiences have proved invaluable. Gospel for Asia now has a team of mature Christian leaders who travel extensively, meeting with and overseeing our 13,000 indigenous missionaries. We have learned what to look for in a man's or woman's character, the nature of their ministries and the fruit that results. Consequently, we can provide support with joy and confidence in the brothers and sisters we serve.

The challenge before us to give wisely and with discernment is not insurmountable. There are steps to take that will ensure accountability, trust and a great deal of satisfaction, knowing that funds are being spent efficiently for the Lord's kingdom.

However, because our investment in evangelizing these countries pushes us abruptly into spiritual warfare, we simply cannot expect a 100 percent success rate. Failures and mistakes will occur. That is why we must move with the Lord's leading. Beyond all that we could ever know, we still need to take that step of faith. As we humble ourselves before Him, seek His guidance and move forward carefully, He will lead us to His servants who need support.

We must understand the missionary or missions board under consideration for support. Three areas need to be covered in the evaluation process: *one,* financial and administrative standards; *two,* personal lifestyle and character and *three,* ministry fruit. (Note: The only exception in the "ministry fruit" category would be a new missionary recruit who has not yet begun his or her ministry.)

Here are questions that should be asked of any indigenous missions group or individual missionary seeking financial support. Answers to questions such as these will give greater insight into the nature and workings of the ministry being considered. Some questions will apply more to an organization than to an individual, and vice versa.

ASK QUESTIONS RELATING TO FINANCIAL AND ADMINISTRATIVE STANDARDS.

1. Is an annual audit done by a certified accountant?
2. Is the audit made available to the organization's constituency?

246 | COME, LET'S REACH THE WORLD

3. Is the ratio of spending for field ministry considerably greater than for administration? (It should be at least 80 percent for actual ministry.)

4. Are all documents, assets and the like in the name of the organization (not an individual leader)?

5. What are the major items of expense? (If funds go primarily for properties, hospitals and schools rather than for actual field evangelism, be *extremely* cautious to check them out.)

6. Is the missionary or group receiving any financial assistance from other sources?

7. Is there a written agreement to declare all sources of income for any given project?

8. Is the group registered with the government as a charitable or nonprofit organization?

9. Are finances and financial records handled only by the leader and his relatives? (If this is the case, then you have good enough reason *not* to support him.)

10. Are the accounts jointly operated (that is, at least two people responsible for handling the funds)?

11. Are written and signed receipts kept for records of how money was spent for any given project or missionary?

12. Who makes decisions that govern the activities of the mission?

ASK QUESTIONS RELATING TO PERSONAL LIFESTYLE AND CHARACTER.

1. Is the missionary involved in full-time ministry (at least eight hours a day) in an unreached area?

2. Approximately how much time does the missionary spend in personal Bible study and prayer?

3. Is the missionary working among non-Christians? (The exception would be a Bible school teacher working with missionary trainees.)

4. How long has the missionary been working on this assignment?

5. What kind of training for ministry has the missionary had?

6. Does the missionary exhibit the qualifications for service listed in 1 and 2 Timothy?

7. Is the missionary sure of a clear call that God has placed upon his or her life?

8. How does the missionary view his or her ministry? (If you sense it is more of a "job" rather than a walk of faith, beware!)

9. Is the missionary living at the level of the people he or she is serving?

10. Does the missionary work well with others, or do you hear of conflicts with his or her coworkers?

11. How long has the missionary been saved?

12. How long has the missionary been in the ministry?

13. What is the missionary's basic doctrinal position?

ASK QUESTIONS REGARDING INDIGENOUS MISSIONARY LEADERS.

1. Are they mature in the faith, having successfully planted churches previously?

2. Are the leaders willing to meet regularly with the indigenous missionaries under them for prayer, fellowship and sharing?

3. Do the leaders display a servant's heart, not desiring direct control over missionaries' lives?

4. Do they care for the spiritual well-being of those under them? (Leaders are responsible to see that indigenous missionaries are qualified for service and remain so in the years following.)

5. Do they have a definite vision for the organization?

6. What standard of living do the indigenous missionary leaders maintain?

ASK QUESTIONS REGARDING MINISTRY FRUIT.

1. Does the missionary have a good testimony among the people?
2. Does the missionary manage his or her own household well?
3. Is he or she a model of sacrificial giving and service?
4. How much Gospel literature has been distributed during the past year?
5. How many have been led to the Lord in the past year?
6. How many have been baptized in the past year?
7. How many have dedicated their lives for full-time service to the Lord in the past year?
8. How many churches were established in the past year? Give such details as name of village, population, major religion, date the church was started, number of believers and place of worship.
9. How many evangelistic meetings were conducted in the past year?
10. What are the ministry goals for the current year? For next year?
11. Does the missions organization have an ongoing reporting/evaluation program that includes unannounced visits to the individual workers to verify the fruit of their ministries?

LET US WORK TOGETHER

Most of us are unable to go in person and inspect the work of indigenous missionaries. Thus, we need to know that the missions organization through which the indigenous missionary works in the West has proper systems and procedures in operation to ensure that effective ministry results from our investment. Ultimately, it is the Lord who must lead us, and He will also provide us with wisdom and discernment as we humbly seek Him.

I trust that I've been able to assist families, small groups, churches and others to gain at least some perspective on the issue. We at Gospel for Asia are ready and willing to offer you further assistance, should you have any questions or need additional information. Please feel free to call on us.

The men and women we support are human. Just like us, they will sometimes make improper choices and will struggle with fleshly motives. But we must remember this: *God has called indigenous missionaries to finish the task of world evangelism in this last hour.* So our response must be encouragement and guidance, when needed, rather than criticism. More than simply supporting them financially, *we must pray for them* that they will not fall prey to the many trials and temptations before them. We must resist Satan on their behalf.

We must pray also for churches, denominations and missions organizations throughout the West to recognize our brothers and sisters from developing countries as coworkers in God's great harvest.

"Speaking the truth in love . . . grow up into him in all things, which is the head, even Christ: from whom the whole body fitly joined together and compacted by that which every joint supplieth, according to the effectual working in the measure of every part, maketh increase of the body unto the edifying of itself in love" (Ephesians 4:15–16).

And as God calls us to further His kingdom through supporting our brothers and sisters in the Two-Thirds World, we will experience afresh what a joy and privilege it is to obey Him.

Thank you for joining in this revolution of men and women who are ready to die, if need be, to reach their own people. I pray that your desire to help reach the unreached will grow deeper in the days to come, as we approach the return of our great God and Savior, Jesus Christ! May the Lord guide and direct your steps as you give of what He has given you.

NOTES |

1 | Calvin Kytle, *Gandhi: Soldier of Nonviolence* (New York: Grosset & Dunlap, 1969), pp. 102–104.

CONCLUSION |

Today, as each second of the clock ticks by, thousands of people in the Two-Thirds World die and go to hell. They slip into eternity before anyone can reach them with the Gospel of Jesus Christ.

What can we do about this?

In this world we can manufacture, produce or buy almost anything. But one thing we are not able to obtain, even with all the money in the world, is one additional minute of time. All we have are the 24 hours that are called today—the same as yesterday and tomorrow.

If there isn't anything we can do to lengthen time, should we give in to the assumption that these thousands of people are beyond our reach? No! There is something we can do—we can make better use of our time. For example, if it normally takes one month to reach a million people with the Gospel, we must find a way to reach them in one day instead.

In order to do this, we would need to multiply all our efforts 30 times. We would use 30 times more people, 30 times greater efficiency, 30 times more equipment and 30 times more money. In this way we would gain 29 extra events instead of only one. We would improve our use of time.

What does it really take, then, to improve our use of time and reach our generation with the Gospel in this decade? It takes desperate people who are gripped by urgency. The cry of their hearts is that there are only minutes left before eternity starts for millions of lost souls!

In my travels, I have met a few people who share this desperation with me. I am cut deeply when I hear how casually God's people, even key leaders, talk about the lost world.

Time is short. We are not engaged in war games—this is real war.

No serious Bible student doubts that we are at a critical turning point in human history. Events and predictions that were once only the subject of idle speculation are now occurring right before our eyes.

The end of this age rushes toward us.

Since first beginning to write these pages, I have seen major changes take place in world evangelism as spiritual revival sweeps nation after nation. The world has turned upside-down, providing us with many opportunities in harvest fields long denied. The events in Israel and elsewhere seem to promise the soon return of Christ. What some might have considered merely academic arguments about strategy are taking on new urgency. The speeding events of history demand that we finish world evangelism in the most effective and efficient way possible and as quickly as possible.

At the same time we must remember that before the Great Commission was made, another command was already in effect: to love. Hours before He made His ultimate sacrifice, Jesus told His disciples, "A new commandment I give unto you, that ye love one another; as I have loved you, that ye also love one another" (John 13:34).

The kind of love Jesus talked about goes far beyond pleasant words and occasional kind deeds. This is the love Jesus displayed when He "made himself of no reputation, and took upon him the form of a servant . . . and became obedient unto death" (Philippians 2:7–8).

Having the love of God in our hearts means a death sentence to our flesh. Just as Jesus gave up His will for the Father's, so we give up any rights to our own plans, our own dreams.

Having the love of God in our hearts means that as we die, He is able to produce fruit through our surrendered lives (John 12:24). His love in our lives will move us to action for the lost world all around us.

Having the love of God in our hearts is the only way we can make a dramatic difference in our world for His kingdom. When His love flows through us, we will reach out to the unreached with the Gospel.

God is continuing to raise up thousands of new indigenous missionaries to complete the task in one closed nation after another. At the same time, we are watching the forces of darkness mount ferocious attacks against the people of God. Sensitive believers realize there is no doubt that Christ will soon return for His Bride and that in fact we are now seeing the Holy Spirit write the last pages of church history.

Time is short. The world is at the brink of eternity. Right now we have the greatest opportunity to rise up and take the victory of the cross to the last corners of this earth. The Lord Jesus is graciously calling a remnant to the joys of simple obedience. For those who respond, I believe there is an opportunity right now to share in the last great move of God before Christ returns.

May I encourage you, my brother or sister, to allow God's love to overcome you and make you truly effective for His kingdom. May God give us the strength and grace to leave behind our apathy and lukewarmness and become desperate enough to "redeem the time" as He has told us to do.

It is my sincere prayer that you will be one of those who will join hands with indigenous missionaries in this last great harvest.

APPENDIX |
EVALUATION QUESTIONS

EVALUATE THE MISSION AGENCIES YOU AND YOUR CHURCH ARE CUR-RENTLY SUPPORTING.

1. Were they formed before 1939?

2. If so, have they altered their policies to include support of indigenous missions in countries closed to Westerners?

3. On the field, is the work headed by Western or indigenous leaders?

4. Are there indigenous churches already existing in the area?

5. If so, how does the missions agency relate to these churches?

6. Is it necessary to have a foreigner doing these tasks, or would it be possible to support an indigenous missionary doing the same things?

7. Are the Western missionaries making disciples to replace themselves?

As you discover the answers to these questions, do you find any patterns of change? Do you see any willingness to be flexible as country situations fluctuate? These are good indications that a missions agency is open to non-Western alternatives. On the other hand, if you sense an attitude of "it worked before, so it will work again" as you evaluate, this agency may need to refocus its priorities.

EVALUATE YOUR CRITERIA FOR SELECTING MISSIONARIES TO SUPPORT.

1. Are there any unwritten qualifications or assumptions for your criteria that are as important as the written ones?

2. Are there "secret standards" for acceptance of missionaries that are not openly acknowledged?

3. Are all your missionaries from the same church, denomination, school or association?

4. Are they all of the same race, language or nationality?

5. Are there standards that are purely cultural?

6. Do you feel they are applied equally and fairly?

7. Are they required of indigenous missionaries as well as foreign missionaries?

8. What percentage of your missionaries are foreign to the field, and what percentage are indigenous?

Ask the Holy Spirit to search your heart and show you if your standards have a real basis in Scripture. If you sense a distrust of indigenous missions and churches in these qualifications or an emphasis on Western importance, these standards are not biblical. Prayerfully consider how to reform these requirements according to Jesus' servant example in the New Testament.

ANALYZE THE JOB DESCRIPTION OF THE MISSIONARIES YOU AND YOUR CHURCH SUPPORT ACCORDING TO THEIR PRIMARY PURPOSE.

Each missionary should be able to fit his or her job description into one of three primary categories: evangelism and church planting, nurturing or developing existing churches and/or nurturing other ministries. Those under the third category should be examined most carefully, asking these questions:

1. What percentage of support is going to social services?

2. Is the relief distributed by local churches?

3. Is the program staff Christian?

4. Has it actually helped the witness of the church in the area?

5. Are medical missionaries and others who are involved in meeting human needs actually able to witness?

6. Have they established churches as a result of their ministry?

If you find that the ministry of social services has become the primary goal of a missions agency rather than a secondary outcome, carefully consider whether your funds are truly being spent for evangelistic purposes.

REVIEW THE BUDGETS OF YOUR MISSION PROJECTS.

1. Is most of the missions money going to support foreign workers?

2. Is it going to help support indigenous missionaries and to purchase the tools and supplies they need to reach their own people?

3. What percentage of your missions giving goes to evangelism, church planting and evangelistic tools?

If you attempt to stay aware of current events and are sensitive to special opportunities that arise on the mission field, your involvement in missions is more than likely meeting the critical needs.

READ THROUGH RECENT PRAYER LETTERS AND ANNUAL ACTIVITY REPORTS OF YOUR MISSIONARIES.

1. How many heard the Gospel as a result of their ministries in the past year?

2. How many converted to Christ and were baptized?

3. How many new churches were established?

If you find that the missionaries you support are not directly involved in or enabling and serving ministries to win souls and plant churches, consider whether these activities are justified by the Great Commission mandate of Christ, especially in light of the billions still unreached.

EXAMINE THE REGIONS OF THE WORLD WHERE EACH OF YOUR MISSIONARIES IS SERVING.

1. Is there a local, thriving body of believers nearby?
2. Could indigenous missionaries from that local church be sent out and supported instead of a foreign missionary?

As you consider these alternatives, they will either clash or agree with your worldview of missions. If you hold to a "field perspective," you will be more concerned about how unreached people groups can best receive the Gospel. If you are only concerned about how you or your church can reach the world, your worldview needs some redirection to the real issue at hand.

EVALUATE YOUR PERSONAL VIEWPOINT AND YOUR CHURCH'S POLICY ON THE ROLE OF THE SUPERNATURAL IN EVANGELISM.

1. Is there any attempt to explain away the occurrence of miracles and other supernatural events?
2. Ask missionaries about their experiences of God's power on the mission field. Have they felt free to share everything that has taken place?

Prayerfully evaluate these policies in light of Jesus' ministry and that of the New Testament apostles. If you sense a resistance to the movement of the Holy Spirit, ask the Lord to open your heart to His plan for the world.

AS YOU EVALUATE YOUR STANDARDS FOR SENDING OUT MISSIONARIES, EXAMINE THE FRUIT OF THEIR LIVES.

1. How much emphasis is put on skills and abilities, and how much on the calling of God?

2. How long has it been since any revisions were made to your policy?

If you see God-given gifts, an uncompromising obedience to His call and a willingness to stand alone for Jesus' sake, you can be assured of their authenticity. If there is an absence of these characteristics, carefully reconsider the qualifications used in sending these missionaries to the field.

If this book has been a blessing to you, please send us a
letter in care of the address below.
Thank you.

GFA Books
1800 Golden Trail Court
Carrollton, TX 75010

a division of Gospel for Asia
www.gfa.org

GOSPEL FOR ASIA

After 2,000 years of Christianity, how can it be that nearly 3 billion people are still unreached with the Gospel? How long must they wait?

This is why Gospel for Asia exists.

More than 25 years ago, God specifically called us to invest our lives to reach the most unreached of the Indian subcontinent through training and sending out native missionaries.

Gospel for Asia (GFA) is a church-planting organization dedicated to reaching the most unreached in the 10/40 Window. Our 16,000 pastors and missionaries serve full-time to plant churches in India, Nepal, China, Bhutan, Myanmar, Sri Lanka, Bangladesh, Laos, Vietnam and Thailand.

Native missionaries are highly effective because they work in their own or a similar culture. They already know, or can easily learn, the language, customs and culture of the people to whom they minister. They don't need visas, and they live economically at the same level as their neighbors. These advantages make them one of the fastest and most effective ways to get the Gospel to the millions who are still waiting to be reached. By God's grace, GFA missionaries have established more than 29,000 churches and mission stations to date.*

However, the young, economically weak Asian Church and her missionaries can't do it alone. The enormous task of evangelizing nearly 3 billion people takes the help of the whole Body of Christ worldwide.

That is why GFA offers those who cannot go themselves the opportunity to become senders and prayer partners of native missionaries—together fulfilling the Great Commission and sharing in the eternal harvest of souls.

To find out more information about Gospel for Asia or to receive a free copy of K.P. Yohannan's best-selling book *Revolution in World Missions,* visit our website at www.gfa.org or contact one of our offices near you.

---

* As of 2005

UNITED STATES 1800 Golden Trail Court, Carrollton, TX 75010
         Toll free: 1-800-946-2742   Email: info@gfa.org

AUSTRALIA P.O. Box 3587, Village Fair, Toowoomba QLD 4350
         Phone: 07 4632-4131   Email: infoaust@gfa.org

CANADA 245 King Street E, Stoney Creek, ON L8G 1L9
         Toll free: 1-888-WIN-ASIA   Email: infocanada@gfa.org

GERMANY Postfach 13 60, 79603 Rheinfelden (Baden)
         Phone: 07623 79 74 77   Email: infogermany@gfa.org

KOREA P.O. Box 984, Yeouido, Seoul, Korea 150-609
         Toll free: 82-80-801-0191   Email: infokorea@gfa.or.kr

NEW ZEALAND P.O. Box 302580, North Harbour, North Shore City 0751
         Toll free: 0508-918-918   Email: infonz@gfa.org

SOUTH AFRICA P.O. Box 28880, Sunridge Park, Port Elizabeth 6008
         Phone: 041 360-0198   Email: infoza@gfa.org

UNITED KINGDOM P.O. Box 166, Winterscale House, YORK YO10 5WA
         Freephone: 0800 032 8717   Email: infouk@gfa.org

CHARTER
ECFA
MEMBER

A higher standard.
A higher purpose.

FREE EMAIL UPDATES
Sign up today at www.gfa.org

Hear from today's heroes of the mission field.
Have their stories and prayer requests sent straight to your inbox.

- ◆ **Fuel your prayer life with compelling news and photos from the mission field.**
- ◆ **Stay informed with links to important video and audio clips.**
- ◆ **Learn about the latest opportunities to reach the lost world.**

GFA sends updates every week. You may cancel your free subscription at any time. We will not sell or release your email address

FREE subscription

FOR YOU AND YOUR FRIENDS

Stay informed! Sign yourself, your relatives and Christian friends up for a FREE one-year subscription to *SEND!*, Gospel for Asia's quarterly magazine, featuring exciting and prayer-inspiring stories and updates from our native missionaries working in Asia. Simply fill out the form below for your free subscription.

Please circle: Mr. Mrs. Miss Rev.

Name _____

Address _____

City _____ State/PR/County _____ Zip/PC _____

Country _____ Phone (____) _____

Email _____

❏ Please send me free email updates

Please circle: Mr. Mrs. Miss Rev.

Name _____

Address _____

City _____ State/PR/County _____ Zip/PC _____

Country _____ Phone (____) _____

Email _____

❏ Please send me free email updates

HA71-PB3G   DOX1-PB3G   ZHX1-PB3G   3HX1-PB3G   LB3R

Include additional names on a separate sheet of paper.

❏ Please identify me as the gift subscription donor.

My name is: _____

MAIL THIS FORM to one of Gospel for Asia's national offices listed on page 263.

MATERIALS FROM GOSPEL FOR ASIA

REVOLUTION IN WORLD MISSIONS

In this exciting and fast-moving narrative, K.P. Yohannan shares how God brought him from his remote Indian village to become the founder of Gospel for Asia. Drawing from fascinating true stories and eye-opening statistics, K.P. challenges Christians to examine and change their lifestyle in view of millions who have never heard the Gospel.

Suggested donation: US $5 / AUS $8 / CAN $5 / €3 / CHF5 / NZ $8 / £3 / ZA R33
Order code: **B1**

AGAINST THE WIND

In this eye-opening book, K.P. Yohannan challenges you to consider how you are running the race God has set before you. Like the apostle Paul, you too can learn what it takes to be able to one day say, "I have fought the good fight; I have finished the race; I have kept the faith" no matter what the obstacles.

HARDBOUND
Suggested donation: US $15 / AUS $22 / CAN $15 / €13 / CHF20 / NZ $22.50 / £8 / ZA R98
Order code: **B6**

SOFTCOVER
Suggested donation: US $10 / AUS $15 / CAN $10 / €9 / CHF14 / NZ $15 / £5.50 /ZA R65
Order code: **B6S**

THE ROAD TO REALITY

K.P. Yohannan gives an uncompromising call to live a life of simplicity to fulfill the Great Commission.

Suggested donation: US $10 / AUS $15 / CAN $10 / €9 / CHF14 / NZ $15 / £5.50 /ZA R65
Order code: **B2**

Order online at *www.gfa.org*

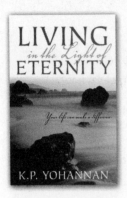

LIVING IN THE LIGHT OF ETERNITY

K.P. Yohannan lovingly, yet candidly, reminds Christians of their primary role while here on earth: harvesting souls. This book challenges us to look at our heart attitudes, motivation and our impact on eternity.

Suggested donation: US $10 / AUS $15 / CAN $10 / €9 / CHF14 / NZ $15 / £5.50 / ZA R65
Order code: **B4**

COME, LET'S REACH THE WORLD

How effective are the Church's current missions strategies? Are the unreached hearing the Gospel? K.P. Yohannan examines the traditional approach to missions—its underlying assumptions, history and fruit—in light of Scripture and the changing world scene. This book is a strong plea for the Body of Christ to partner with indigenous missionaries so that the whole world may hear.

Suggested donation: US $10 / AUS $15 / CAN $10 / €9 / CHF14 / NZ $15 / £5.50 / ZA R65
Order code: **B3**

REFLECTING HIS IMAGE

K.P. Yohannan takes us on a journey back to God's original purpose for each of our lives: to reflect His image. This book is a compilation of short, easy-to-read chapters that all deal with following Christ closely.

Suggested donation: US $10 / AUS $15 / CAN $10 / €9 / CHF14 / NZ $15 / £5.50 / ZA R65
Order code: **B5**

Order online at *www.gfa.org*

EXCITING DVDs

THE CALL TO HARVEST

In this 25-minute DVD, you'll meet the people who are near to the Father's heart: the unreached. See them through the eyes of native missionaries like Titus and Joseph, who face danger and hardship to preach the Gospel in Asia. As the life-giving presence of Jesus transforms lives and families daily, the Lord is calling His people everywhere to come and share the joy of this harvest.

Suggested donation: US $10 / AUS $15 / CAN $10 / €9 / CHF14 / NZ $10 / £5.50 / ZA R65
Order code: **DVD9**

CHRIST'S CALL: "FOLLOW MY FOOTSTEPS"

In this compelling 41-minute DVD, K.P. Yohannan challenges us to follow in Christ's footsteps—steps that will deliver us from our self-centeredness and cause us to impact the lost millions in our generation.

Suggested donation: US $10 / AUS $15 / CAN $10 / €9 / CHF14 / NZ $15 / £5.50 / ZA R65
Order code: **DVD1**

TO LIVE IS CHRIST!

Feel the passion of K.P. Yohannan as he describes the life-giving power of total commitment to Christ in this 55-minute DVD. Be amazed by stories of missionaries who risk their lives to preach the Gospel. Weep with him as he recalls his mother's years of sacrifice that changed lives for eternity. Many people search in vain for the path that leads to the abundant life that Jesus promised. K.P., through the Word of God, uncovers that path in this inspiring and challenging message.

Suggested donation: US $10 / AUS $15 / CAN $10 / €9 / CHF14 / NZ $15 / £5.50 / ZA R65
Order code: **DVD8**

Order online at *www.gfa.org*

OPERATION BOOT CAMP

This 15-minute DVD will transport you to India and take you inside one of Gospel for Asia's intensive training centers. Learn why the training is so challenging. Meet young men who are willing to lay down their lives to reach the unreached of Asia.

Suggested donation: US $10 / AUS $15 / CAN $10 / €9 / CHF14 / NZ $10 / £5.50 / ZA R65
Order code: **DVD4**

BUILT ON THE SOLID ROCK

This 15-minute DVD will show you the fruit of Gospel for Asia's church-planting ministry in living color. See lives that have been eternally and completely transformed by the love of Jesus.

Suggested donation: US $10 / AUS $15 / CAN $10 / €9 / CHF14 / NZ $10 / £5.50 / ZA R65
Order code: **DVD6**

WORLD MAP

Allow God to burden your heart for the lost with GFA's *Pray for the World* laminated map.

WALL MAP   21.5 x 36 inches
Suggested donation: US $10 / AUS $15 / CAN $10 / €9 / CHF14 / NZ $10 / £5.50 / ZA R65
Order code: **MAPL**

PLACEMAT-SIZE MAP   11 x 18 inches
Suggested donation: US $3 / AUS $4 / CAN $5 / €6 / CHF10 / NZ $5 / £2 / ZA R20
Order code: **MAPM**

Order online at *www.gfa.org*

JOURNEY WITH JESUS SERIES

vol 1

VOLUME ONE

Living by Faith, Not by Sight (56 pp) — *Order code:* **BK1**
Journey with Jesus (56 pp) — *Order code:* **BK2**
That They All May Be One (56 pp) — *Order code:* **BK3**
Principles in Maintaining a Godly Organization (48 pp) — *Order code:* **BK4**
ALL FOUR BOOKLETS — *Order code:* **JBKS1**

SUGGESTED DONATIONS	PER BOOKLET:	US $3 / AUS $4 / CAN $4 / €3 / CHF5 / NZ $4.50 / £1.50 / ZA R20
	PER VOLUME:	US $10 / AUS $15 / CAN $10 / €10 / CHF16 / NZ $15 / £5 / ZA R65

vol 2

VOLUME TWO

Dependence Upon the Lord (48 pp) — *Order code:* **BK5**
Seeing Him (48 pp) — *Order code:* **BK6**
The Way of True Blessing (56 pp) — *Order code:* **BK7**
A Life of Balance (80 pp) — *Order code:* **BK8**
ALL FOUR BOOKLETS — *Order code:* **JBKS2**

vol 3

VOLUME THREE

The Lord's Work Done in the Lord's Way (72 pp) — *Order code:* **BK9**
The Beauty of Christ through Brokenness (72 pp) — *Order code:* **BK10**
Learning to Pray (64 pp) — *Order code:* **BK11**
Stay Encouraged (56 pp) — *Order code:* **BK12**
ALL FOUR BOOKLETS — *Order code:* **JBKS3**

Order online at *www.gfa.org*